SANDRA RENEE APPET

EVERNIGHT PUBLISHING ®

www.evernightpublishing.com

SANDRA RENEE APPET

DEDICATION

For Audrey
Thank you for your words of encouragement.

SANDRA RENEE APPET

FIRE AND MIDNIGHT

Sandra Renee Appet

Copyright © 2016

Fire and Midnight is a delightful story full of characters you won't soon forget. I didn't want it to end!

—*New York Times* bestselling author Stephanie Evanovich

Chapter One

Maybe she should adopt a cat, Jane mused as she unlocked the door. Drops of water rolled off her jacket onto the worn wood floor. Leaving her shoes on the mat, she flipped the light switch illuminating most of her cozy apartment, which was a far cry from the spacious home she'd left behind. The silence was the hardest thing to get used to. A clang echoed off the bare walls as she dropped her keys on the counter next to the copy of her divorce decree. She figured the signed copy had hit her lawyer's desk that morning. She shoved the bundle of papers in the nearest drawer. "Out of sight. Out of mind," she mumbled and padded with stocking feet to her bedroom and changed into a pair of sweats and her old Rutgers t-shirt.

She checked her phone as she headed back to the kitchen and opened the fridge to survey her options. No messages or texts from Tyler. She pulled out some leftovers and a bottle of Cabernet Blanc and turned on the news. The drone of the television was a welcome diversion. Empty Nest Syndrome had arrived earlier than she had expected when Tyler, her only child, had jumped at the opportunity to take a summer class and move into his college dorm early. Her phone buzzed on the counter next to her plate. She glanced at the screen, hoping for a text from her son but smiled at the message from her friend, Charlotte.

I have a surprise for you. Check your email.

Charlotte had a way of lightening Jane's mood even when she wasn't around. Jane uncorked the bottle and poured a generous glass. She left the food container on the counter, carried her wine to the desk in the living room, and flipped open her laptop.

"What's up her sleeve now?" Jane took a sip, logged into her e-mail and clicked the subject line: Giddy Up.

Jane,

You're my best friend in the world and I love you to pieces, but all work and no play has made Jane a dull girl. It's time to get back in the saddle and what better place to do it than on your trip to San Antonio? So pour yourself a glass of wine (or two) and click this link. For once in your life, do something completely selfish. Do it for you...

Xoxo ~ Char

P.S. I've already signed you up (user name: JaneK PW: RideEm). Don't bother to call and yell at me. I'm boarding a flight to LA.

Intrigued, Jane clicked the link and was directed to a landing page containing a picture of a cowboy hat and boots along with the words:

The Cowboys, A Personal Service: Are you searching for a companion with no strings attached? Look no further than our cowboys for hire.

"What the heck?" Jane explored the website and discovered a whole new definition of a cowboy. The cowboys on the website didn't wear dusty jeans and ride horses. They wore well-cut suits and drove sports cars. They spoke a range of languages, were versed in opera, wine, and art, and were perfect companions during getaway weekends or cocktail parties … at a cost.

The Cowboys was a high-end male escort service.

Jane poured another glass of wine. She took a healthy gulp and leaned back in her chair putting distance between herself and the screen. A bundle of emotions, mostly anger, raced through her veins. Charlotte, her happily single best friend, always had a steady stream of men at her door. Did she think Jane was so pathetic she had to *pay* a man to take her out? A vision of a greasy guy wearing a shiny shirt and gold jewelry flashed in her mind.

"No way." She shook her head and clicked around the site looking for instructions for deleting her account. Charlotte was damn lucky she was thirty-five thousand feet in the air because Jane had a few choice words for her. Jane clicked "About Us" in hopes of finding a phone number to call. No number was listed, but she jotted the e-mail address and continued reading.

According to the website, escort services were legal as long as the escort was not compensated for sexual services. It went on to say if chemistry developed between the two parties, romance might occur, but it was never contracted.

A few client testimonials followed…

I travel all over the country on business. When I need to kick off my shoes (and other articles of clothing),

I call The Cowboys. Their escorts are as charming and intelligent as they are good looking. I've never had a bad experience.

Instead of a spa weekend, I schedule a date with Paul from The Cowboys. My tension automatically melts when I'm with him, and he gives a great massage.

I'm recently divorced and had been feeling unattractive and unwanted. Jack from The Cowboys treats me like I'm the only woman in the world. One evening wasn't long enough, so I booked him again for next weekend. The entire weekend.

She hovered the arrow over the "Meet Our Cowboys" page and clicked. A half-dozen pictures of men filled the screen, many appearing to be not much older than Tyler. She was about to close the site when brilliant blue eyes leaped from the screen and caught her by surprise.

She drank in the image as she refilled her glass. A shock of dark hair framed his chiseled features. He wore a gray t-shirt that teased the promise of warm skin and thick muscles. Mr. Tall, Dark, and Incredibly Sexy poked at her long neglected fire that had turned into a pile of barely warm coals. She clicked his picture, which opened his bio and more images.

"Hello there, Ryan Zeigler," Jane slurred.

Chapter Two

A familiar pickup truck squealed to a stop in front of Ryan Zeigler's house.

"Hey, buddy!" Joe shouted, as Ryan dropped his gym bag onto the backseat of his convertible.

"Morning, Joe. To what do I owe the honor of seeing you this early in the morning?" Ryan asked, knowing too well what his brother-in-law wanted.

Joe cut the engine and stepped out of the truck, slamming the rusty door behind him, with two disposable coffee cups in either hand. "I have a job down the road and thought I'd bring you a cup o' joe from Joe, you know?"

"Thanks." Ryan took the cup and waited for the inevitable request.

Joe's gaze darted over Ryan's yard. "You can use a good weeding and mulch. Want me to send one of my guys over?"

Ryan breathed out slowly. "What do you want, Joe?"

"I'm a little short this month again. Got hit with some unexpected things. Isabel needs braces, and Maya's throwing another damn party."

"You're not drinking again, are you? If you are I'll kick your—"

Joe held up his hands. "No, Ry. I'm clean. I swear."

Ryan studied his face. "Gambling?"

Joe shook his head. "It's nothing like that."

Ryan rubbed the back of his neck. "I told you after the last time I gave you money, that was it."

"I know, and I didn't think I'd have to ask you again. I feel like such an asshole for doing it, but I don't have another choice. I hoped you were still…" Joe had always acted uncomfortable with Ryan's profession as a male escort, but he never seemed to mind asking for the money Ryan earned doing just that.

"Gave it up. The restaurant takes all of my time now."

Joe shrugged. "I don't know how you can walk away from all that cash."

"I have to. I need to separate from it, and I need to do it now." Ryan's heart raced as the words tumbled from his mouth. It was the first time he'd admitted it to anyone except Camille. Not that there were many people to tell. Ryan kept that part of his life from everyone close. His brother-in-law had discovered Ryan's secret quite accidentally.

"You gotta do what you gotta do, you know? Don't worry about us. I'll figure something out." Joe shuffled to his truck and yanked the door open. The screech of metal against metal tore through Ryan's head.

"Hey. I should be able to help. We can't have Izzy running around with crooked teeth, can we? I'll get back to you later."

The lines around Joe's eyes softened. "You're the best, Ry. I'll pay you back someday. You know that, right?"

"Sure, Joe. I'll call you later." Ryan had a better chance of making a clean break from The Cowboys Escort Service than he would recouping the borrowed money. His brother-in-law knew how to pull at Ryan's heartstrings. He'd do anything for his sister, Maya, and his niece, Isabel. Family was family after all. Ryan climbed into his convertible and started his drive toward the tall office buildings and hotels dotting the morning San Antonio skyline.

****

Ding. Ding. Beep. Ding. Ding. Beep.

Ryan remembered a time when that familiar rhythmic ring had sent electricity through his veins. The excitement of what followed that call was close to what he'd imagined being high felt like. Now he dreaded the sound of the unique ringtone he'd assigned to The Cowboys. He pulled his phone from his pocket and glanced at the display, not that he had to. He knew Camille was on the other end of the call, tapping her red fingernails on her desk, waiting for him to answer. He considered sending the call to voice mail, but Camille was a piranha when she wanted something, and she'd call incessantly until he answered. He'd given his notice the same night he'd broken off their twisted relationship. The problem was Camille didn't believe him. In the past, she'd contacted Ryan for two reasons, and it was too early in the day for a booty call. By process of elimination, Ryan deduced she had a client waiting in the wings for his services. He poked the screen and raised the phone to his ear.

"Hoping I was just kidding about quitting the business?"

"How's my favorite cowboy?" Camille purred.

"Ex-cowboy."

"You'll always be a cowboy to me."

"Is the word 'no' in your vocabulary?" Ryan descended the stone steps to San Antonio's River Walk as the early morning sun chased the chill from the air. With the exception of a few joggers, the walkways were empty, showcasing the waterfalls, gardens, and nooks and crannies that made the River Walk one of a kind.

"I didn't get to where I am by taking that word seriously. If I did, I'd still be slinging drinks at a local dive. Come to think of it, so would you." Camille never wasted an opportunity to remind Ryan of her part in his rise to the most sought after male escort south of Dallas.

He often wondered if he would've been better off without her help.

"How's business?" Ryan asked, changing the subject.

"Booming, which is the reason for my call."

"I figured you weren't calling just to hear my voice."

"You do have the best bedroom voice in the business. If I'm not mistaken, it's the first thing I noticed about you."

"Before you corrupted my morals," Ryan said, wishing he were joking.

"You mean before I made you a lot of money."

"More like before I made you a *ton* of money." The truth was, their partnership had been mutually beneficial. She was right. Without Camille, he'd have spent years dancing and tending bar to save the capital necessary to open his restaurant, but anything to do with Camille came at a cost.

"It must be expensive owning a restaurant with equipment and food to buy and people to pay. How's it going?"

He rolled his eyes. "Come on, Cam. You don't care how Vine is doing. What do you want?"

"I have an opportunity you won't want to pass up."

"I've heard those words out of your mouth before, and look where that got me."

"Let's see. Where did it get you, Ry? Rich, fucked, and richer."

"You've always had a way with words." Ryan crossed the brick patio and stopped in front of slatted double doors. With the phone sandwiched between his shoulder and cheek, he slipped the key into the lock of Vine. He pushed the door open and surveyed the quiet elegance of his restaurant. He was still in awe of the place and the fact it was his. It was very different from the dive bar where he'd met Camille.

He recalled the first time he'd seen Camille LeVan. She'd stood out in Le Tigre like a five-hundred-dollar pair of designer shoes in a row of flip-flops, and for good reason. She owned the place along with a host of other strip joints in the vicinity. The clubs did well, but it didn't take Ryan long to discover Camille's real reason for owning the establishments. They provided her with a free flowing inventory of recruits for her online escort service, The Cowboys. It wasn't long before Ryan became her protégé. At twenty-six, Ryan had had a few years on most of the fresh-faced boys who crossed through the doors of Le Tigre looking to make a quick buck on their gym-built physiques, unlike Ryan, whose muscles were sculpted from framing houses and laying roof shingles under the sweltering summer Texas sun. Five years passed, and before he knew it, Ryan was Camille's next in command, charged with training new recruits, not to mention fulfilling Camille's every sexual whim and fetish.

"We made an unstoppable team," Camille said in the same tone she'd use to order her lunch.

"At one time that was true."

"It still could be," she snapped back.

Not a chance. A vision of walking in on Camille straddling one of the new dancers continued to taunt him. She'd tried to compare the situation to Ryan sleeping with a client. "It was just business," she'd explained. The scene served as a beacon signaling Ryan to rise above the murky darkness of sex and deceit masquerading as passion and love.

Ryan took a deep breath. "As you always say, time is money, and I have a restaurant to run. Get to the point."

"Fine. I'm in a bit of a bind. I have a last-minute weekender coming into town. She's a new client, and she requested you."

"You didn't take my picture down yet?" His free hand rolled into a fist. He should've done it himself before he quit.

"Haven't gotten around to it yet. I've had a hard time keeping up since you left. You should've given me more notice," Camille said.

"I gave you plenty of notice to train a new boy toy. What about the guy you were treating to a personal new hire orientation a few months ago?"

"Zackary? He's just a baby. He's not you."

"A guy half your age is good enough to take to bed, but not good enough to handle your website?"

Camille laughed. "You're getting cranky in your old age. Do me a favor and take this client for me. I still owe you last quarter's commissions. I'll double the payment as a bonus."

"You're like a lioness in heat."

"You know I like to make the impossible possible. So you'll do it?"

He turned the key and pulled the door handle. "Whoa. I didn't say that. Give me a second to check my calendar to see if it's possible to make the impossible possible." He strode pass the bar toward the hallway that led to his private office, unlocked his office door, and flipped the light switch before sinking into a chair and opening the date book on his desk, the one reserved for private and large-party bookings. Ryan made a habit of jotting any personal appointments and dates in it, as well, not that he had many. "Okay. When?"

"This weekend, but you'd do the initial meet and greet Friday night over drinks."

He leaned back in his chair. "Friday as in tomorrow?"

"You got it. Are you in?"

He raked his fingers through his hair and glanced at the curly handwriting in Sunday's box on his date book. His sister, Maya, had charged in last week to remind him about the date. "There's no getting out of the party, little brother. I'm writing it in your book." He'd been dreading the date for weeks. One of the curses of being not only the youngest, but also the only male sibling was that he'd always had more than one mother. His oldest sister, Susanna, had married a Marine and moved out of San Antonio, so Maya had taken over as mother hen. He loved his sisters, but didn't love their Spanish Inquisition about how he worked too long and played too hard. Even his sex life was up for discussion, as far as they were concerned.

"I have plans on Sunday."

"Take her with you," Camille countered.

He tapped a pen on his agenda book. Entertaining Camille's client would earn him enough money to solve Joe's current dilemma. Plus, he'd have enough left over to buy the floor-to-ceiling wine bottle chiller display case he'd had his eye on for Vine. His gaze moved across his desk to the brochure left by the commercial bar-equipment salesman.

A beep signaling another call interrupted his thoughts. "Send me the details and I'll give you an answer by lunch," he said before ending the conversation with Camille and connecting the second call.

"Boss, I'm at the fish market, and the scallops are the size of quarters. We can't run the special today. They won't do," Chef George barked.

"How's the shrimp look?" Ryan asked.

"Shrimp! Where's the shrimp?" George called. A rumbling of voices flowed through the phone. "Ah, here they are. They're beautiful and plump."

"We'll do coconut shrimp instead of bacon-wrapped scallops today. Get as much as we need," Ryan directed.

"Got it, Boss. See you in a few."

Ryan dropped his phone on the desk. The scallop crisis was one of at least fifty split second decisions he was sure would come his way that day. He understood why some owners couldn't handle it, but for Ryan the pressure fueled his fire.

He opened his laptop and made the change to the specials before sending the daily menu to Gretchen, Vine's general manager, for printing.

Ryan rose from his chair to brew a pot of coffee in the kitchen when his phone sounded again. He peered at the caller's name on the screen and dreaded taking the call almost as much as Camille's. He swiped his finger over the screen and tapped the speaker button. "Hey, Joe."

"Hey, Ryan. Look, I'm sorry about steamrolling over you this morning. That was shitty of me."

"It's all right, man. I'll have the money for you next week."

"Thanks. But I don't want you to do it at a cost to yourself, if you know what I mean. If you feel like you can't do it, don't go against your principles for me."

"I don't know what my principles are anymore," Ryan muttered.

"What was that?" Joe asked as a motor revved in the background.

"Nothing. Sounds like you're on a job site. I forgot to ask you how things are going with the business." Ryan almost hated to ask. He'd injected Cortez Construction with a large capital investment. Joe promised to turn the business into a profitable venture or sell it and find employment elsewhere.

"Well, I'll start with the good news. The new crew you helped me hire is doing great. I'm even pulling in some referral work. Business is picking up slowly."

"I told you it'd pick up if you stayed on course." Ryan said, softening his words. Not too long ago he'd put his brother-in-law up against a wall and told him he'd kick his ass if he didn't stop drinking and started paying attention to his construction business, which was bleeding red ink. He'd made Joe a deal. Ryan would pay his way out of debt if Joe sobered up. Ryan had made good on his word, and he hoped Joe continued his end of the bargain.

"I am. I swear. But after paying the crew there's not much left over to live on. I'm having a hard time keeping the lights on at home, and Maya insists on hosting every family party. Something's got to give."

"Have you told her that?"

"Seriously? You know Maya. She'd overreact. Anyway, it's just temporary. Construction is on the rise. I'm sure I'll be making bank in the next year or two. I couldn't do it without your help, and I appreciate you not saying anything to Maya about the money. I'll pay you back as soon as I can. Everything. With interest."

"No problem. I can do it. I'll send a case of wine over for the party and will see you Sunday," Ryan said and headed to the kitchen to prepare for his staff's arrival.

****

Well?

The one-word text was his only message when Ryan checked his phone after the lunch rush. He ran his hand through his hair. "Gretch, keep an eye on things. I have to make a call."

"No problem," she called to him from the bar.

Ryan closed the door to his office, flipped open his laptop and clicked the unopened message from Camille.

Here you go. I'm counting on you…
Jane Keegan, 39
Divorced
In town on business
Preferences: 35-45, dark hair, tall, medium build.

Photo attached

Ryan wasn't an exact fit within Ms. Keegan's parameters. Thanks to his Spanish-German genes, he'd inherited a shock of thick, almost black hair from his mother and his over six-foot stature from his dad. To his sisters' horror, Ryan was the only Zeigler sibling to inherit their father's blue eyes. He'd argue that his build was on the higher side of "medium", thanks to muscle built through years of working construction. His age tipped below her range, having just celebrated his thirty-second birthday a few months before.

He clicked the .jpg file attached to Camille's e-mail and stared idly at the screen as the picture loaded.

Ryan sucked in a breath and held it for a few moments when the image finally appeared on the screen. He blinked a few times before pushing the air from his lungs slowly through his teeth. Glossy golden brown hair tumbled in controlled waves over her shoulder as she shot a staged smile at what looked to be a selfie picture with the second woman cropped out of the shot. As attractive as she was, her grin never quite reached her eyes. The green-flecked hazel eyes were etched with a sadness she'd tried to hide. He wasn't a stranger to that look. Faces like hers stared at him from the other side of the bar on a daily basis.

Baggage. He could tell Jane Keegan had lots of it. He had hoped the new client was a lonely corporate executive looking to blow off steam for the weekend, possibly topping it off with a sizzling night between the sheets. The woman staring back at him was in search of much more. Closure. Acceptance. He wasn't sure exactly what motivated her to shell out big bucks for a weekend with a stranger, but after five years of working as an escort, he'd learned how to read people. Contrary to what other people thought of the profession, an escort was more than wining, dining, and seducing. He'd played the roles of shrink, best friend, confidant, daddy, lover, and bodyguard, among others.

Ryan shook his head, realizing he'd been staring at the picture while thinking of all the troubled women he'd serviced over the years, and, most importantly, why he quit the business. "I hope I can help you find what you're searching for, *Querida.*"

Click. Her picture disappeared from the screen, and he tapped a text message to Camille.

I'll do it for you as long as my picture is taken off the website. I'm no longer a Cowboy.

Camille responded immediately.

Consider it done.

Chapter Three

Ryan made his rounds, greeting the hungry and thirsty Friday night patrons with an extra bounce in his step. From the moment he woke, Jane Keegan's intriguing eyes hadn't been far from his thoughts. Maybe because he knew it was his last assignment, but he couldn't remember a time when he looked forward to meeting a new client as much as he had that day. He'd checked The Cowboys website, and surprisingly, Camille had made good on her promise. His pictures and bio were gone. Jane would be his last client.

"What are you so jazzed about today?" Gretchen asked, interrupting his thoughts.

"Jazzed?"

"Yeah, jazzed. You're bouncing around like a kid before Christmas. And you're smiling. You never smile. You feeling okay?" she asked narrowing her eyes.

"Never better. Remember, I'm heading out early tonight. You're okay to close up?"

She snapped her fingers. "Ah, that's it. You have a hot date. Anyone I know? Is she a customer?"

Ryan stifled a chuckle. If she'd only known what type of "customer" he was scheduled to meet. "Sorry, Gretch, no hot date. Just meeting a friend of a friend who's in town on business." It was an easy alibi he'd used over the years when he had to explain his whereabouts.

She eyed him suspiciously. "Uh-huh. Well, try to have a little fun. You've been stressed out lately."

Ryan resisted a retort in the interest of showing up on time. He double-checked the text message from Camille, even though he'd memorized the details: Nine o'clock at the Omni Hotel's second-floor lounge.

Ryan stepped outside and headed toward the

Omni, leaving Vine in Gretchen's care. Convention season had just begun, and the River Walk was crawling with tourists. As he passed the countless rowdy themed restaurants and bars that dotted the sidewalks, he appreciated the subdued elegance of his own establishment.

Finally, he turned toward the entrance and pushed open Omni's heavy glass door. As he did, an unexpected slew of memories flooded his mind. He couldn't begin to count the number of women he'd escorted through those doors over the years.

Bypassing the bank of elevators, he turned toward the stairs instead, jogging up them two at a time leading to the lounge on the second floor.

Ryan slowed his pace as he entered the bar, letting his eyes adjust to the dim lights. He scanned the bar, looking for a dark head of shoulder-length hair, and spotted her instantly at the end. He'd already figured, from her picture and the scant information listed on her bio, that she wasn't the "look at me" type. He'd expected someone like Jane Keegan to find a seat off to the side, where she wouldn't be the center of attention. Her unassuming ensemble of jeans, sandals, and black blouse confirmed his assumption. There were things about Jane that hadn't been evident from her bio and picture, like how even the dim lighting of the lounge picked up the brilliant highlights in her hair as she twirled a lock around her finger and let it spring back. Or the way she nervously kept her hands busy by circling a fingertip around the rim of her wine glass. Or the way her blouse hugged the curve of her waist. One look confirmed his initial impression of Jane Keegan. The difference between Jane and the majority of his escort clients over the years was like the difference between a multi-layered Napa Merlot and a bargain bottle at Wine Depot. He was convinced there was much more to Jane Keegan than her profile and picture.

He stopped just inches away, close enough to inhale the clean citrus scent of her perfume. "Jane?"

As she swiveled her seat, he knew he had the right woman. Her eyes were just as sad as they had seemed in her picture, although she tried to mask them with a friendly smile.

"I'm Ryan," he said, and offered his hand.

She took it in her own, the warmth of her flesh capturing his as she squeezed lightly.

"Hi," she said, locking gazes with him for a moment before a laugh bubbled up to her lips. At the sound of it, her palm shot up to cover her eyes. "That was brilliant, wasn't it? I'm not good at stuff like this."

Ryan chuckled, enjoying the pink rising in her cheeks. "Believe it or not, neither am I," he said. Gesturing to the stool next to hers, he took a seat.

"I don't believe that for a moment," she said, and picked up her wine glass.

"No really. I suck at the introduction phase."

"Well then, we can suck together," she said, then slapped her hand to her mouth. "Oh my God. I can't believe I just said that. Please order a drink or something, and put me out of my misery."

Ryan ordered a beer before he met her stare. "Something wrong?"

"At first I wasn't sure if you were the same guy I saw on the website, but you're definitely him. I can tell by the scar on your cheek." She pointed to the left side of his face.

"Football injury. You should see the other guy." He shot her a crooked smile.

"Bad?"

"Not a scratch on him." They both laughed,

lightening the mood.

"I tried to find your picture again so I'd recognize you and it wasn't on the website, so I figured you wouldn't be the one showing up. I thought it was some kind of bait and switch thing."

"Not much of a trusting type, are you? You must be from New York."

"No fair. You knew that." She tucked a lock of hair behind her ear and laughed.

"I can't get anything by you." He winked. "So, what brings you to San Antonio?" he asked, avoiding the subject of the disappearance of his image from The Cowboys website. "Okay, now who sounds like a dork? The 'what brings you here' pick-up line must be the oldest in the book."

She smiled and glanced down. Her dark eyelashes fanned over her cheeks that were pink with a growing blush. "Here's the thing. You don't need to use a pick-up line on me." She leaned forward and lowered her voice. "Apparently I'm a paying customer."

Ryan chuckled. Most of his escort dates stuck with the premise of a real date. Jane's candor was refreshing.

She smiled again, and this time her eyes crinkled at the corners in a way that enhanced her natural beauty. "I'm here on business. But you probably already know that, along with my height, my weight, what I had for breakfast this morning, and whatever else Charlotte added to my bio."

"Charlotte?"

"My meddling but lovable friend. This was all her idea. She's the one who signed me up for this," Jane admitted, and laughed. "It seemed like a bad idea then, and an even worse idea now."

Ryan feigned a look of shock. "Am I that bad?"

"No, not at all. Really. It's not you, it's me."

He smiled. "Ah. The 'it's not you, it's me' line."

She shook her head. "I'm sure you can tell that I've never done anything like this before." She took a sip of her wine, then another, seemingly relying on it to pump her with courage. She pointed at the glass. "I shouldn't be drinking this. Wine is the reason I'm here. I believe I drank a whole bottle before confirming the weekend date with the service. This whole thing is just not me. I'm not sure how women do this."

Ryan tilted his head. "Wine makes a great scapegoat. I'm curious. What do you think *this* is?" he asked, genuinely interested in her answer.

She shifted in her seat. "Well, for starters, women pay you to treat them like they're beautiful and desirable. I suppose I understand the appeal of it, but I'm too much of a realist. In the back of my mind, I don't think I could get past the fact that it's just pretend. The fantasy would be lost on me."

"I think that's where you have it wrong. Yes, women are paying for companionship, but the arrangement is very real. I couldn't be with a client I didn't find attractive. That's why the client and escort meet before the session ever begins, like we're doing now, to make sure it's a good match for both parties."

"So why do women choose to hire an escort?"

Ryan took a sip of his drink before answering. "Lots of reasons. Some do it just for the good time. It's a chance to have a little fun, with no strings attached. Some use it as a stress reliever. They just want to blow off some steam. Others are coming off a bad relationship and need a session with an escort to get back in the saddle, so to speak." He'd experienced them all.

Jane narrowed her eyes. "I think my friend Charlotte used that same expression."

"Is it safe to say you're in the last category, then?"

She nodded. "I've been separated for almost a year, but my divorce became final recently. Charlotte thought this would help me jump back into dating. I'm just not sure this is the right way to do it." Jane's gaze moved to her drink. "I'm a real downer, aren't I?"

"Not at all. Your life is in a state of upheaval. What you're feeling is completely normal. Maybe you're not saddle-ready yet," Ryan said, sensing she was about to give him the boot. It had only happened a couple of times in his career.

She smiled. "Actually, I think I am, but not like this. I'm sorry. I'm sure you're a hot commodity and women throw themselves at you, but like I said—"

"It's not for you," he said with a smile.

"Exactly." She tilted her head. "I deserve to be with someone who wants to be with me, not who's getting paid to be with me. I'm going to hold out for that person." Jane pulled the strap of her purse, which hung on the back of the chair, and fumbled with the clasp. "It was nice meeting you."

"Have you eaten yet?" Ryan asked, even though he was sure she'd drunk the glass of wine on an empty stomach by the way she wobbled on the heels of her sandal as she stepped from the stool.

"Um, no. I just got into town a few hours ago. I'll just grab something."

"Have you ventured down to the River Walk yet?"

"Out there?" She pointed to the bank of windows. "My room overlooks that area. It seems a little crazy."

"It can be, but it also boasts the best places to eat in town. Care to join me for dinner?"

"You do understand that I just canceled the date, right?"

"Officially, yes. That doesn't stop me from asking

a hungry out-of-towner to dinner and because I want to, not because I'm being paid," he said, purposely using her words.

He enjoyed watching her shift from foot to foot considering his invitation. "You don't have anything better to do on a Friday night than hang out with a stranger?"

"Frankly, I can't think of anything else I'd rather do." Ryan hooked the strap of her purse under his thumb, slid it over her shoulder and tossed a few bills on the bar.

"Shall we?" Ryan offered her the crook of his elbow. After a moment of hesitation, she accepted, sliding her small palm around his arm.

Chapter Four

Ryan led Jane to the bustling walkway, and he studied her face as she scanned the crowd.

"You'd never know how loud it is out here from inside the hotel." Jane shouted.

Ryan bent his head to get closer to her ear. Her hair caressed his cheek as a faint scent of citrus tickled his nose. "You're lucky you're staying at the Omni. The nicer hotels do a great job of shielding their visitors from the frenzy down here. This section of the River Walk gets to be overwhelming, especially in tourist season, or when the big conferences are in town."

"This section? Is there more?"

Ryan pointed as they continued walking. "It extends for twenty-one miles that way. The original plan was a big sewer project to control flooding of the river, but the city's conservation society decided it should be a beautification venture and the River Walk was born. Most of the stretch isn't like this, but when out-of-towners hear 'The River Walk', this is what they expect."

"There's certainly a lot going on," Jane said as they passed a group of people circling around a lively mariachi band.

"Something for everyone. You can get Mexican, German, Italian, Irish, Spanish, Greek, or plain old American food here. If you want to dance, sing, yell, wear your napkin on your head or take a boat ride, there's a spot for you. Anything and everything goes here."

They turned to the right and headed across one of the many bridges over the river. Jane stopped at the middle and watched as a gondola filled with people floated under them.

"What are you in the mood for?" Ryan asked.

"You're the resident expert. What do you recommend?"

"I've been to them all. Let's walk around and you choose. After you." Ryan's fingertips brushed her shoulder. He followed her across the crowded bridge to the other side, using the opportunity to get a glimpse of her curves as she made her way to the sidewalk. Jane stopped at a few restaurants as they walked, but nothing seemed to interest her enough to stay.

They continued on the path along the river where the bar noise faded into gurgling fountains among lush greenery. "How about that place?" Jane pointed ahead.

Ryan smiled. "Good pick. What caught your attention?"

Her gaze washed over the exterior as they approached. "I don't know. It's quiet, but it has an inviting vibe. It's almost as if the others were trying too hard. This place says 'Come on in, and you'll be happy you did.' Have you eaten here?" she asked, flashing a quirky grin that warmed his insides.

"A few times. How about a table outside?" Ryan waved his hand toward the brick patio.

"Perfect."

Ryan turned toward the hostess stand and pointed at a free table at the end. "Gretch, is that table available?"

Gretchen's gaze bounced from Ryan to Jane and back to Ryan. She shot him a grin that warned him she'd grill him for information. "Sure. I'll send Victor out to take your order."

Ryan grabbed a menu from the stand and led Jane to the table. He held her chair for her and placed the menu on the table in front of her.

"I take it you come here often."

"You could say that. I own it."

Jane stared at him. "You own this place?"

He smirked. "You sound surprised."

"Only because I am." Jane turned in her chair and surveyed the restaurant, giving it an appreciative nod as Victor approached the table and filled their water glasses.

"Good evening. May I interest you in a bottle of wine or a cocktail?"

"Do you like sangria?" Ryan asked Jane.

"Love it."

"Please bring a large carafe of our new summer sangria."

"Right away, boss."

Jane was still wide-eyed.

"You're surprised that a guy who rents himself out to women owns a place like this?" Ryan asked, chuckling to soften the bite of his words.

Jane lifted her water glass. "Actually, that's not it at all. What surprises me is that you didn't lead me here. I chose it from all the other restaurants and bars we passed, and you own it." Her eyes narrowed. "Wait, don't tell me. You're some eccentric billionaire, and you own *all* the restaurants here, but you pose as an escort to screw with lonely women's heads."

Ryan laughed, genuinely amused. "Great story, but nope. Just this one, and that's enough. I don't think I'd have the energy for another, even if I had the funds. But I'm amazed you picked Vine, too. You made my night."

Jane smiled and picked up the menu. "What do you suggest?" she asked Ryan.

"Any food allergies? Vegan? Gluten-free?"

"No, no, and no."

"Great. Then this will be easy. Leave your palate in my hands. You won't be sorry." Victor returned and served the sangria. "Let's start with the tomato crab gazpacho, some of the Louisiana oysters, and two filet tenderloins." His gaze flicked to Jane. "Medium okay?"

"That's how I like it."

He could almost see her stress melt and her posture relax as he kept the conversation moving and light. He entertained her with stories about opening Vine a few months previous.

"I take it this is the reason your listing is off The Cowboys site."

"In a nutshell, yes. Opening a restaurant has been my dream for a while, but I wanted to do it on my own and not have to answer to investors. So I worked a bunch of different jobs to earn quick cash."

"How did you get into escorting anyway?"

He chuckled. "One of my jobs was at a male revue joint. The owner, Camille, recruited me into The Cowboys, and everything fell into place. I was able to gather the start-up money in just a couple of years."

A smile played at her lips as her cheeks turned a rosy pink. "You used to strip?"

"Yup. I was a dancer for a short time, but I mostly tended bar there. It wasn't my scene, so I jumped at The Cowboys opportunity."

"Do you think you'll miss it?"

"Escorting? Nah. I like meeting new people, but the hours aren't a good fit with running a restaurant. This place takes up a lot of my time, especially on the weekends."

"I'm sure it does. I guess me canceling on you was convenient."

He smiled and met her gaze. "Actually, I cleared my schedule and had plenty of coverage. I was looking forward to spending my last weekend as an escort with you."

Jane shifted in her seat and rested her gaze on Vine's exterior. "You did a great job on the place. You should be proud of what you accomplished. I've always wondered what it would be like to run my own business."

"Sounds like you've given it some thought," Ryan said.

Jane shrugged. "I went back to work when my son Tyler started high school. I thought about opening a graphic design business from home, but Nick thought it was more practical to work for a company. You know, the 'regular paycheck and benefits' thing." She shrugged. "I guess he was right."

"Nick?" Ryan asked, even though he knew she was recently divorced. He felt guilty knowing more about this woman than he should.

"My ex," she said lifting her glass of white sangria filled with mango, grapes, and strawberries.

Sangria was too sweet for Ryan, but he was sure Jane would like it. It was quickly becoming a favorite with his female patrons. Ryan lifted his to Jane. "To new friends and good food."

"I'll drink to that." She seemed happier each time she smiled. She opened her mouth to speak but closed it and covered her grin with her glass.

"You were about to say something," he said.

She shook her head, but her grin held back a secret. "This is going to sound really weird." She waved her hand. "Never mind."

"I've heard a lot of strange things in my day, and I'm sure yours isn't as weird as you think. What's on your mind?"

"I was just thinking how I have the entire weekend free and you went to the trouble of freeing your schedule. Maybe we should go through with the weekend after all. I mean, if you want to." A glimmer of doubt flashed in her eyes like she expected him to reject the idea.

"Why the change of heart?"

She took a deep breath and leaned back in the chair. "I haven't felt this relaxed in a long time. I'd forgotten what it was like to just *be* with someone. I don't know if it's this place, the wine, or the fact that I've been wound so tight for so long that I've forgotten what it was like to have a good time." She leaned forward and shook her head. "Does that make any sense, at all?"

"It makes a lot of sense." He was being honest because he'd felt the same way lately. "Looks like we're back on. You'll love what I have planned for tomorrow."

She rubbed her hands together. "What is it?"

"You'll have to wait and see."

"Tease." Jane laughed. It was a deep belly laugh from someone comfortable in her own skin, not the typical high-pitched giggle his ears had suffered through from countless clients.

"So tell me, Ms. Keegan, what type of business has brought you to my fair city?" Ryan asked, wanting to keep her talking. He loved how her eyes were starting to come alive, sparkling under the twinkle lights in the trees.

It soon became clear that he'd found the right conversational gambit. Jane talked about her job and new account through dinner.

"Just listening to how you work with your clients tells me you'd do very well with your own business. You shouldn't give up on that dream. Now, how about dessert? Our crème brûlée is out of this world."

"I don't think I could eat another bite. Everything was delicious. I should probably head back to my hotel." Jane reached for her purse, but Ryan caught her hand. When she didn't pull away, he stood and helped her to her feet.

"I do have one surprise for you tonight. I promise it won't take long, and it will deliver you to your hotel. Your chariot awaits."

She cocked her head. "Chariot?"

He couldn't get enough of her smile.

"Well, not exactly a chariot, but I'll show you one of the reasons I chose this location for Vine." He placed his hand at the small of her back, a gesture that felt completely natural to him.

He waved good-bye to Gretchen on their way out. "See you Monday." She called to him in a sing-song voice. He'd better be prepared for rapid-fire questions from his general manager. "It was nice meeting you, Jane."

He guided her toward a narrow pathway. Greenery and fountains decorated the edges of the walkway. "This is my favorite stretch of the River Walk," he confided.

"It's absolutely beautiful. What's that ahead?" She pointed to a path lit by dim lights resembling candles.

"Your chariot," he said, gesturing.

An old man looked up from his newspaper, and his face brightened. "*Hola*, Reyo, my boy. Good to see you."

"How's business, *Tio*?"

The old man grunted. "Slow tonight. I need to put some ads in the paper or something," he said pointing to the newspaper.

"No one reads the paper anymore. You need a website."

"Meh." He waved a wrinkled hand at Ryan. "The only webs I know about get swept from my boat every morning with a broom. I'm too old for websites. And where are your manners, boy?" he demanded, turning his attention to Jane.

"This is my friend, Jane. Jane, meet my Uncle Pascal. He runs the only private gondola company left on the River Walk. Franchises bought up the rest of them, but Uncle Pascal wouldn't budge."

"It'll take more than them throwing a few bucks my way to move from my spot," Pascal said, swatting his hand as if he were shooing away a fly.

"I think the last offer was more than a few bucks, *Tio*. You may want to reconsider, one of these days."

"Never. Anyway, it's a pleasure to meet you, *Señorita*."

She extended her hand, but instead of shaking it, he brought it to his mouth and kissed it.

"It's Jane's first time here," Ryan said. "I hope you might give her the special scenic tour, ending at the Omni."

"Say no more. Hop in and we'll be on our way," Pascal invited, gesturing at the sole gondola bobbing in the water.

Ryan climbed aboard. Out of habit, he planted his feet far apart in the middle of the boat, steadying it as he helped Jane. He'd had plenty of practice helping people on and off the boat. Paddling it, too. In his youth, he'd spent his summers working for his uncle, carting tourists up and down the river.

He guided Jane to a seat in the middle of the boat and sat next to her. Pascal untied the rope from the dock, stepped to the front of the boat, and pushed against the dock boards with his paddle, sending them toward the middle of the river. He paddled slowly as he sang a song Ryan remembered from childhood.

Relaxing, he pointed out various places of interest along the way. "On the right, we'll pass Marriage Island," he told Jane, nodding toward a large tree that appeared to be growing from the middle of the river.

Pascal stopped singing. "We'll do more than pass it. We're going to stop."

Ryan eyed his uncle. "Is a stop at the island part of the tour now, *Tio*?"

Pascal shot him a smile. "No, but I don't think the *Señorita* will mind. They made some improvements to the dock, and I want to see them up close. I have a wedding booked in a few weeks. You don't mind, do you, Jane?"

"Of course not," Jane said, her gaze bouncing from Ryan to Pascal.

Ryan helped his uncle tie the gondola to the dock. "Improvements, huh?" Ryan murmured, his gaze washing over the weathered and warped boards.

"Hmm. They must be doing them next week," Pascal said, and winked. "*Señorita*?" Pascal offered Jane a hand as she stepped onto the deck.

Ryan watched as she took in the scenery. It had been a while since he'd set foot on Marriage Island, but it was exactly as he remembered. Not much changed in San Antonio.

Jane walked to the opposite side of the tiny island. Ryan followed her to the sign beside a sculpture.

Jane pointed at the plaque. "The island was built to preserve the tree?"

Ryan smiled. "Yes, back before saving trees was fashionable. You'll find that throughout the city. Preservation of nature and history is important to the locals. Don't even get my uncle started on the Alamo. You'll get an earful."

Jane walked to the old cypress and placed her palm on its bark. "This tree has seen thousands of weddings."

"Maybe millions," Pascal said from behind them. "It's believed this tree brings lifelong love to all couples who walk under it." He looked from Jane to Ryan, and nudged his nephew.

Jane cleared her throat.

"I think that's for couples who are married under it," Ryan said with a chuckle. "Let's get a move on. I'm sure our guest is tired from her long day of traveling."

Pascal did most of the talking during the ride to Jane's hotel. He explained the history of the River Walk and how it had been a part of Franklin D. Roosevelt's New Deal, to help residents get work during the Great Depression.

"I never realized how rich San Antonio's history was. Thank you for the tour, Pascal," Jane said as she stepped off the boat in front of her hotel.

"My pleasure, *Señorita*. It's not every day Reyo introduces me to a beautiful woman like you. I hope to see you again soon." He turned to Ryan. "Do you need a ride back to the restaurant, *Sobreno*?"

"*Gracias, Tio*, but I'm headed home now. Thanks for the ride." Ryan hugged his uncle.

"I'll see you at Maya's on Sunday," Pascal replied, and Ryan noticed that it came out as a statement, not a question.

"Of course," he replied. "She won't let me miss it."

Pascal's gaze shifted to Jane, and he opened his mouth to speak. Ryan knew his uncle was about to invite Jane to the party, but Ryan didn't want to put her on the spot. The Rosales family could be pushy. "Good night, Uncle."

Pascal shook his head. "Good night," he said, but he muttered something about youth being wasted on the young, fortunately in Spanish, as he released the rope and pushed off from the dock.

"He's sweet," Jane said, watching the boat disappear in the darkness. "Is your real name Reyo?"

"It's my given name."

"I get it. You use Ryan as your escort name so no one can look you up and stalk you after you break their heart." She lifted her eyebrows.

Ryan chuckled. "That's quite a story, but no. My mother started calling me Ryan when I began school. It was important to her that her children grew up American. She made sure we knew our roots and culture, but she wanted to give us every advantage America had to offer, especially me as her only son. She felt I would be treated differently with a Spanish name, so I became Ryan. The Rosales side of the family still calls me Reyo."

Ryan held the door as she walked into the hotel lobby. Jane hesitated when Ryan guided her to the bank of elevators with his fingertips at the small of her back. "When I said I wanted to continue the date, I didn't mean..." She lifted her gaze to meet his, and soft lines formed on her forehead.

"I knew exactly what you meant. Don't worry. Your virtue is safe. I have no plans to hit on you upstairs, *Querida*. However, I will escort you to your room to be sure you get in safely. It's in the escort handbook." He poked the up button.

"It is not."

"Maybe not, but it's in *my* handbook," he said as they stepped into the empty elevator. "Floor?"

"Eleventh. What does *querida* mean?" Jane asked and moved to the opposite wall facing him.

"Its English translation is darling or dear."

"You must use it on all of your clients so you don't have to remember names."

Ryan's gaze washed over Jane as she straightened her back rising to her full height, which couldn't be more than a few inches over five feet. He shook his head. "No. I can't recall anyone else I've ever called *querida*. It was a term of endearment my father used to use for my mother."

"Oh." She turned away. Ryan was sure she was trying to decide if she believed him. He'd bet she didn't.

The doors opened, and he followed Jane to her door. "Well, Ryan Reyo, thank you for the lovely evening."

He smiled at the way she rolled her "R" imitating his uncle. "You're good at that."

"High school Spanish class. We got extra credit if we rolled our Rs." Jane laughed and pulled her hotel access card from her purse and offered him her right palm.

Instead of shaking it, Ryan gently turned it over and kissed the top of her hand.

"Is that a San Antonio thing? I don't think I've had my hand kissed twice in one day ever."

"Not a San Antonio thing. It's a Rosales thing. The Rosales men are *caballeros*. Gentlemen." He took the access card from her and opened the door. "I'll pick you up right here at ten o'clock tomorrow morning. Thank you for a great evening."

She stepped into the room and spun around. "What should I wear?"

"Something comfortable with shoes meant for walking."

A slow smile formed on her lips prompting a sudden urge to pull her into his arms. "Where are we going?"

"That's a surprise. But I promise you by the end of the day, you're going to know more about San Antonio than most locals. Are you up for it?" He tilted his head and captured her gaze.

She raised an eyebrow. "Can't wait," she said and gently closed the door. Ryan waited until he heard the click of the lock before heading to the elevator, leaving one of the most captivating women he'd ever met.

Chapter Five

Jane pivoted on her toes a few times, checking her reflection in the hotel room's full-length mirror. She admired the only dress she'd brought for the trip as it swirled around her knees. Suddenly self-doubt reared its ugly face. Why did she suggest they continue the date? Date. It really wasn't a date at all. It was a business arrangement. Why was she trying so hard? She paced the floor and stopped at her opened suitcase. He'd take one look at her dress and would think she was trying too hard. A knock at her door interrupted her thoughts as she dug through her suitcase for a pair of jeans. "One moment," she called, and then caught a glimpse of herself in the mirror again. She looked good. Damn good. "Screw it. At least, if I embarrass myself, I'll never see him again," she muttered, and tucked her jeans back into her luggage.

She strode to the door, flipped open the locks, and swung it open. "Hi." She gave Ryan a slow up and down perusal, quelling any doubts she had about spending day two with Ryan the almost ex-Cowboy. After all, she'd consumed more wine and sangria than usual the night before. Her tipsy state, the dinner, and the romantic gondola ride could've clouded her judgment. The thought had crossed her mind that her Spanish prince could have actually been a frog. A really good-looking frog.

Her breath caught. If he was part of the amphibian family, he was the hottest and sexiest specimen she'd ever seen. His chiseled features were more defined in daylight. His blue shirt turned his eyes an even darker shade of delicious, if that was possible. A pair of khaki shorts showed off his tanned legs, with a smattering of dark hair. Her pale legs were a stark contrast to his golden skin. She hitched her thumb toward her suitcase. "I was thinking about changing into jeans."

"It's a beautiful day, and you look amazing just like that." Ryan wasn't shy in the way his gaze trailed down her body. "Ready to go?"

"Ready." Jane grabbed her purse and caught another glimpse of her body. Her eyes were bright and her cheeks were flushed. She almost didn't recognize the happy young woman who gazed back at her. She couldn't remember a time when she'd felt so carefree.

He guided her toward a sleek black convertible. What was it with men and cars? At least it wasn't red like Nick's new toy. A muffled ring sounded and he reached into his pocket. "This is the one and only call I'll take today. I promise," he said, pulling out his phone.

"No problem," she mouthed.

"Hey, Gretch. ... No sea bass left? We should've sent Victor to the market early. I had a feeling you wouldn't get there in time..."

Then his gaze met hers, sending a warm tingle through her body. She was sure her embarrassment must show on her cheeks, but his smile was worth it.

"No, it's fine, get the cod, but call George and let him know he needs to come up with a kick-ass cod dish for tonight's special." Ryan held her gaze as he opened the passenger door. "Don't forget to pick up the shrimp and scallops... Yeah, I know you're not stupid. Thanks. See you later." Ryan chuckled as he ended the call and closed Jane's door.

"Everything okay?" she asked when he slipped into the driver's seat and turned on the engine.

"Everything's fine. I sent Gretchen to the seafood market for the first time, and she got there a little late for sea bass, which was supposed to be one of tonight's specials. The good thing about fish is there's always a substitute."

"I'm keeping you from your restaurant responsibilities, aren't I?"

He shot her another warm smile. Damn, she could get used to those lips, preferably on hers. "My staff keeps telling me I need to take time off and give them more responsibility. A few of them, like Gretchen, Victor, and Chef George, have been with me from the beginning. I trust they can take care of things when I'm not there. This is good for them and good for me." His fingers grazed her hand before he palmed the stick shift. "Are you ready to start the adventure?"

"Oh yeah. Where are we going?"

"You can't visit San Antonio without touring the missions. First stop is Mission San Jose." He revved the engine, and they were off. The ends of her hair floated around her head as they drove out of the city. She couldn't help stealing an occasional gaze at his muscular thighs as the sun beat down on her cheeks. She wasn't sure if it was what Charlotte had in mind when she suggested Jane jump back in the saddle, but Jane couldn't think of another place she'd rather be.

****

They bypassed the reception desk and opted to tour the grounds on their own. Ryan rattled off interesting facts as they walked, and Jane soon figured he must know more about the missions than some of the guides. She couldn't help but stare at him in wonder as he explained the significance of the famed Rose Window.

"I'm boring you, aren't I? There's a great shopping area not far from here—"

Jane placed her hand on his shoulder. "I'm not bored at all. It's just that you have such passion for this place. You make it come alive."

"It's funny you say that. Uncle Pascal used to take my sisters and me here all the time. 'You must understand your roots,' he'd say. At the time, I used to be bored out of my mind, but as I got older, I understood the importance." His eyes scanned the crumbling buildings of the Mission. "I take Isabel here all the time."

"Isabel?" Jane fought a twinge of envy niggling at her belly. She had no right to be jealous of a woman in Ryan's life. The weekend was a business arrangement.

"My niece. My sister Maya's daughter. Although you would never know it. Maya's very serious. I'd guess you'd call her rigid, if you're being nice. I bet most people think she's something that rhymes with witch. But Izzy's such a happy-go-lucky little girl. She's a lot of fun."

Jane studied his face. "She must take after her Uncle Reyo." She wondered if Ryan was putting on a show or if he was the real deal.

She must've stared at him too long.

"What are you thinking?" he asked.

She smiled. "I was wondering what it was like to have such a rich family history. I guess you could call me a mutt. Part Italian, part German, with some Scots and Irish sprinkled in."

"That explains those adorable freckles." He tapped the tip of her nose, and she felt the heat rise again in her cheeks.

"It also explains how everyone around me knows when I'm embarrassed." She turned in an attempt to hide her blush.

"That's pretty adorable, too." His fingers grazed her back. "How about we head to lunch? I know a great place for empanadas, best in town, and it's right down the street."

"Then what are we waiting for, Reyo? Let's go," she said, and impulsively grabbed his hand. She froze and glanced at his hand in hers. When did she become bold?

"Shall we?" His lips curved into a grin that almost turned her bones to chocolate pudding. She tried to pull her hand away, but he held on.

****

He loved the way his given name rolled off her tongue, and he wondered what she would sound like when he kissed her … or touched her … or…

Whoa. Reel it in. He steadied his breath and concentrated on navigating the streets. Within a few minutes he pulled into the dirt lot, parked under the chipped hand painted sign and cringed. "I'm sorry. I've been here so many times and the food is so good, but I forgot what a dive it was. We can go somewhere else." He shifted the car into reverse.

"Are you crazy? It looks fantastic. You can't tease a girl with promises of the best empanadas and then take her somewhere else," Jane said, lifting her hands up.

Ryan shifted back to park and laughed. "Okay. *Besos* it is." He strode to the passenger side and opened the door for Jane. "It's not much better inside." He pointed to the restaurant's exterior.

"Not every place can be as nice as Vine," she said with a wink as he pushed the door open.

"Sit anywhere you like," the waitress called from her perch at the bar. "I'll be over with some menus."

Ryan chose a booth away from the other diners.

The waitress followed and handed them two plastic menus with frayed edges. "What can I get you to drink?"

His eyes tipped to Jane. "Their sweet tea and margaritas are equally great here."

Jane's gaze trailed along the drink selections. "A Cadillac margarita please, on the rocks."

"Salt?" The waitress questioned.

"Of course."

Ryan smiled. "Make that two."

Jane smiled after the waitress left. "I don't often drink in the middle of the day, but, I don't know, I'm kind of in the mood to celebrate."

He folded his arms. "And what are you celebrating?"

"I'm celebrating the ability to kick back, have some fun and relax. It's been a while since I've had the chance to do any of that." Her shoulders seemed to relax, and he loved the smile that appeared on her face. He could get used to that smile.

Their drinks arrived, and Ryan raised his glass, realizing he'd been in the same boat. He couldn't remember the last time he'd taken a day off. "To working hard but playing harder." As the words left his mouth he had a vision of what it would be like to play with the woman sitting across the table. He had a feeling her mind went in a similar place as her glass met his with a heavy clink and her gaze moved to his mouth.

"Know what you're having?" the waitress interrupted.

Jane cleared her throat and scanned the menu. "It all looks good. Why don't you order for the two of us?"

"Can't go wrong with the empanada platter for two."

"Sold." Jane plucked Ryan's menu from his fingers and handed them to the waitress. She turned back to Ryan after the waitress left the table. "I'm having a great time. Thanks for showing me around. San Antonio is really a special place. I can see why you've never wanted to leave."

"Actually, I spent some time away from this place. Had a full ride to UCLA for football."

Jane smiled and tipped her glass to him. "Impressive."

"I always knew I wanted to run my own restaurant, so I majored in hospitality. After graduation a couple of the guys asked me to go into a restaurant deal with them in L.A., and it was a great spot. But in my heart I knew L.A. wasn't for me. Plus, my brother-in-law needed help in his construction business. So I came back home."

"Do you ever regret your decision?"

Ryan pinned her with his eyes and smiled. "I make it a rule not to regret anything in life."

Their gaze was broken by the appearance of a platter filled with an assortment of empanadas accompanied by side dishes of rice and black beans.

"It smells amazing," Jane said.

"Tastes even better. Dig in." Ryan watched as she took the first bite, closed her eyes and groaned. He loved her appreciation for good food. They chatted about their visit to the mission while polishing off the platter.

"I've never tasted anything as good as this." Jane popped the last morsel into her mouth.

Ryan smiled and finished his last bite. "I know my empanadas. So, now that we're sufficiently nourished, want to continue the tour?"

"I don't think I can move," Jane said and laughed. "You certainly know how to show a girl a good time. Mind if I ask you a semi-personal question?"

Ryan folded his arms and leaned back. "Shoot."

She straightened her back and looked him in the eye. "Are you the real deal, or are you just playing the role of attentive escort? Either way is okay, but I need to know."

Her gaze darted away for a split second but returned to meet his stare.

"I've enjoyed every minute of our time together, and that's not an act," Ryan said.

Her eyes softened, and she nodded once seemingly accepting his answer. "So what's the business really like? Do you ever blur the lines between what's real and what's not?"

"Sometimes it didn't feel like a job at all, and sometimes it was the worst job possible." Ryan was about to tell her the real reason he'd left the escort service when the waitress approached the table.

"Can I get you anything else today?" the waitress asked.

"The churros here are incredible," Ryan suggested to Jane. "Do you have a sweet tooth?"

"Of course I do, but I'm stuffed."

"Just the check, please," Ryan said to the waitress. She ripped a slip of paper from her pad and left it on their table. "In that case, I have other plans for dessert," Ryan told Jane with a grin.

"I figured you did or I'm sure a plate of churros would already be headed our way." She tilted her head. "You seemed like you were about to say something, before the waitress came by."

"It was nothing."

"Come on. Out with it. You already know far too much about me, since you were privy to my bio. Now it's your turn."

He rested his elbows on the table. "Fair enough. The main reason I'm leaving the business was exactly what you said. There's a blurred line between what's real and what's not. I started to feel hollow."

Jane searched his face. "Like you were just filling obligations?"

"Sounds like you know something about that."

Jane nodded. "Sadly I do. Even though Nick was the one who cheated, I felt like the bad guy for breaking up our marriage. He just threw the whole situation in my lap and wiped his hands clean. He was like: 'Here you go, Jane, clean up my mess.' Honestly, it would've been easier—cleaner—if he'd just left me."

"You didn't leave him right away?"

She shook her head.

"I took the coward's way out. I did nothing for a long time, almost as if it hadn't happened. Then something snapped. I remembered how happy I'd been the year before, and I realized the bastard had already been cheating on me at that time. There I'd been, in oblivious bliss with my doting husband and perfect family, and he was buying his girlfriend lingerie for their next rendezvous. It really pissed me off, pardon my crudeness. When I finally told him that I was filing for divorce, I think he was relieved. We both were." Jane managed a smile.

"There was nothing cowardly about what you did. Everyone deals with things differently." He'd had many clients who stayed with cheating husbands for a number of reasons. He could never understand how a man could disrespect his wife in that way. He'd happily trade a case of his best wine for a few minutes alone with Jane's asshole ex-husband.

"It was just a matter of survival and doing the right thing for my son." She shook her head. "I don't know about you, but I'm ready to move on. What's next on the tour?"

"Well, just like me, this is a multi-heritage tour of San Antonio. How would you like to taste the most amazing strudel in America?"

"We're eating again? I hope there's a stop at a gym, at some point."

"No gym, but I promise we will get some exercise."

"Very well. Lead the way."

****

They were soon in the middle of one of his favorite parts of San Antonio where well-maintained houses with manicured lawns and picket fences lined the wide streets. "This is known as the King William District. Lots of Germans settled here in the early 1900s. It's where my father's family lived, and where he met my mom when he returned from serving in the Air Force. It's also the home of the best bakery around." He parked on a side street, and they walked a few blocks before stopping in front of one of the more modest houses. "This was my grandparents' home. I remember climbing that tree with my cousins." He pointed to an old elm tree in the front yard. "I was the youngest of the bunch, so they'd make me climb up, then leave me there until one of my sisters came to rescue me. They said I always needed to be rescued. I swear, they still think so."

"One of those families, huh? Well, you're lucky to have them. I'm an only child, and my father died when I was little. My mother worked a lot, so I felt pretty much alone during most of my childhood."

Ryan's gaze moved from the house to Jane. "Whether you have a big family or none at all, I think everyone feels alone sometimes." He laced his fingers with hers and gave her hand a tug. "How about that strudel?"

He led her around the corner to the largest home on that street, which had been converted into a restaurant.

"I forget how busy this place gets." People stood along the porch and walkway leading to the entry. "Stay here a sec and I'll check the wait time," Ryan said, and squeezed her hand gently before letting go. He charmed his way up to the front of the line, hating to leave Jane alone. He'd hoped an old family friend was working the hostess stand and could pull a few strings for him. No such luck. The wait was so long, he could bake his own strudel in the amount of time it'd take them to get seated, but he thought of another plan as he returned to Jane. "The wait's at least an hour, but I have another idea. Come with me." Ryan winked and slid his hand into hers, startled by how natural it felt to hold her slender fingers in his. He led her to the back of the restaurant and in through a side door. "Most people don't know you can get pastries to-go back here." A small counter in the back held a glass case filled with cheese, apple, and berry strudels, sticky buns and muffins. "What will it be?" Ryan asked.

Jane's gaze swept over the glass case. "Everything looks delicious! What do you suggest?"

"My favorite is the traditional apple strudel."

"You read my mind."

Ryan handed her the bag containing the pastry, forks, and napkins as he grabbed two coffee cups. Once outside, he nodded to the river beyond the restaurant's flower garden. "I know the perfect place, and I don't think it will be crowded."

They took a seat on an empty bench overlooking the river. He pulled one fork from the bag as Jane opened the container. The scent of warm apple and spices filled the air. He sank his fork into the flaky pastry and offered her the first bite, then found that he couldn't help staring at her lips as they closed around the tines of the utensil.

She shut her eyes and groaned. "This is the best thing I've ever tasted." She licked her lips, and Ryan could have sworn the temperature rose twenty degrees.

"You said the same thing about the empanadas," he teased and offered her another forkful of the sinful strudel.

Jane slid her hand over her stomach. "I don't think I can—"

"Eat another bite?" he interrupted with a smile. "I hope that's not true. I'd love it if you would join me for dinner tonight, unless you're getting sick of me?"

Jane laughed. "Hardly, but I have some work to do and I bet you've been ignoring your responsibilities at Vine."

Responsibilities. Ryan pulled his phone from his pocket. "That reminds me. Gretchen has texted me about a hundred times."

"See? You need to get back."

He glanced at the most recent texts, and saw that there really were legitimate matters that needed his attention. Normally, he enjoyed the thousand little decisions that went into keeping Vine in top form. Today, however, he was genuinely torn. Capturing Jane's gaze, he said, "How about this. I'll drop you off at your hotel for a few hours, but only if you agree to meet me at Vine at eight o'clock. I'll bet you'll be hungry by then. Deal?"

"Deal," Jane conceded, and Ryan felt a stab of pure relief. He had no intentions of saying good-bye to her anytime soon.

"There's something else," Ryan said. The idea had been swimming around in his head all day. "I want to officially cancel our date as far as The Cowboys is concerned. I'll make sure your money is refunded." He knew Camille would be furious, but he didn't care.

Jane's brows bunched together. "Why? I don't understand."

"I want to go on a real date with you. Not because you're paying me but because we want to spend time together."

"I'd really like that."

Ryan couldn't think of a better way of breaking free from Camille and The Cowboys for good.

Chapter Six

"Are you back in the saddle yet?" Charlotte's voice sounded through the phone.

Jane poked the speaker button and towel dried her hair. "What, no 'Hello, how's your trip'?"

"Okay, girl. Hello. How's your trip? Did you get laid?"

"No, but I saved some money. The arrangement has been canceled."

"You didn't! Why—"

"Hold on. Before you get all over my case, I spent last night and most of the morning and afternoon with the cowboy anyway. Well, he's not exactly a cowboy anymore…" Jane gave Charlotte a recap of the past twenty-four hours.

"My little Janie is growing up. I'm proud of you!"

"Seriously, it's no big deal."

"I hate to tell you this—actually I love telling you this: It sounds like a very big deal. Enjoy your cowboy. I mean it. *Enjoy* him."

Jane laughed. "I gotta go, Char."

"Ride 'em, cowgirl."

As Jane slipped on a pair of jeans and a white blouse, her thoughts drifted to Ryan. She felt as if she were in her own fairytale. But, like every other fairytale, hers would be over soon. Which was too bad. She could easily get used to a guy like him.

****

Snaking her way through the crowded walkways of the River Walk, Jane smiled when she spotted Vine's brick-cover façade with traces of ivy crawling up the walls. Gretchen greeted her at the hostess stand and showed Jane to the reserved table for two at the back of the restaurant. A bottle of wine was already perched in an ice bucket, with two wine glasses beside it.

Gretchen pulled a corkscrew from her apron and started opening the wine. "Ryan will be out soon. He had to take care of a few things in the kitchen." She drew the cork from the bottle and poured a glass for Jane.

"Thanks. Ryan tells me you've been with him since the restaurant opened."

"Yup. Ry's a great boss. Easy to work for. How long have you known each other?"

"We just met yesterday, actually," Jane confessed.

"Really? You must've made quite an impression. He never takes time off like this."

"Are you telling my deepest and darkest secrets?"

Jane's gaze moved to the owner of the deep voice that had suddenly spoken behind Gretchen. She realized her stomach must have missed hearing his voice for the couple of hours they were apart, because it did cartwheels as he spoke.

"Nope. Just some girl talk." Gretchen winked at Jane and stepped aside so Ryan could take a seat.

"Girl talk, huh? I think there are some customers waiting to be seated," Ryan said.

"I'm going. I'm going. Good to see you again, Jane."

Jane waved good-bye to Gretchen and returned her gaze to Ryan, noticing the fine lines that creased his skin at the outer edges of his eyes. "You look tired."

He poured a glass of wine for himself. "Nah, I'm fine. Just got off the phone with my sister. She's having a big family party tomorrow, and she won't let me out of it, no matter what excuse I throw at her. She's relentless."

"Not a fan of family parties?"

"Don't get me wrong. I love my family, but they get to be a little much after a while. They go all out. Live music, a million kids, and what seems like ten generations of Rosaleses."

"Sounds like fun," Jane said, and meant it.

Ryan's eyes brightened. "Come with me tomorrow."

"What? No. I couldn't impose on you and your family."

"You'd be doing me a favor. Maya always complains how I never bring a date to these things. It would win me a reprieve from her constant nagging. Come with me. Please."

She stared into his blue eyes and forgot every reason why she should say no. She forgot that she was getting far too attached to the man before her, this sexy man with eyes the color of a calm Caribbean ocean. She forgot her flight home in three days, and the fact that she'd never see him again. She even forgot why she was in San Antonio, repressing all thought of the meeting prep she was ignoring while spending her time with him.

"Sure," she said. "I'd love to."

****

The next morning, Jane woke early and hit one of the shops on the River Walk before Ryan picked her up. Besides the dress she'd worn the day before, she had packed nothing else suitable for a party. She opted for a gauzy pale-yellow skirt and a white tank top, with sand-colored sandals. It was a significant departure from her usual black and gray wardrobe, but it felt right for the occasion.

When she answered the knock at her door, there stood Ryan, holding a beautiful gardenia the exact shade of her skirt.

"I picked it on the way over. Thought it would look nice in your hair." He tucked the stem behind her ear and grazed her cheek with his thumb. Her stomach fluttered from his touch.

"Beautiful," he said. "Thanks again for doing this."

Her gaze washed over his casual white button-down shirt, with the sleeves rolled up to expose tanned and muscled arms. "Thanks for asking me." She hooked her hand around his arm, feeling like a teenager on a first date.

They drove to a neighborhood similar to the one they'd toured the day before. He turned onto a car-lined street and parked.

The soft notes of guitar music filled the air as Ryan helped Jane from the car. Suddenly her heart began to hammer in her chest, and she froze. What was she getting herself into? She could've stayed safe in her comfort zone and spent the afternoon perfectly happily, curled up with a book beside the hotel pool. Instead, she had let herself be swayed by a sexy grin.

Ryan seemed to sense her hesitance. "Come on. They won't bite unless provoked. And don't worry. If you're not having fun in an hour, we'll leave. That's usually when my head starts to hurt anyway." His expression became a little less carefree. "Oh, and my family doesn't know what I used to do for a living."

Jane tilted her head. "They don't know about the cowboy thing?"

"The only person who knows is my brother-in-law, Joe." Jane noticed the subtle clench of his jaw.

She raised her eyebrows. "What's it worth to you? I see a year of empanadas and apple strudel in my future."

His expression softened. "That could be arranged."

Jane nudged him in the ribs. "Your secret's safe with me."

"I'll be eternally grateful. Ready to meet the crew?"

There was no graceful way to turn back, at that point. "Ready if you are."

The music grew louder and louder as they walked toward the house on the corner. Instead of going up to the front door, Ryan guided her around to the backyard. "I like to sneak in through the back, to avoid any verbal attacks from the hens in the kitchen."

Jane laughed. "Sounds like you've been to a lot of these things."

"Too many to count."

"Uncle Ryan!" a high-pitched voice called from overhead.

Jane looked up to see a young girl with dark pigtails smiling down at them from a tree.

"Isabel! What are you doing up there?" Ryan asked, and held up his hands to her.

She jumped into his arms. "Waiting for you. Mama promised you'd be here."

"I wouldn't miss it," Ryan said, lowering her to the ground.

"Who's that?" Isabel asked, smiling as she pointed at Jane.

"This is my friend, Jane."

Isabel's brown eyes widened, and she opened her mouth, revealing a missing tooth. "You have a girlfriend?"

"Well, I didn't say that exactly. But Jane is a girl, and she is my friend."

Isabel giggled and skipped into the backyard, singing, "Uncle Ryan's got a girlfriend."

He smiled at Jane, looking only slightly abashed. "That was a preview of the Rosales family circus. Ready for the show?"

"Let's do this," Jane said, and stepped into the backyard.

Colorful lights were strung along the fence, and a band played in the middle of the yard. All around them were partygoers, old and young. Jane estimated that there were at least a hundred people gathered there. "All of these people are your relatives? How do you keep them straight?"

Ryan scanned the crowd. "Some of them are relatives, some are family friends, and I have absolutely no idea who the rest are. But there's a familiar face," Ryan said, and led Jane to where Pascal was manning one of the grills.

Before she had a chance to say hello, Jane felt a tug at her skirt, and looked down to see Isabel with a bunch of daisies in her hand, which looked to be freshly picked from the patch along the backyard's fence. "These are for you, Miss Jane."

Jane bent as Isabel passed her the handpicked bouquet. "Thank you so much! How sweet," Jane said, and watched as two women approached Ryan.

"There you are, little brother! I almost began to think you weren't coming. Look who's back from graduate school? You remember Tilly."

Jane stood holding the flowers. Her eyes landed on a beautiful young girl with long dark hair who was staring wide-eyed at Ryan.

"Sure. Of course I remember. Hey, Tilly. Welcome home," Ryan said. He snaked a hand around Jane's back. "And this is Jane Keegan."

The woman Jane assumed was Ryan's sister narrowed her eyes. "Ryan, you should've mentioned you

59

were bringing company." Her gaze moved to Jane. "He never brings anyone to these things. I'm Maya."

"Nice to meet you both." Jane turned her attention to Tilly, who looked as though someone had stolen her last lollipop. "What did you study in school?" she asked.

"Communications," Tilly said with a pout.

"My good friend is an entertainment reporter in New York. Are you looking to go into broadcasting?"

"I-I don't know," she mumbled, and Jane wondered if Tilly had chosen the right field of study.

The four stood in awkward silence for a moment. Then Ryan cleared his throat and pointed to something across the yard. "I see you received the case of wine I sent over."

Maya turned in the direction he was pointing, where a crowd stood around tables holding platters of food, and nodded. "The wine's always a big hit."

"Happy to oblige. And now, if you don't mind, I'm going to get some. I told Jane all about it in the car, so I'd like her to have a taste. Can I get you two a glass?"

Maya and Tilly declined, and Ryan grabbed Jane's hand, leading her firmly away from the two women. "That was awkward," he muttered when they had made their escape.

Jane was beginning to love the feel of his hand in hers. "No big deal. I'm an unexpected visitor. This is Maya's party. You really should have told her you were bringing a guest." Summoning her courage, she asked, "Does your sister try to set you up often?"

"Every once in a while. But she usually warns me before doing something like that. And with Tilly Sena? I don't understand what Maya's thinking. I remember that girl running around with dolls and pigtails when I was in high school."

"She's very pretty." Jane suddenly felt old and frumpy in her mid-calf-length skirt, compared to the woman whose skimpy sundress barely covered her perfect, can't-be-a-day-over-twenty-five-year-old ass.

"Hey," Ryan said, while his thumb traced the inside of her wrist, sending goosebumps up her arm. "She's not even in your league."

Jane offered him a grateful smile. "You always seem to know the perfect thing to say, even if you don't mean it."

Ryan pinned her with his stare and drew her close. "I don't say things I don't mean. Ever. Now, how about that wine?"

****

Jane managed to have a great time at the party. The only one who kept her distance was Maya, yet Jane caught Maya staring at her more than once, as afternoon shaded into evening. Between Ryan being adorable, Uncle Pascal's jokes, and the great food, Jane's cheeks hurt from smiling so much.

When Jane finally did check her watch, she was shocked to see it was so late.

Taking her cue, Ryan wrapped his arm around her shoulder. "You have an early meeting in the morning, as I recall. Let's get out of here. We'll sneak out the same way we came in," he said, and guided Jane toward the side of the house.

"Uncle Ryan!" Isabel's voice yelled from the window of the house as Jane and Ryan left the party.

"Aren't you supposed to be asleep, Isabel?" Ryan's voice was stern, but he was smiling as they moved closer to the window.

Isabel's bottom lip shot out. "How can anybody sleep, with all this party stuff going on? I just wanted to tell you I had fun tonight, and I have a secret to tell you, but you have to come closer."

Ryan walked even closer to the house. "What is it, little one?"

"I like Jane," Isabel said in a whisper loud enough for Jane to hear.

"I do, too," Ryan replied, mimicking the girl's tone, which made her giggle. "Now go to sleep before your momma gets mad at both of us."

Isabel nodded and waved at Jane before disappearing from the window.

Ryan strode back to Jane's side. "I love that kid."

"I can see why. She's adorable."

"Hard to believe she's her mother's daughter," Ryan said with a chuckle.

"Well, they both love you fiercely. Don't be so hard on Maya. She just wants what's best for you."

"Maya wants what *she* thinks is best for me. Did you have a good time despite her evil eye?" he asked.

"You caught that, too? I wasn't sure whether it was just my imagination."

"Unfortunately not. I plan to have a talk with her about it. But not tonight." He pushed the button on his key fob, and the headlights provided a path to his car.

"Please don't do that on my account. She's your sister, and I'm just…" Her face flushed. Jane hoped it was dark enough to hide her embarrassment as they stepped to the passenger's side. *What the heck am I?*

Ryan eased her body against his car. Warmth from the metal of the door seeped through her thin skirt, doing nothing to cool down her heated skin. "You're sexy, intelligent, and a hell of a lot of fun, and it's taking every ounce of self-control for me to not kiss you, right here and now," he said, his voice low and silky.

The air slipped from Jane's lungs. She searched his face, wondering if he meant the words as a joke. She tried to look away, but his body was so close to hers that he dominated her field of vision, from the white shirt stretched over his broad shoulder, with a smattering of dark hair peeking from his unbuttoned collar, to his stubbled jaw and his full lips.

God, those lips. She needed him to kiss her more than she needed to draw a fresh breath of air into her lungs. But what if she wasn't good at it? She hadn't kissed any man other than Nick in … how long? Almost twenty years?

"*Querida*." He hooked his thumb under her chin, challenging her to meet his gaze.

"I love when you say that," she whispered.

"*Querida*," he repeated slower and trailed his fingers up her cheek and threaded them through her hair to the nape of her neck, pulling her closer.

She froze.

"What's wrong?" he asked, capturing her stare.

"It's just…" Truth seemed to be her only option. "This is embarrassing to admit, but I haven't kissed anyone else in a very long time."

"It's just like riding a bicycle."

"That's easy for you to say."

"And it'll be easy for you to do, especially with those lips." The palm of his free hand cupped her face, and he traced her bottom lip with his thumb. "Like I said, I've wanted to kiss you all night. Actually, all day *and* all night."

Everything became dark as Ryan leaned in closer. His intoxicating scent overpowered Jane's senses as his lips brushed hers, feather-soft, as if he was testing her. She opened her mouth just a little as a slow heat blanketed her body.

"Just like a bicycle," he repeated and reclaimed her lips.

As if they knew exactly where to go, her hands snaked around his back, locking her body into his embrace. She whimpered into his mouth as his tongue began a leisurely exploration of her mouth.

Holy crap. Not only had it been a long time since she kissed someone else, it had been a very long time, maybe never, since someone had kissed her like *that*.

After a minute, Ryan pulled away but kept his hand on her chin. "Well, was it?" he murmured.

Jane's eyes were still closed as she savored the kiss. "Was it what?" she asked, wishing time would stop so that they could remain leaning against his car on this quiet street forever.

"Was it just like riding a bike?"

She smiled. "I'm not sure. I think you'd better try it again so I can take off the training wheels."

She wasn't sure how long it was until she heard voices headed toward them, growing louder. She savored the warm buzz of being thoroughly kissed as Ryan helped her ease into the passenger seat.

They rode in silence until the sleepy lights of the city came into view. Then the realization that her time with Ryan had come to an end crept painfully into the pit of her stomach.

"What time do your meetings start?" Ryan asked.

"Nine," she replied, and glanced at the clock on his dashboard.

"I kept you out too long, didn't I?"

Jane laughed ruefully. "You're a bad influence." As Ryan's car turned in at the parking lot of her hotel, she added, "You don't have to walk me in. Since you're technically not a cowboy any longer the rulebook doesn't apply." It wasn't that she didn't trust Ryan, but she didn't trust her own actions if he came back to her hotel room.

Ryan parked and cut the engine. "Sorry, but that rule comes from *my* book." He smiled as he opened his door and strode to the passenger side. Jane's gaze was glued to him. He offered his hand as he helped her out of the car, not letting go until they had crossed the lobby, ridden up in the elevator and walked the length of the hallway to the door of her hotel room. "Any chance I can tear you away for dinner on your last night?"

Jane sighed, more disappointed than she wanted to admit. "I have dinner with my client tomorrow."

Ryan shot her a crooked smile. "I shouldn't have asked." His index finger traced a line up her arm, and then touched her cheek. He leaned over, and she inhaled his scent, capturing it, committing it to memory. She licked her lips, raising her mouth to his.

Instead, he placed a gentle kiss on her forehead. "Thank you for the best weekend I've had in a long time, *Querida*."

She didn't want the night to end. She tried to summon the courage to ask him inside. *I can do this. I can...*

He squeezed her hand, released her fingers and turned to leave.

"Ryan?"

He turned around, but she couldn't seem to say the words. She watched as he stuck his hands in his pocket and pinned her with his stare.

Her breath escaped in a rush. "I don't want to say good-bye."

"I don't want to say good-bye, either. But tomorrow's a big day for you, and I don't want you to regret a single moment of the time we've spent together. So, for now, goodnight."

He was right. He was so very, very right.

"'Night," she said, almost in a whisper, and forced herself not to look back as she stepped into her empty, lonely room and closed the door.

Chapter Seven

A muffled beep woke Jane from a restful sleep. She fished her phone from the sea of pillows, and she peered at the display.

Well, five hours of sleep were better than none. She'd stayed up until almost one, prepping for her first meeting, but it was time well spent. She strode confidently into her client's office building overlooking the River Walk. The full day of meetings with the company's executives proved fruitful. They loved her campaign ideas and were ready to take their advertising nationwide.

As focused as Jane was on her client, Ryan and the last kiss they'd shared were all she could think about. Knowing he was only a few yards from her made the fact she'd never see him again even harder to face.

In all honesty, she wasn't sure exactly why he had chosen to cancel the escort arrangement and to spend the weekend with her anyway. Maybe he felt sorry for her. Maybe he was trying to prove some kind of point to the owner of The Cowboys. Or maybe, like her, he was just lonely. Whatever the reason was, it didn't matter. It was over. She had to put it behind her, no matter how sweet it had been, and concentrate on her career. After her meetings wrapped up, she checked the time of her early morning flight out the next day. She'd be back in cowboy-free New York before she knew it, and her weekend with Ryan would be a distant, but wonderful, memory.

"Are you ready for dinner? There's a great place on the River Walk we thought you'd love."

James, her account's CEO, jolted Jane from her thoughts.

"Sounds great. I explored the River Walk over the weekend. Which one?"

"Grande Mexico. Their enchiladas are the best in town."

Jane felt a twinge of disappointment run through her body as she nodded. "I'm ready when you are." She pulled her bag over her shoulder, and felt her phone vibrate through the leather.

"I'll gather the troops. Wait here," James said, and strode away.

Jane slipped her hand into her bag and pulled her phone from the pocket, then tapped the screen to open two unread text messages. The first was from Tyler.

School's going great. Hope your trip is too. Don't forget to get me a shirt!

The second was from a number she didn't recognize.

I can't stop thinking about you. If you feel the same, meet me in the hotel lounge after dinner. Ryan

Her heartbeat drummed in her chest, and she couldn't control the wide grin that took control of her mouth as she reread his text.

"Good news?" James asked, followed by a parade of executives.

Jane slipped her phone back into her purse as she tried her best to tone down her goofy smile. "My son. He's doing well in college. Wants me to pick him up a souvenir before I leave."

Over the course of the next hour, she barely tasted the best-enchiladas-in-town enchiladas. She was fairly confident she nodded and laughed at the right times during the conversation, but internally she was counting down the minutes to seeing Ryan again. At meal's end, she finalized the project plan with James and agreed to the date of her future visit, in six weeks' time, to deliver the final draft of their ad campaign.

"With your fresh ideas, I foresee a great partnership with you, Jane."

"Thank you. It's been a pleasure, and thank you for the wonderful dinner, but I'm going to head back to my hotel now. I have an early flight in the morning. I'll be in touch once I'm back in the office."

Jane said her good-byes and made a stop in the ladies' room to run a brush through her hair before meeting Ryan. When she consulted her reflection in the mirror, she hardly recognized the person staring back. Even her eyes were smiling. Confidence radiated from the woman in the mirror. After years of feeling not quite good enough, it was a rush to know she was not only good enough, but was also wanted by a sexy-as-sin man who was willing to wait all night for her.

She swiped a coat of gloss over her lips and spritzed her neck and wrists with perfume when it dawned on her that she might be about to get naked with Ryan. With perfect, looks-like-a-Greek-god, Ryan. How long had it been since she'd had anything resembling a flat belly?

You're getting ahead of yourself, Querida, she told herself, then wondered, *and when did you start calling yourself Querida?*

She giggled at her own foolishness, and closed her purse. She'd worry about her insecurities later. Right now, she had a hot guy waiting for her, back at her hotel—that fact put an even bigger smile on her face.

Chapter Eight

Jane took a deep breath and stepped into the Omni's lounge, slowing her steps as she scanned the bar. She spotted Ryan sitting on the exact bar chair she'd occupied on the night they met. His arm was casually draped along the back of the seat. His posture straightened when he spotted her, and his gaze washed over her body, slow and hot. Definitely hot.

She closed the final distance between them, and he stood to greet her.

"Hi," he said.

"Hi, yourself."

He leaned in, so that his mouth was close to her ear. "I wasn't sure you'd come," he murmured, and his gravelly whisper sent her libido's motor into overdrive. "Do you want something to drink?" he asked, and pulled back to search her eyes.

Jane shook her head. Her leg pressed against his, and her gaze darted from his eyes to his lips. She wanted him more than she'd wanted anything in a long time. Suddenly, the people standing near them seemed like an intolerable invasion of her space. "I'd rather go upstairs."

Ryan nodded and left a couple of bills on the bar. He slipped his hand around her waist, his hand resting low on her hip.

They walked to Jane's room in silence, but her body buzzed as his thumb caressed her waist with slow strokes, promises of what was to come. Warmth flooded her with each step closer to the private oasis of her room. Ryan's fingers brushed hers as he took the access card from her hand, opening the door with a soft beep.

As soon as they were inside, the door slammed shut, and her purse and computer bag dropped to the floor as his hands ran the length of her ribcage. All available air left her lungs, and she gave herself up to Ryan's kiss as he steadied her face in his hands, his lips sweeping along the seam of her mouth.

He shifted her to the foot of the bed his hands traveling up her blouse. As he fingered the first button on her blouse, she glanced at the lamp blazing in the corner. "The light."

"What about it?" His breath heated her skin.

"Can you turn it off?"

"Not a chance. I've waited days to unwrap you. I'm not doing it in the dark."

"You don't understand. I've had a kid. I don't live at the gym. My body is not what you're used to," she said, averting her gaze.

"Look at me, *Querida*."

Recovering her nerve, she met his gaze.

"I want everything about you," he said firmly. "I haven't been able to take my eyes off you. I love your body, and you will, too. Turn around."

Her eyebrows shot up as he spun her so that her back nestled into his chest, and the reflection of the large mirror above the dresser stared back at her. "You're going to see exactly what I see." He slid his hands around her waist and released the bottom button of her blouse before moving to the next.

"Ryan."

"We're going to play a little game. There are two rules. First, you're going to keep your eyes on my hands. You're going to see and feel everything they touch, everything they do. Second, you're going to do this without judgment. No negative thoughts or feelings about what you see. Agreed?"

She studied his face in the mirror. Could she do it? She wouldn't forgive herself if she didn't at least try. She mustered a smile. "Agreed."

"This is going to be fun and incredibly sexy," he said with a grin. "Starting now. Eyes on my hands."

She complied, and her gaze rested on his hands as they deftly traveled up her blouse, unbuttoning as he went. Her instinct was to wrap her arms around her middle, but he seemed to know what was in her head. "There's another rule. Your arms must remain at your sides."

"No fair. You're changing the rules."

"Nope. Just adding to them," he said huskily in her ear.

She played by his rules and kept her gaze on his fingers as they trailed up her arm, pulling the fabric of her blouse aside to expose her white shoulders. She held onto her shirt, not allowing it to fall to the ground, and sucked in a breath as she glanced at her belly.

Ryan kneaded her shoulders, his hands warm and gentle. "Let the shirt go. Eyes up here, *Querida*."

"This is harder than I thought," she said, but she did as he asked, trying to focus on nothing but his touch.

He gathered her hair into a ponytail and pulled it over her shoulder, then kissed the exposed skin of her neck. His breath blew hot on her flesh as she leaned into his body. His mouth found a sensitive spot right under her ear, and she gasped as heat flooded her belly and traveled south along with his hands, which were at the closure and zipper of her dress pants.

Before she had time for doubts, her pants dropped in a sea of fabric at her feet.

Jane glanced at her body in the mirror, and couldn't help but notice the stretch marks below her belly button. Her hands moved instinctually to shield her stomach from view.

"You know what happens when you don't follow the rules?"

Her gaze flicked to his in the mirror.

"I'll tell you what happens—another rule gets added. Arms up."

"You're not playing fair," she pouted, but she couldn't lie. She was warming up to the game. At least, with her hands up, her breasts wouldn't look droopy.

"I think you like when I change the rules."

"Maybe I do." She winked at his reflection.

He chuckled. "In that case, I think you're ready for more." He slid his hands along her stomach and up to her bra-covered breasts. His fingers traced circles over the silky fabric, and soon her nipples were straining, as if begging for their share of attention. She was sure he was deliberately avoiding touching her hardened peaks. Instead, his fingers whispered along her ribs, following the outline of her bra. Then he released the snap.

Her breasts bounced free from her bra, and he whisked the scrap of fabric up and over her arms.

Exposed, Jane sucked in another breath and closed her eyes.

"Not playing by the rules again?" Ryan teased. "Good. I'm going to enjoy this next rule."

She swallowed hard. "What is it?"

"I'll show you." His hands were once again on the move. Every touch sent tingles along her flesh. He played her body like an instrument as his fingers traced up her arms and laced them with hers. He lowered her arms but not to her sides. Instead, he turned her palms so they were facing her, and guided her hands to her breasts. "Touch yourself like you'd want me to touch you. But instead of watching my hands, now I want you to watch yours." She almost lost her footing, and his hands moved to her waist steadying her. "We're both going to watch you."

"I—" Jane was sure she shouldn't want this as much as she did. Her hands hovered, unmoving, over her breasts.

"No words. Just feeling. When's the last time you felt like this?"

"Never," she said breathlessly without a second thought, and her gaze moved to her hands. The pads of her fingertips brushed over her sensitive flesh, enticing her nipples into tight knots. She traced lightly over one bud, and the thrill of sensation it awoke elicited a soft moan.

"You're driving me crazy," Ryan murmured in her ear.

She felt his hips move, and the length of his arousal pressed against her back, making her smile and lean into his warmth.

"I swear, *Querida*, I think you *like* driving me crazy."

And, damn it, she did. It had been so long since she'd felt wanted that she'd almost forgotten what it was like.

Ryan's hands covered hers and guided them over her head to his shoulders. "My turn."

Her head fit perfectly into the space along his neck right under his jawbone. She lifted her hands to run them through his hair, loving the sensation of it between her fingers as he began to caress her skin with purpose.

She'd already had the feeling he'd be an excellent lover. She doubted whether he could have been a successful male escort if he fell short between the sheets … but holy hot hell! Either she had seriously underestimated his abilities or it had been far too long since her engine had been this finely revved.

"Eyes on my right hand," he said, and his graveled voice rumbled through her body. His left hand crossed her body and rested on her breast, while his other hand began its descent down her stomach and stopped on her lower belly. She sucked in her breath and held it. "This is one of my favorite parts of you."

She blew out her breath in a small chuckle. "Are you kidding? Those are my battle scars. It's the area I try the hardest to hide." She could never understand how one pregnancy had managed to stretch her skin so far beyond repair.

"Call it what you want. I call it beautiful. This makes you a woman. A soft, sensual, amazing woman." His fingers grazed her skin, causing her to squirm against his thigh. His hand inched lower, and the pads of his fingers traced the lacy line of the top of her panties.

Jane's breath hitched, and she threw her head back as he began to venture inside.

"Eyes on my hand, baby. I want to see you watch me while I make you come undone."

She thought her knees would give out on her when his finger slid between her delicate folds. At this rate, there was no way she'd last more than a few strokes of his hand.

"I want you inside me," she whispered. She didn't want to embarrass herself by coming too soon.

But Ryan had other plans. "We have all night, and I plan to spend most of it buried deep inside you, but first you're going to unravel for me, here and now."

"But—" She took a deep breath. "I don't want this to end, and … well, I'm not one of those multi-orgasmic women. I'm more one and done."

His gaze pinned hers in their reflection, and a deep laugh erupted from his lips. "I intend to prove to you that you *are* one of those women. You just haven't had the right partner. Trust me, by the time the sun rises, you'll lose count."

Jane gulped, but her insecurities and inhibitions began to flutter away, along with the butterflies in her belly, as his fingers did magical things under her panties. She didn't recognize the sounds coming from her own throat, but she was pretty sure the entire hotel floor must have heard her as she surrendered to the mother of all climaxes. At least, that was what it was in Jane's book, not that her book had too many pages. All of her past noteworthy orgasms had come from the touch of her own hand, after a glass of wine or two.

As the spasms of ecstasy subsided, Ryan withdrew his hand and sent her panties floating to the floor. Then he scooped her up and lowered her gently onto the bed, giving her shaky legs a much-needed reprieve.

Jane was grateful. It took all the strength she could muster just to stay standing. If the touch of Ryan's hand had reduced her to a state where she'd nearly melted into a lusty puddle at his feet, she shivered at the thought of what the rest of his body might be able to do.

As if he could read her mind, he began to release the buttons of his own shirt, quickly revealing his trim and sculpted chest. If it were any other day in the life of Jane Keegan, she would have been mortified to have a man as perfect as Ryan staring down at her naked body. But basking in the afterglow brought on by Ryan's capable fingers, with the promise of more yet to come, she could forgive the stretch marks on her tummy and the fact that her breasts were not as perky as they once had been, and simply enjoy stolen time with the man who was quickly becoming the center of her universe.

He lifted an eyebrow as he stripped out of his white button-down shirt. "What's going through that busy mind of yours now?"

She hitched up on her elbows and brazenly allowed her gaze to travel down his chest and come to a halt at his belt. "I was thinking one of us has too many clothes on. Since I'm already naked, that must be you."

Yup. Jane the vixen is coming out to play.

He chuckled. "If I'd known an orgasm would melt your inhibitions so efficiently, I would've tried at the bar on Friday night."

"I'm pretty sure we would've been thrown out. I'm a little loud," she reminded him, and giggled.

"It would've been worth it."

She narrowed her eyes. "Now, about those pants."

"Want to help me out of them?"

It wasn't an invitation she intended to ignore. Fixing her gaze on the package she couldn't wait to unwrap, she sat up, swung her legs over the edge of the bed, and pulled him forward to stand between her knees.

Ryan relaxed his arms at his sides, clearly waiting for her to explore on her own.

Jane trailed her fingertips up the fabric of his pants to his bare waist. Then she reached higher, running her palms up his warm flesh to the planes of his chest, decorated with a smattering of hair. She drew invisible lines, circling around his nipples before she began a slow descent toward his stomach. Closing her eyes, she drew a heavy breath in through her nose, enjoying the heady scent of fire and midnight. She wasn't sure one *could* smell midnight, but she as sure as hell felt as if she did, and it was fabulous. The erotic journey of her hands made a temporary stop at his belt, toying with the buckle, but her inner vixen became bolder. Through the fabric of his slacks, she cupped his hard length against her palm.

Ryan sucked in an audible breath, and the corners of Jane's mouth turned up in a satisfied smile.

Boxers or briefs? she mused, and felt her own pulse quicken. *Boxers, I bet.*

Slowly, she unfastened his belt and drew it out of its loops, one by one, before dropping it to the carpet. Next, she unfastened the waistband of his pants, and lowered the zipper of his fly, tooth by tooth, gradually exposing a pair of silky blue boxer shorts.

I win, she thought, and knew that it was true in more ways than one.

Finding the slit in the fabric, she dipped her hand inside and wrapped the fingers of one hand around his erection, pulling him a step closer with the other. With a little squeeze that sent a shiver through him, she released him and slid her hand free so that she could run both palms up and down along his back. Sliding them lower, she slipped them beneath the waistband of his boxers.

Ryan's groan injected her with the courage to boldly continue her exploration. Her body tingled as she lowered his pants and boxers and let them fall around his ankles. Leaning close and reaching around him, two-handed, she fingered the crease between his backside and his muscular thighs. The move brought her ever so close to where his length stood proudly in front of her, and she found herself licking her lips in unexpected anticipation.

Ryan ran his fingers along her jawbone, gently tipping her face up to meet his fevered stare. "If you don't take pity on me and take me inside you in the next few minutes, I may not survive, *Querida*."

He bent and captured her lips with his, his tongue running along the seam of her mouth, coaxing it open.

Jane buried her hand in his hair and met his strokes with her own tongue.

She supposed she should be hitting the brakes. This wasn't the conservative Jane Keegan she thought she knew. But something about this magnificent man made her mind turn from reasonable thought. Even if her sensibility dared to protest, her body begged for more.

He urged her toward the middle of the bed, and she moved there willingly, but a shaky breath escaped from her as his knees nudged her legs apart. "Condoms," she gasped. "Tell me you have them."

"I wouldn't let it go this far if I didn't." He rolled to the side of the bed and pulled his pants from the floor, palmed the fabric and hastily extracted his wallet. He pinched the sliver of silver peeking from inside and tugged at the foil before dropping his wallet to the floor. Ripping open the square, he rolled the condom on his length. Her hips lifted off the bed as he caged her between his muscled arms. She pushed all lingering doubts out of her head as she wrapped her legs around his hips. If this was going to be her best worst decision, she was going down in a flaming ball of sizzling sex.

He guided his length to the entrance of her heated core, pausing to kiss her.

"Don't tease me, cowboy." She lifted her hips and bucked to welcome his thrust as he filled her need.

Together, they moved, finding their rhythm, then quickening the pace as their excitement built. Jane welcomed him deeper, desperate for his touch, his strength, his ardor as he clung to her, driving into her as if she were the answer to all his dreams. Oh, yes. It was her best worst decision indeed, she thought as she tasted the salty sheen on his shoulder. Grabbing a fistful of the bed sheet, she cried out as she fell into a dizzy abyss of passionate completion like none she'd ever experienced. A moment later, she felt his entire body lock in a shudder of pleasure as he, too, found his release.

And then there was peace, a bone-deep peace that swept over her like an ocean wave.

Dazed, she realized it had taken her almost forty years to find out earth-shattering, toe-curling sex was not an urban legend. She lay sleepy and blissfully sore, in Ryan's most capable arms. Their breathing lulled her to the edge of slumber, until he brought up the subject she'd tried so hard to ignore all evening.

He wrapped his arms around her midriff. "I hate to ask," his husky voice broke the silence, "but what time's your flight?"

Damn, he had a sexy bedside voice. "Early. Too early." She palmed the bedside table, in search of her phone, and checked the display. "My flight's in five hours."

Ryan took a deep breath and pulled her into his chest. "Right. Let's sleep for a little while. You need some rest."

****

Soft beeps from her phone woke her from the best dream she'd had in years. Jane kept her eyes closed and enjoyed the wonderful sensation of warm hands trailing down her body. She wasn't dreaming after all.

His stubbled chin tickled her shoulder as he found her ear. "Morning already."

She took a deep breath, before reaching for her phone. "I have to go."

He pulled her back. His warm breath blanketed her cheek. "Stay for a few more days, so we can explore where this is going? I want to get to know you better."

Jane opened her mouth to speak, but he slid the pad of his thumb gently over her bottom lip.

"Don't say anything now. Think about it. If you feel the same way, meet me at Vine, later. If not … well, if not, thank you for an incredible few days, *Querida*." His lips grazed her cheek before he sat up and climbed out of the bed.

She watched him dress, trying to memorize every inch of him. Then he crossed the room and, with one last glance back at her, opened the door. "I hope you decide to stay," he said and left, closing the door behind himself with soft finality.

Chapter Nine

Jane paced the lobby, glancing through the glass doors as a cab rolled to a stop. Her fingers fidgeted with the jacket Ryan had left in her room. She considered calling him to meet her in the lobby to claim his jacket, but seeing him again would make another good-bye awkward. She decided it was less messy to send it to the restaurant after she returned home.

At least that's what she told herself. In reality, she wasn't ready to part from the physical proof of her passion-filled weekend in San Antonio or the man who captured her heart.

"May I help you with your bag?" The voice interrupted her fast-forward review of the past few days. Startled, Jane nodded and followed the bellman resolutely to the cab.

The driver opened the door and waved his hand. "No traffic this morning. I'll have you to the airport in no time."

Jane slid into the cab. The stench of stale air combined with traces of cigarette smoke turned her stomach. Taking shallow breaths, she peered out the window and spotted the sun rising over the top of the Alamo, with the promise of another beautiful day in San Antonio.

Jane pressed the button on the door's armrest, but the window didn't budge. "Can you open my window, please?"

"Sorry, window controls are broken, but I'll send some A/C your way. Give it a minute to cool down," he said, and shifted the cab into gear.

Jane stared ahead through the smudged windshield, but her head began to pound as she inhaled the offensive air. "Stop!"

"Ma'am? Did you forget something?"

"Pop the trunk. I'm not going to the airport after all." She handed the cabbie a ten-dollar bill, pushed the door handle, and climbed out.

Stepping up onto the curb, she drew in a long, deep breath of fresh air.

An invisible weight slid from her shoulders. No longer did she need to suffocate, lost and alone, weighed down by the expectations of others. For the first time in Jane's life, she would do what she wanted, right or wrong.

"Says she's not going," she heard the cabbie mutter through the passenger-side window, which was now open. It figured he had lied to her about the window controls being broken. She seemed to be a magnet for deception.

Jane turned to the bellman. "Would you hold my bag for a while?"

"Of course." The bellman handed her a claim ticket. "Would you like to leave your jacket?"

She looked down at her arm and smiled as she tucked the ticket into her back pocket. "No thank you," she said and headed toward Vine. Ryan had mentioned his daily routine during the Mission tour. If she were to guess, he'd returned home from his run and was on his way to Vine. It made her smile to imagine his muscles flexing as his feet pounded the pavement, his body aglow with light sheen of sweat. Jane licked her lips, remembering how she had touched her tongue to the curve of his shoulder as they made love, savoring the faint taste of salt on his skin. Oh yes, Vixen Jane had well and truly come out of hiding, and she wasn't going away anytime soon.

The shops and restaurants lining the walkways of the River Walk were beginning to open. Shop owners were out setting up tables and watering planters overflowing with flowering greenery. The carved Vine sign came into view as she walked over the same bridge where she and Ryan had first brushed hands. Had that been his advance or hers? She wasn't sure, but the way his crystal-blue eyes had darkened with a sensual hunger was an indication that he'd felt the same jolt of heat and connection that had raced through her.

Jane slowed her pace as she approached his restaurant, noticing little details she hadn't seen before, like the flowers that dotted the manicured ivy partially covering one of the brick walls, and the way the wrought-iron light fixtures outside the front doors mimicked the shape of the candleholders on the tables. She ran the palm of her hand along the soft ivy, sensing the pride Ryan had for this place, and how he loved his restaurant and staff. She peeked in the window and spotted Ryan. His back was toward her, but she'd know his broad shoulders and shock of thick, dark hair anywhere. Jane wrapped her hand around the brass door pull when a voice sounded behind her.

"I thought *you'd* be long gone by now."

A woman's sharp voice with a hint of a Spanish accent startled Jane. She spun around, and her gaze landed on a figure she recognized, seated on a bench facing the restaurant, half-hidden behind a cactus plant.

Jane squinted in the direction of the voice. "Maya? What are you doing out here?"

Maya stood. "Waiting for Ryan. His attention is a bit taken right now." She folded her arms and nodded toward the window. "Haven't you used up all of the time on your weekend special package?" she spat, pinning Jane with a hostile glare.

"Excuse me?"

Maya pushed out a sarcastic laugh. "I know what my brother does for a living, even though he tries to hide it."

"Your brother owns and manages this successful restaurant. That's what he does for a living."

"Yeah, that and whoring himself to a bunch of lonely women looking for a good time." Maya raised her eyebrows at Jane as she walked past her, then stopped in front of the restaurant and placed her hands on her hips. "He'd never taken one of his jobs to a family event though. I guess you should consider yourself lucky. Or maybe he just ran out of things to do with you."

"I'm not sure what you think you know, but you couldn't be farther from the truth," Jane said icily, although she knew there was a thread of truth in Maya's accusation.

"Really? So you didn't come to San Antonio to get lucky over the weekend? Because that's Ryan's specialty, you know." Maya raised one manicured index finger into the air. "First, he wines and dines them on Friday, leaving them at their hotel door with a hint of what the weekend will bring." She formed a V with her middle and index finger. "The next day is a 'get to know you' activity, balloon ride, Mission tour, a stroll through the market. Something about his damn blue eyes makes them think they're special. Depending on the woman, there's a touch here, a kiss there. By that time, they're usually panting like a bitch in heat." Three deep-red fingernails flashed angrily in Jane's face. "Then, on the last day, he goes in for the kill. I hear he has some skills. Aren't you a lucky lady? I bet you paid big for the Ryan Special."

"It wasn't like that." But, except for the fact that he said he'd refund her money, it had been exactly like that. She wasn't special at all. She was just another lonely woman in his long line of conquests.

"No? Then what was it like, 'Jane'? Is that even your real name?"

"Of course it is. And I don't think your brother would appreciate the way you're talking about him."

"Don't pretend you know anything about my brother. What you had with him isn't real, and now it's over. Time to crawl back to your real life and unhook your claws from Reyo. I know what's best for him."

"I may not know Ryan like you do, but you're wrong about a number of things. And I know this—if you keep sticking your nose into his business like this, you'll lose him one day."

A shadow of worry floated over Maya's face for a split second. Then her expression hardened again. "Do him a favor and get out of his life. This career of his has only brought him pain and loneliness. He needs to find someone and have a real relationship, not one formed out of a sick fantasy."

Jane froze. Was that what their weekend had been? A fantasy? Had she been so stupid to think she could have a relationship with this man? She opened her mouth to defend her position, but the words wouldn't come. Something else had been bothering her that morning. She had checked her bank balance before checking out of the hotel and was surprised the refund hadn't been processed yet. Maya was right, and Ryan had played her for a fool.

But he said he wanted her to stay. She needed answers. Jane marched to the front door.

"What do you think you're doing?" Maya demanded.

"Ryan's in there. Let him clear this up."

"I wouldn't do that. See that woman he's chatting with?" Maya pointed to a woman sitting at the bar. Jane hadn't noticed her when she caught sight of Ryan. She had long blonde hair that she kept sweeping off her shoulders with a manicured hand. Graceful long legs hung crossed from the edge of the barstool. "She's Ryan's next date. They're going over the details now. She was so excited, she came to the restaurant to see him before even checking into her hotel."

Jane spotted the black rolling suitcase next to the stool. Her gaze moved to Ryan who sat next to the blonde. He was leaning forward and flashing his you-are-the-most-special-woman-in-the-world smile. Jane couldn't take anymore.

"Did you think you'd come down here and scoop up your little Boy Toy and cart him back to New York with you, Jane?"

Even if what Maya said was wrong, what type of future did Jane have with him anyway? He wasn't moving away from his business, and she had her job in New York. Any relationship they'd attempt would be doomed before it even began.

Jane pressed her lips together and turned toward Maya's angry face. "Please give this to your brother and tell him good-bye for me." She pushed the jacket into Maya's hands.

As she began the weary walk back to her hotel, she heard Maya mutter "Good riddance" behind her back.

Chapter Ten

Jane kept her window down after paying the airport parking fee and took a deep breath, inhaling New York's crisp early autumn air. She glanced at the t-shirt she'd bought for Tyler at the airport peeking from her purse on the passenger seat. Just what she needed, a reminder of her days in San Antonio. Not that she needed a souvenir. That weekend would remain with her forever. Regardless, she'd hoped Tyler would lose the t-shirt before returning home for the summer.

Another tear followed the wet path of the first. She wasn't sure if it was a happy or a sad tear. Maybe it was a little bit of both. Instead of wiping it away, she let it roll off her jawbone and land on her arm as she turned into the parking lot of her apartment complex.

A cherry-red sports car was idling next to the entrance to her apartment.

What the hell is Nick doing here?

Her imagination flashed to a million different scenarios as she parked and climbed out of the car.

Nick was already striding across the parking lot toward her.

"What's going on?" Jane asked and stopped in her tracks as she saw a haze of worry in his eyes.

Nick took another two steps, until he was only a few inches from her. There were new lines in his forehead and around his eyes. "There's been an accident."

"Please don't tell me something's happened to Tyler." The words came out in a whisper. But it had to be Tyler. Nick wouldn't be standing in front of her if it had been anyone else.

Her very soul seemed to rise up in protest. She could get through anything—anything except something terrible happening to her son.

"He's at the hospital," Nick said. "They're assessing him now. I just got off the phone with the doctor when you pulled up."

"What happened?" Jane asked. Her purse dropped from her shoulder and she felt her knees begin to buckle.

Nick reached around her and provided much needed support. "He was driving to the store with his roommate. Another car ran a red light and hit theirs. They know he's got some broken bones and bruised ribs. They're evaluating him for internal injuries."

"Why didn't anyone call me?"

"We tried, Jane. The hospital. Me. Your phone's off."

Damn it. She'd forgotten to power it back on after getting off the plane.

Nick picked up her purse from the ground and handed it to her without a word.

Jane fished her phone from the pocket and turned it on. She closed her eyes as the screen loaded. What a terrible mother they must think she was. She opened her eyes. Fifteen missed messages.

"I need to talk to someone." She frantically scrolled through the missed calls, trying to determine which one to return first, but her hand was shaking too badly, refusing to cooperate.

Nick took the phone from her and dropped it into his shirt pocket, then wrapped his hands around her forearms. "I know you want information. I do, too, but standing here calling the hospital so they can give you the same information I just got from them doesn't make sense when we have a three-hour drive ahead of us. Let's move your suitcase to my car, and we'll drive to the hospital together."

Say what she might about Nick, he always kept his cool, no matter how grave the situation. Jane nodded and opened the trunk of her car. Nick pulled her luggage out and extended the handle, while Jane locked her car. As they walked, the only sound was the low murmur of the suitcase wheels rolling along the blacktop. He poked his car remote and the trunk door opened.

Jane's gaze landed on Nick's suitcase.

"You could've left without me."

Nick picked up her suitcase and laid it next to his. "I knew he was in good hands at the hospital, and I worried you'd be a mess when you found out. So I waited for you."

"How'd you know when I'd be back?" she asked, settling into the passenger seat.

"I called your office." Nick put the car in motion. "They told me your travel plans, after I explained the situation." He glanced over at her. "I wished you'd tell me when you're going away, in case of emergencies like this. We may be divorced, but we still have Tyler."

Jane nodded. She'd been so focused on hating him and his new life in New York, she'd never thought to give him the heads-up that she would be away, just in case. She'd told Tyler, but that didn't do her or Nick any good in this situation. "You're right. I'm sorry."

"I'm sorry, too. About a lot of things."

Jane stared at the sea of brake lights as they pulled onto the highway. "Rush-hour traffic. We'll be lucky if we make it there by nine."

"The hospital has my number. They promised to call if there's any change in his status."

Jane took an unsteady breath. "I'm so scared, Nick. If anything happens to Ty, I don't know what I'd do." Tears stung her eyes.

Nick found her hand and gave it a squeeze. "Everything's going to be all right. I know it will. He's as strong as an ox."

Jane nodded, picturing her almost-larger-than-life son. Tyler was big from the minute he was born. She remembered the nurses joking with her about her baby boy barely fitting in the hospital's newborn bassinets. "We're going to need a crib for this kid if you don't take him home soon," they'd teased when they wheeled him into her room.

Ty had always looked years older than his actual age. Strangers used to shoot her dirty looks when he acted up at restaurants. "He's only three," she'd wanted to say.

When he hit high school, coaches clamored to have him on their teams. Jane pushed out a shaky laugh. "I always worried about him getting hurt during football." Tyler had been offered several partial athletic scholarships, but it had been his choice to stick to academics. "I was so relieved when football was over and he got though it without a concussion. I figured my days of worrying about injuries were over." Jane sucked in a breath. "He doesn't have a concussion, does he? I should call and make sure they check him." She knew she was rambling.

"The car he was in had side airbags. They were hit on Tyler's side, but the airbags did a good job of protecting his head." He pulled her phone out of his pocket and held it out to her. "But you can give them a call, if it will make you feel better."

Nick's smile comforted her as she scrolled through her missed calls and found the hospital's number. After sitting on hold for a good twenty minutes, Jane heard little beyond the same information Nick had already told her: Tyler was resting comfortably but was still being evaluated for internal injuries.

"They said he didn't show signs of a concussion," Jane said after she broke the connection.

Nick nodded. "Looks like traffic is opening up a little. We'll make better time now."

Miles passed filled with switching radio stations, comments about the weather and long silences. After one particularly lengthy break in conversation, Nick said quietly, "It's not too late for us, you know."

Startled, Jane turned to study his face. "What? Where the hell did that come from?"

"I've been giving it a lot of thought, Jane."

She huffed out a laugh. "You're serious?"

"Of course I'm serious. Look, I know you can't forgive me for what I did, but is living separate lives better than being together? Don't just think of the present. What about the future? Tyler will eventually have his own family. Do you really want to be alone?"

Jane narrowed her eyes. "I'm not afraid of being on my own, and I don't think that's a valid reason to get back together." She paused. "Besides, what makes you think I'll be alone?"

"Oh, come on. You haven't dated in decades. The bar scene's not your thing, and I hardly see you as the type to resort to online dating. It's not so easy to meet people at our age, you know."

"Really?" Jane folded her arms. "Well, thanks for the advice, but I don't need it. I'm doing just fine in that category."

"What's that supposed to mean?"

"It simply means I've still got it, buddy. Thanks to your indiscretion, I was feeling pretty crappy about myself, but I've met someone who doesn't make me feel that way." The statement wasn't entirely true, but at least, for a little while, Ryan had made her feel wanted and desirable.

Nick looked shocked. "You met someone?"

"I did."

"You're lying. What's his name?"

"Believe what you want. His name is Ryan. He's handsome, fit—" Jane's gaze flicked down to where Nick's belly extended over the seatbelt. She could've sworn he sucked it in for a moment. "And he's in his early thirties." She'd only then realized she'd never asked him his age.

Nick turned his head and stared at her for a moment, seemingly assessing if she was telling the truth. "There are a lot of leeches out there. Seriously, you have to be careful. I've heard about men who scam older women and take everything they have."

Jane laughed. "You just can't believe someone wants me for myself, can you? For your information, Ryan owns a very successful restaurant. He hardly needs or wants my money—not that there's much of it anyway."

Instead of rising to her anger, Nick sighed. "Hey, I'm sorry. I just didn't expect you to move on so fast."

Jane turned and met his gaze. She raised her eyebrows, and he turned his attention back to the road. "Shit," he muttered.

"You gave up the right to know anything about my love life the second you cheated on me, Nick."

"You know I'm sorry about that. It was the worst mistake I've ever made. If I could take it back, I would. People do make mistakes. I'm not asking for your forgiveness because I don't think I'd ever get it. What I'm asking is for you to consider getting back together. I still love you. I've never stopped."

She had often wondered if she should forgive Nick, until the day when she'd finally realized forgiveness wasn't an option. He was right. She doubted she'd ever forgive him for betraying her trust. "Yes, people do make mistakes. Unfortunately, I can't see past yours."

"Don't hate me for what I'm about to say."

Jane braced herself. "Do I even want to hear it?"

"Probably not, but here it goes anyway. The way I see it, we're even, now. We've both had our flings, but now we can choose to go back to being the team we once were. Think about it, Jane. We're in the prime of our lives. We have no money issues. We can do what we want. Go on vacations, eat at great restaurants, buy anything we want. You have to admit, it's a pretty attractive option. Plus, it'd make Tyler happy."

Jane thought about his words for a moment. "You don't get it, do you? We're not even. Not at all. You committed adultery. I didn't. You had your fling while we were married. That's very different from me dating someone, now that our divorce is final. And how low can you go by bringing Tyler into this argument? Besides, what makes you think mine is just a fling?"

"I'm stopping for gas. I used most of mine idling in your parking lot, waiting for you to get home." That was Nick-speak for *I'm not winning this debate so I'm changing the subject and will try to make you feel bad about it*. He took the next exit and pulled into the nearest gas station.

Jane rubbed her temples when he was out of view. Why did she let him get under her skin? Like it or not, she knew Nick's ways almost as well as she knew her own. She shouldn't let him get to her.

Minutes passed, and Jane tried not to fidget, begrudging this albeit necessary delay. When she heard the gas cap screw into place, she took a deep, relieved breath, and braced herself for Round Two.

But Nick, sliding back into the driver's seat, only said, "All set. We have another hour or so to go. Why don't you try to close your eyes until we get there?"

Jane turned away from him and gazed out the window, but instead of sleeping, she found herself thinking about what her life would be like if she reconciled with Nick. Sure, they'd be free of money issues. She made a good income, and Nick made a great one. They'd live in New York and would probably eventually buy a condo in Florida or somewhere else warm. She'd treat herself to days at the spa, go shopping on Fifth Avenue, and have lunch with friends. But would she ever truly trust him again? Could she ever relax into the luxury of knowing that she was his only interest?

No. She knew she'd never look at him and see the same man she'd married. And the prospect seemed intolerable.

But then new questions wormed their way into her brain. How many longtime married women still actually trusted their husbands? How many turned a willingly blind eye to their mate's indiscretions, in exchange for financial stability? How many traded away their sense of self-worth for the sake of the creature comforts of a secure home and the public façade of a long-term marriage?

She had tried to sweep it under an ugly rug of lies and deception, but it never went away. In the end, the price had been too high, the sacrifice too dear. Lonely but resolute, she had turned away from the hollow shell of her empty marriage.

And then she had met Ryan.

As bitter as it had been to stand and listen while Maya stripped away the lovely illusion of what her weekend in San Antonio had really meant to him, Jane found that she couldn't wholly regret her experience there. Even though her time with Ryan had turned out to be a wonderful fantasy that came to life, he'd helped open her eyes to a fresh sense of who she was and who she might yet become.

Oh, Ryan...

Her heart ached, and she could beat herself at having been such a naïve and self-deluding fool. But she and Ryan had still shared moments of kindness, and of pleasure, and of passion.

However high the cost to her pride, those were the memories she would continue to treasure.

Chapter Eleven

Jane woke with a jolt. Straightening in her seat, she blinked the sleep from her eyes.

The lights of an imposing EMERGENCY sign glared back at her, reminding Jane abruptly of the reason she was at a local hospital in the sticks of Pennsylvania.

She assessed the exterior of the sad building, but it was devoid of anything uplifting. Her heart began to beat hard and fast in her chest as her mother-bear instincts took hold. Her baby was hurt and alone in a place that didn't even care enough to plant some early fall flowers in its chipped cement planters. But she was here, now, and she would protect him.

"We're getting Tyler transferred to a bigger hospital. Maybe in Philly, or one of the New York hospitals," Jane said as she unfastened her seatbelt, pushed the car door open, and stood. Every joint hurt. She hadn't realized how stiff she had become, folded into Nick's answer to his midlife crisis.

"Let's not get ahead of ourselves. They seemed pretty competent on the phone," Nick answered as they headed toward the sliding glass doors.

Inside, a pleasant-looking woman manned the front desk. She smiled at them. "How can I help you?"

"We're Tyler Keegan's parents. He was in a car accident."

The woman checked the computer monitor. "He's in Room Ten. One moment and I'll get someone to take you back."

After a few minutes a woman in scrubs approached and led Jane and Nick through a heavy door and down a short hallway. "Tyler? Your parents are here."

Jane took a look at her son and breathed deep, steadying herself. His face, bruised and swollen, looked like it had been stitched under his eye, and his arm was in a sling. The last thing she wanted to do was scare him by having a horrified look on her own face, so she plastered on her best smile. "Tyler."

"Mom." His voice was muffled through his fat lip. "I'm sorry."

"It wasn't your fault, sweetheart."

"I know how worried you get."

"Are you in pain?" she asked. If she could, she'd absorb every bit of his discomfort.

"Nah. I'm okay. If you think I look bad, you should see the other guy."

Jane laughed. It was their inside joke. Whenever Tyler had come home with bruises from football, he'd said the same thing. Bless his heart, he always knew how to take the edge off of her worry, even the time he'd broken his ribs... *His ribs!*

"Did you tell them you broke your ribs a couple years ago?"

Tyler grunted and nodded his head. "I think I re-broke them."

Jane's gaze moved to the bandages on his chest, as Nick moved to the other side of the bed. "Hey, champ."

"Hi, Dad."

Nick reached down and squeezed Tyler's uninjured hand.

"Do you know how Mark is?" Tyler asked. "They told me he was okay. He was able to get out of the car after the crash. He was still trying to get me out when the police came."

"We haven't heard, yet. Dad and I are going to talk to the doctor so we can find out what's going on. But we'll be back, okay?"

Tyler nodded. "I'm a little tired."

"Close your eyes and rest, sweetheart." Jane pressed a careful kiss to his forehead, and followed Nick from the room.

"He's going to be okay," Nick said.

"I know he is. Thank God." Tyler looked broken and bruised, but she knew the minute he'd started talking that he would be okay.

Jane walked with Nick to the nurses' station, where a set of parents stood next to a boy in a wheelchair. Jane recognized the boy from when she'd moved Tyler into his dorm. "Mark?"

"Mr. and Mrs. K! I'm sorry. The guy came out of nowhere and hit us. There was nothing I could do," Mark explained. "How's Ty?"

"Some broken bones, but he's going to be just fine. How are you?"

"I'm okay. Tyler got the worst of it. The guy hit us on his side. Good thing he's such a monster," Mark said, and chuckled. Jane compared Mark's slight frame with her son's, and figured Mark probably wouldn't have been as lucky as Tyler if he'd been in the passenger seat.

Jane turned her attention to Mark's mother and father. "I'm Jane, and this is Nick. We're Tyler's parents."

"These kids certainly know how to give us gray hair. It's nice to meet you. We're glad Tyler's going to be okay. Please let us know if there's anything we can do," Mark's mother said. She had dark circles under her eyes. Jane supposed she was sporting her own baggage, too.

Jane turned to face what looked like a fresh-faced kid in a white coat.

"I'm Dr. Peters, the attending ER doctor. I've been with Tyler since they brought him in. He's a lucky guy. And you two look like you could use a cup of coffee. If you'll come with me, I'll fill you in." Dr. Peters lead them to a small waiting room attached to the ER, where he carefully explained Tyler's injuries. "He's stable, now. We'll move him to a room upstairs in the morning and monitor him over the next day or two. If all checks out he can go home soon."

"Thank you," Nick said. "We'll check into a hotel and come back in the morning. I think we could both use some sleep."

Jane finally allowed the fear she kept lodged in her shoulder blades to begin to melt away. Relief left her feeling spent and empty. She dropped her paper coffee cup into the trash and rubbed her eyes. She'd have preferred to curl up on one of the uncomfortable chairs and spend the night at the hospital with Tyler, but she knew she'd need to be alert and focused in the morning. Besides, she didn't have the energy to argue with Nick tonight, about the hotel or anything else. Tyler was going to be fine. It was all that really mattered.

They said good night to Tyler and drove in silence to the same hotel they'd stayed in when they visited during their college search. Back when Tyler's school choice was the most important thing on her mind. Back when she was oblivious to her husband's infidelity. Had she been too focused on other things, treating Nick and her marriage as an afterthought? Was that why he'd strayed?

Jane's exhausted body begged her to keep her mouth zipped. A hot shower and a comfortable bed were all it could handle, at the moment. But her pride reared its fierce head.

"What made you do it?" she asked, breaking the silence.

"Hmm? Do what?" Nick asked, shifting his car into Park.

"What made you have an affair?"

Nick's eyes widened. "You want to talk about this now?" He turned the engine off and pulled his key out of the ignition.

"No, I don't want to 'talk about' it. I just want a simple answer."

"There is no simple answer."

She felt her temper stir. "Give me something. The first thing that comes to your mind."

"I don't know. The excitement, I guess."

Jane nodded. After almost twenty years of marriage, "exciting" wasn't in the top ten qualities she'd have used to describe their relationship. Wasn't that true of most people, unless they were one of those couples that did crazy stunts like base diving together? "Fair enough."

"I said it before, and I'll say it again. I'll never stop caring about you."

She opened her car door. "Flip the trunk of your midlife crisis, please."

A hearty chuckle escaped from Nick, a sound she'd missed over the past few months. He pulled their suitcases out of the trunk and stacked hers on top of his. Then the two of them shuffled into the lobby and stepped to the front desk. "We need a room for two nights," Nick told the young woman behind the desk.

"Two. We need two rooms, please," Jane said.

The desk attendant's gaze bounced from Jane to Nick.

"Are you sure you want to be alone?" Nick asked.

"Quite sure."

"Jane—"

She turned to him, and her eyes burned with anger.

He nodded and flipped his credit card on the counter. "We'll take two adjacent rooms, if you have them. Both can go on this card."

The woman slid two sets of room access cards across the counter. "Take the elevators on the right to the third floor. You'll find your rooms on the left. Complimentary breakfast starts at seven. Enjoy your stay."

Jane followed Nick into the elevator, then stole a glance at him from the opposite side. He looked tired, with his hair slightly mussed and his clothes rumpled. She was sure she looked even worse. "Thanks for picking up my room."

"Not a problem," he muttered.

"And thank you for waiting for me, today. You're right. I would've been a mess, driving out here on my own."

"That wasn't an option, as far as I was concerned." The elevator doors opened, and Nick dragged their suitcases down the hall. He left Jane's luggage in front of her door and moved to the next room. "Good night, Jane," he said, and closed the door without waiting for her response.

****

"What a difference a good night's sleep makes," Jane said, dropping her purse on the chair next to Nick's in the hotel lobby. "I called the hospital earlier, and the nurse said Ty's on his second breakfast." She didn't mention that she'd called the ER before she went to sleep.

"I spoke to them, too. Maybe we should coordinate before calling, so we don't waste their time relaying Tyler's status twice," Nick said from behind the newspaper he held close to his face.

Mister "I'm Feeling Young in My Red Sports Car" must've forgotten his reading glasses, Jane reflected wryly, then said, "I don't think it'll be an issue, since he'll have a room today. We'll be able to call him directly. I'm just going to grab a cup of coffee to go, and we can head over."

Nick was quiet in the car on the way to the hospital, but his funk seemed to lift once they found out that Tyler had already been moved to a room and his condition downgraded. Nick and Jane got to his room as the doctor was making his rounds. He'd examined Tyler and seemed pleasantly surprised by how well he was coming along.

"When can I get out of here, Doc?" Tyler asked.

"I'll come back tomorrow morning. If all is well you can probably leave tomorrow with restrictions. You'll have to take it easy while those ribs heal. You're a very lucky man. Don't press your luck and try to do too much or you'll end up back here."

"Got it. But is there anything you can do about the food in this joint?"

As if on cue, Tyler's roommate, Mark, walked in with bags of what smelled like greasy burgers and fries.

"Dude!" Ty exclaimed, brightening. "You brought me Curly's?"

"Since we never made it there yesterday, I figured I owed you."

Jane stood from one of the two chairs in the room. "You have lunch with Ty and Nick and I will check out the hospital cafeteria."

It was a choice they soon regretted. In the end, they each filled Styrofoam containers with greens from the salad bar and found a table.

"So," Jane said as she speared a cherry tomato with her fork, "what are we going to do about Tyler?"

Nick looked up at her blankly. "Do? What's to do?"

"He may want to come home for a while to heal. Maybe we should talk to the school about freezing his status and letting him take the rest of the semester off."

"Don't you think you're getting ahead of yourself?"

"I have to think ahead, Nick. I'm a single parent now. It's not like he has the option of staying at your one-bedroom bachelor pad."

Nick shoved his salad away and shifting closer to her. "It doesn't have to be this way," he said, resting his elbows on the table. "You've made your point. Now, let's stop this charade and get back together. Things would be much easier."

She stared at him in disbelief. "'Convenience' is not a reason to get back together."

Nick shrugged. "Realistically, it is. Chances are pretty slim that you or I will find someone else, especially…" Nick's voice trailed off, and his gaze moved from her to his hands.

Jane stiffened. "Especially … what? Especially *me*?"

"I didn't say that."

"No. But you were about to." Counting to ten did no good at all. Jane pushed back her chair and stood up. "I'm going to the ladies' room. I need to cool down, before I take action on a sudden desire to pour my soda over your head."

Turning on her heel, she stormed away, pushing the bathroom door open hard enough to make it bang against the wall.

Mercifully, the stalls were all empty. Jane clasped both sides of the sink and stared at her reflection. Dark circles still decorated the thin skin under her eyes. She sighed. Maybe a dab of concealer would make her look slightly more human.

Jane felt for her purse, which usually sat on her hip when she crossed it over her chest, and realized she'd forgotten it at the table, in her haste to remove herself from Nick's venom.

It was the final straw. As hard as she tried to resist them, hot tears stung her eyes. She fled into the farthest bathroom stall and locked its door, shutting herself away from prying eyes as the weight of the past day and a half caved in upon her, forcing sob after sob from her aching chest.

Chapter Twelve

Ryan strolled the same path each morning to Vine, but his steps weren't as light as they'd been a few days ago. Reality had set in. Jane had gone and not taken him up on his offer to try to make things work between them.

A long-distance relationship would have been possible, if they'd both been willing. He'd been very willing, but she obviously wasn't, or she would have met him at the restaurant instead of taking yesterday's flight.

For one magical second, Ryan's breath caught in his chest as he approached Vine and saw a set of women's legs extending from the bench outside. Unfortunately, the legs belonged to his sister, Maya.

Stung by disappointment, he made no secret of the anger that still churned in his belly over the way she'd treated Jane at the party. "What do you want?"

His sister looked startled. "Still mad, are we? I'm sorry, Reyo. I was just surprised you brought a date to the party. You always come alone. Besides, Tilly was so excited to see you," Maya confided with a wink.

"Tilly needs to find someone a little closer to her own age," he said as he slipped the key into the lock and opened the door.

"I could say the same thing about you. How old is what's-her-name, anyway? She must be pushing forty-five."

"Her name is Jane, and she's nowhere close to forty-five. And even if she were, who cares? I don't, so why should you," Ryan bit out and shook his head. "Why do you have to be such a bitch, Maya?"

"I'm only looking out for your best interests. You're a good-looking, successful business owner and a hot commodity." She laughed. "My girlfriends drool over you. All women do. Can't you see that? You should be out partying every night with young beautiful girls, not entertaining aging businesswomen who come to town looking for a good time."

Ryan glared at his sister. He wasn't in the mood to battle with her. "What are you doing here anyway?"

"We have to talk about Tio's seventy-fifth birthday. I tried stopping by yesterday morning, but you were busy with some blonde. You do move on quickly, little brother. At least that one seemed closer to your age. Anyway, I think we should have his party here—"

Ryan shook his head in confusion. "Hold on. I don't know what you're talking about. What blonde?"

"The one with the suitcase. She was sitting right there at the bar." Maya pointed toward the window.

"That was Gretchen's sister. She just got into town and was waiting here for Gretch. You really like to jump to conclusions. What do you think, I'm some sort of man-whore?"

Maya raised her eyebrows, and Ryan was about to give her a piece of his mind when his gaze rested on the bag she'd set on the floor. He bent and pulled the jacket from the bag. The last time he'd seen it, he'd draped over Jane's shoulders at the hotel. His mind raced. "How'd you get my jacket? Wait. Was Jane here, yesterday?"

Maya's gaze wandered around the bar, and Ryan could almost see her mind at work, cooking something up. After a few seconds, she blew out a breath. "Yes, she dropped by to see you, yesterday, but, like I said, you looked like you were busy. She and I had a little talk, and then she left for the airport."

"What'd she say? Or maybe the better question is what did *you* say to *her*?"

"Look, Reyo, it's time we stop pretending. I know you're one of those male escorts and she was your client.

I think she was getting pretty attached to you, so I explained the deal to her."

Ryan narrowed his eyes. "What makes you think I'm an escort?"

"A friend of a friend told me, a while ago. They were set up with you through a service. She recognized the last name and asked me if we were related. Damn it. You couldn't at least have used a different last name?"

"First of all, I *was* an escort. 'Was' as in past tense. I did it for a while, to raise cash to buy the restaurant, and, well, for other things." He was so close to informing Maya how much she'd benefited from his work. "Second, Jane was not an escort client."

"Really? She certainly didn't seem surprised when I started talking about it. She tried to be all self-righteous, telling me she wasn't the type to do that and I needed to stay out of your business, but then she just got real quiet, like it all made sense. And then she left."

Ryan paced the floor. So much pent-up anger flowed through him that he wanted to punch something. "She was right. You need to stay out of my business. Get out, Maya," he said coldly, and glared at his sister.

She looked unfazed. "I'm sorry, but it was for the best. She's not in your league. Now Tilly, for example—"

"Out! Get out of my restaurant." Ryan had never laid a hand on a woman out of anger, but at that moment he wanted to grab her arm and push her out the door.

Fortunately, Maya seemed to realize that he was serious. She shuffled to the door like a scolded puppy, then turned at the threshold. "I suppose this isn't the right time to talk about the party."

If Ryan had been capable of shooting daggers from his eyes, his sister would be pinned to the wall. Without another word, he strode to his office, slammed the door and locked it to be sure he wouldn't have to see her face again anytime soon.

His thoughts moved to Jane. More than twenty-four hours had passed since she left, and he could only imagine what she was thinking. He wasn't entirely sure what Maya had said to her, but he knew it wasn't good. Maya could be downright vicious.

Ryan pulled out his phone and scrolled through his contacts. He'd saved Jane's number, even though he'd told her he wouldn't. After making his feelings clear, he had left the decision of whether she wanted to continue seeing him up to her.

He ran his fingers through his hair. Why hadn't Jane walked in and confronted him instead of believing Maya's lies? Damn, he needed to know what was going on in that beautiful head of hers.

He tapped her number, and the phone began to ring. And ring. And ring. He supposed he should hang up, but the thought of hearing her voice, if only on her voice mail recording, made him stay on the line.

"Hello?" a man's voice answered.

Ryan checked the screen to confirm he had the right number. "Hello. May I speak to Jane, please?"

"Jane's not available. May I ask who's calling?" the voice asked. Was it his imagination, or was it tinged with a slight edge?

"This is Ryan Zeigler. Do you know when Jane will be available?"

A long pause followed. "Listen, Ryan. I know who you are, and you need to leave my wife alone. Our son was in a car accident, and she's dealing with a lot, right now."

"Your wife?"

"That's right."

Jane was still married? He rubbed his palm over his face. "I'm sorry to hear about your son."

"Our hands are full. It would be best if you didn't contact her again."

"I'd like to hear that from Jane."

"Look, I'm her husband. I think I know what's best for her. Don't call her again."

Click.

She was still married? He dropped the phone on his desk. Why hadn't he seen this coming? Jane saw him as a male escort, a man whose sole purpose was to help her escape from her everyday life, nothing more.

She didn't want him. She never had.

She'd only wanted the fantasy. Just like Camille. Just like all the others.

Chapter Thirteen

Jane found Tyler sitting up in bed, finishing his breakfast. She moved to the side of his bed and kissed the top of his head. "Looks like you're getting used to hospital food."

Tyler laughed. "It's so bad, I'm actually looking forward to eating at the school cafeteria again."

It was the first time here that she'd heard him laugh without a pained expression. "Feeling better?"

"Much better. Doc said I can get out of here today."

"Yeah, we should talk about that." She sat on the edge of the bed. "I think you should take the rest of the semester off and come home with me to recover. You can go back in the spring."

Tyler pushed his tray away. "What would I do at your apartment? I don't know anyone there. I want to stay at school. My friends will help me. Mark even stopped at Student Life and told them about my accident. They said they can make some accommodations for me while I heal, like letting me do some of my work online until I'm okay to walk around campus for the whole day."

It wasn't what Jane wanted to hear, but she had to admit what he said made sense and she was pleasantly surprised he had taken the initiative to figure it all out. "Sounds like you've given it some thought."

Tyler nodded. "When you guys sold the house and moved into your own apartments, I felt a little lost. But I like it here. It's where I belong right now."

A twinge of guilt slithered up her spine as Nick walked into the room. "They're discharging him later today. The nurse gave me a couple prescriptions for Tyler."

Jane squeezed Tyler's hand and stood. "Let's get them filled and pick up a few things before he's released." With a wave to her son, she led the way to the parking lot.

Over the course of the past couple of days, Jane had seen to it that most of her conversations with Nick occurred in public places. Now, she chose the privacy of the car to unload the emotions boiling up within her.

"Tyler wants to stay at school, and I'm perfectly fine with that, but let me make one thing clear. Under no circumstances will you and I be getting back together. Last night, you tried to tell me we'd be better off together than apart, and I disagree. I'm better off without you. You chose someone else over me. Well, guess what? Now I'm doing the same thing, but that 'someone else' I'm choosing is *me*. I'm doing fine on my own. Whether I choose to share my life with someone else in the future or not will be my decision." She took a steadying breath. "You and I have known each other a long time, and we created a wonderful son together. We'll always have that bond in common, but you need to understand the husband-and-wife part of our relationship is over. I won't be changing my mind, and I won't be taking you back." She let the final words tumble from her lips, and braced herself for his rebuttal.

"You're wrong," Nick said quietly. "I miss you. I'm lonely without you, and I think you're lonely, too."

Jane looked out the window. She knew about loneliness. She'd suffered her own case of it, more times than she could count. "That may be true, but it's not a valid reason to get back together. We both deserve more than that." She turned to Nick. She stopped herself from touching his arm.

"I'll never give up hope that you'll come back to me, you know," Nick said.

Hearing that, the old Jane would have had second thoughts, wondering if she was making a mistake by not going back to Nick. But the new Jane knew she'd be just fine without him. She slipped her phone from her purse and checked for messages. None. What did she expect? Ryan had moved on. Not only had he moved on, from the looks of her bank account on her smart phone app, he'd also kept the fee he'd said would be refunded. Jane dropped her phone back into her bag and shook her head. How had she been so stupid? Fortunately, she had a boatload of work to dive into, over the next few weeks. She knew that she would need all the strength she could muster when work returned her to San Antonio, the city that had both energized and destroyed her.

Chapter Fourteen

The plane's wheels touched down waking Jane from her Chardonnay induced nap. In an attempt to keep her time in San Antonio to a minimum, she'd taken a late flight, which gave her just enough time for a restful night's sleep before her meeting the next day. She'd hoped the pain would've eased after six weeks, but the tightening of her throat signaled something different. She was back, and the sting of Ryan's deceit and rejection were just as raw as the day she left.

Her pity party would have to wait. Jane pulled her carryon from the overhead compartment and followed the passengers to the gangway as she mentally reviewed her presentation. Jane was in town to help pitch the plan for a nationwide advertising campaign to her client's Board of Directors. There was a lot riding on her trip. The Board's consent would not only open the door to a multi-million-dollar marketing budget for her client, but her boss also promised Jane a substantial bonus for her work.

The familiar lights of San Antonio illuminated the inside of the cab as it pulled up to the entrance to the Omni Hotel. She tried not to think about the last time she'd checked into the hotel when she was filled with the excitement and anticipation of meeting her cowboy. As she stepped to the registration desk, the only thing she felt was hunger, and her stomach grumbled a reminder she hadn't eaten since noon.

"Welcome to the Omni. Are you checking in?" the woman behind the desk asked. A nameplate marked "Candy" hung from her blouse.

Jane nodded and handed Candy her driver's license and credit card. "Is the restaurant still open?" Jane asked.

"Sorry. I'm afraid it closed at ten, but the lounge is still serving from the bar menu until midnight," Candy said handing Jane her room key.

"The lounge."

"Yes, it's right up the escalator to the second floor." Candy's too-sweet smile became brighter as Jane's mood turned darker.

"I know where it is. Thanks," Jane muttered. It was the last place she'd like to be. Maybe she could wait to eat until morning. On cue, her stomach protested with a loud rumble. Well, the lounge *was* on the way to her room on the second floor. Her hunger, combined with velvety piano music, beckoned her toward the lounge as she pulled her carryon onto the escalator. Avoiding the spot at the bar where she'd rendezvoused with Ryan, she chose a seat at a small table near the piano and ordered a glass of Chardonnay and a Caesar salad. As her eyes adjusted to the dim lights, she scanned the lounge and spotted a head of dark hair. Her gaze wandered to broad shoulders wrapped tightly in a black t-shirt. Could it be him? A flutter danced in her empty stomach, and her heart pounded in her ears.

"Your Chardonnay, Miss. Your salad will be out in a moment. Will this be on your room?" the waitress asked.

"Um. Yes, please. Room two-ninety-four." Jane turned her attention back in the direction of the dark haired man and found only an empty chair. She blinked back tears and took a few gulps from her wine glass. It was going to be harder than she'd thought.

****

Her fingers raked through dark hair as his warm breath caressed the curve of her neck. Her body melted into his, and she whimpered when he entered her, inch by inch, with a soft groan. A swell of wet heat flooded her core as his muscles flexed under her fingertips, and she traced the dips and planes of his back. Wrapping her legs around his backside, she invited him deeper, filling her completely. His tongue parted her lips, and she tasted a hint of spice and wine as she met every stroke from his mouth. Rocking her faster, he carried her deeper into the wave of pleasure taking over her body. His forehead touched hers. She yearned to watch him as he brought her to the brink of spiraling out of control.

"Ryan?"

She opened her eyes expecting to see crystal blue eyes gazing back. Instead, the air left her lungs as she woke with a gasp. Her legs were tangled in bed sheets and strands of hair stuck to her damp cheeks. She sat up and scanned her surroundings, illuminated by the slice of sunlight peeking through the drawn drapes framing the single window of her hotel room. She propped the pillows against the headboard, pulled the sheets up and placed her palm over her chest. Her quickened pulse beat against her hand as she tried to hold on to the feeling Ryan evoked, even if it was just through an exquisite dream.

"Get it together," she mumbled before throwing her legs over the edge of the bed and trudging to the bathroom to run a very cold shower.

****

Her presentation was flawless. As she flipped through the advertising designs on the screen, Jane cited test market results and demographic data for her client's target audience. She was excused from the room after her part, and the executives and Board members met in a private session. Jane paced the conference room floor waiting for the boardroom door to open. She glanced out the window to the busy River Walk below. Colorful gondolas filled with tourists floated down the river, and a small boat caught her eye. Jane moved closer to the window, and a grin played at her lips. She'd know the man standing proudly on his boat anywhere. He appeared to be serenading the young couple in the gondola. Jane's mind flashed to the magical night she'd met Ryan and their gondola ride to Marriage Island. She could almost hear Pascal's song over the murmur of gurgling water against his oar as he rowed. Jane touched her fingertips to the window. "Take care, Tio," she whispered. It wasn't until that moment that Jane realized she not only missed Ryan, she missed the total package.

She turned as the conference room door flew open. "The Board approved it. We got the funding!" James said as he stood in the doorway.

"Yes! That's great news!"

"We have a lot of work ahead of us, but today we're celebrating. I've given everyone the rest of the day off, and we're heading downstairs to Rio Iguana for margaritas. Are you up for it?"

Jane grabbed her purse. "Lead the way."

They took the elevator to the River Walk level and walked a few feet to the brightly painted bar with fake cactuses welcoming patrons to the entrance. Sounds of loud music, laughter, and cheers directed at the soccer game on the television screen filled Jane's ears. Many of her client's office staff were already present and in celebration mode. Jane found an open seat at the bar next to James's administrative assistant, Donna.

"What'll it be?" the bartender asked.

She pointed to Donna's fruity concoction. "I'll have what she's having."

"Make that two," James said before turning to Jane. "I can't thank you enough. We couldn't have done it without you, Jane. The Board was impressed with your designs and market expertise. In fact, one of them said we should hire you before you're snatched up by someone else." Two icy drinks complete with pineapple chunks skewered to paper umbrellas appeared. James picked up a glass in each hand and gave one to Jane. "To bright futures for all of us."

"Cheers," she said, and the three glasses met with a clink.

James turned to Donna. "Let's set Jane up with a dedicated workstation. She'll be spending a lot of time here over the next few months while we get ready for the launch."

Jane nodded with a tight grin. As happy as she was about the deal, the thought of making regular trips to the city that had caused her much pain and embarrassment was daunting to say the least. She didn't know how much more of San Antonio she could take.

"James! Over here!" A voice called from the other end of the bar.

"Excuse me a moment," he said.

Jane turned her attention to Donna, when a familiar face caught her eye. Through the crowd she spotted his profile. Ryan was seated at a high-top table no more than twenty feet from her. Luckily, a crowd entered the bar and stood in twos and threes in back of the barstools hiding Jane from Ryan's view. Her gaze caught his rolled shirtsleeve and exposed muscular forearm prompting her mind to race to the sultry dream she'd had the night before. She couldn't stop her eyes from trailing to the dimple that decorated his stubbled cheek. She watched the corner of his eye crinkle as he smiled and wondered who was the receiver of his crooked grin. She tilted her head to get a better look but a waitress serving him a series of shot glasses blocked her view. When the waitress finally stepped away, Jane understood why Ryan was so happy. He appeared ready for a fun night of shots with a petite blonde in a low cut blouse.

"Something wrong?" Donna asked following Jane's gaze.

"I think I need some air." Jane slipped off her chair and snaked through the crowd to the door. She sucked in a deep breath when she stepped outside. Any lingering doubts she had about Ryan were put to rest. She hated to admit Maya had been absolutely right about Ryan. Jane took off as fast as her high heels would allow.

****

"This place is poppin'! See, if you carry my line of flavored tequila, your bar could be poppin' too," said Dylan McGuire, one of Vine's liquor reps.

Ryan chuckled. "I don't think Vine needs to be popping."

"Sure it does. Look at all these people spending their hard earned cash one ounce at a time." She picked up one of the many shot glasses on the table. "Try this one. It's coconut flavored."

He downed the shot and grimaced. It tasted more like suntan lotion than anything else. He placed the glass on the table. "Look, Dylan. I understand what you're trying to do bringing me here, but I'm still not interested in making Vine into a cheap shot spot. There are enough of these types of places here." He shook his head as the remnants of coconut-flavored tequila burned his throat. He pointed to the bar. "I'm gonna grab a glass of water. Want one?"

Dylan shrugged. "Sure."

Ryan inched his way to the packed bar when he picked up a distinct scent of citrus. He stopped and inhaled again. It was the unique scent of Jane's perfume.

It couldn't be, he thought. But he remembered she had a client in town. Was she back? Ryan scanned the bar

119

and caught a glimpse of a woman with her same golden highlights heading toward the door.

"Excuse me," he said, pushing through the crowd. He reached the walkway and circled the area once.

Twice.

She was gone.

Chapter Fifteen

Thanks to modern technology, Jane managed to keep her trips to San Antonio at a minimum while working on her client's national advertising campaign. However, James insisted she attended the kick-off party. She followed the directions to the event on her phone and found herself in a familiar stretch of the River Walk. Jane stopped in her tracks when she spotted Vine's ivy covered façade.

"Miss Jane! Miss Jane!"

Jane recognized the excited voice, as well as many of the faces of the people laughing, eating and drinking on Vine's patio. She tried to make a clean getaway by crossing the bridge to the other side of the river, where she'd hoped she wouldn't be seen. But the effort had proved futile. Of all the places on the River Walk to have a party, why did it have to be a few doors down from Ryan's restaurant? A minute before, Jane had thought nothing could be more awkward, but then the little voice called out to her and proved her wrong. Jane tried to ignore it, quickening her walk. She was already a few feet beyond the restaurant, almost out of the woods. Almost.

"Miss Jane?" The high, piping voice was coming from behind her now.

Jane hesitated, then stopped, closing her eyes as she prayed for strength to turn around. She could picture the smile on the face of the little girl running toward her.

Then small hands tugged at her skirt. "Miss Jane! I knew it was you! Do you remember me?"

Jane opened her eyes and returned the child's smile. "Of course I remember you. How could I forget a sweet girl like you? How are you, Isabel?"

"I got an A on my science project. Uncle Ryan helped me. I asked him where you were, but he said you had to go home." Isabel gnawed her bottom lip. "I missed you."

Jane tucked in a strand of hair that had come free from the girl's ponytail. "I've missed you, too. It looks like quite a party. Are you having fun?"

Isabel's head bobbed up and down, and her pigtails swept over her shoulders. "It's *Tio's* birthday." She crooked her finger, gesturing Jane closer.

Jane stooped so she was on eye level with Isabel.

"He's old," Isabel whispered followed by a giggle. "Momma says I'm not allowed to say that out loud, but you won't tell on me, will you, Miss Jane?"

"My lips are sealed," Jane assured her, and turned a pretend key at the seam of her mouth.

"Sounds like there are some heavy-duty secrets going on here," a deep voice said from above them.

Jane closed her eyes, then reopened them to blue eyes even more delicious than she'd remembered. He was mimicking Jane's stance, kneeling just inches from her. His familiar scent wafted up her nostrils. The added aroma of olive oil and his favorite cabernet made her mouth water.

He raised his eyebrows. "Hi there."

"Hello." Warmth flooded her face, and she stood up, hoping for a breeze to cool her flaming cheeks. No such luck.

"Look, Uncle Ryan. Miss Jane is back!" Isabel cheered, hopping back and forth between them.

Ryan's gaze didn't leave Jane's. "So she is, little one. Why don't you go back to the party before your mom starts to worry? I'd like to talk with Miss Jane."

"Okay, Uncle Ryan. Don't let her leave again. I don't like it when you're sad."

Jane and Ryan watched Isabel skip back to the restaurant.

"Out of the mouths of babes," Jane said.

Ryan crossed his arms. "What are you doing here?"

"I … I'm—" His tone caught her off guard. "I have a client here, remember? Why do you sound so mad? I'm the one who should be angry." This time, it was she who mimicked his body language, folding her arms and straightening her spine.

"You? Why should you be angry?"

"Make that royally pissed off. You really pulled one over on me. Not only did you make me think you actually cared, you scammed me, too."

"Whoa. Hold on. Scammed you? What are you talking about?"

"What I don't understand is if you never intended to refund the fee, why did you offer?"

His eyes widened. "You didn't get the refund?"

"No."

He rubbed his palm over his face. "I can't believe she did that. I told Camille to refund you the entire amount and to take her fee from the amount she still owed me. Seems like she took my fee and yours too." Ryan shook his head. "Look I'm sorry about that. I'll get it taken care of right away." His eyes softened, and somehow she knew he was telling the truth. "I know you came here the day you left and had a run-in with Maya."

"Yes, your lovely sister had a few words for me. By the way, she's on to you and The Cowboys."

"I know. I set her straight about my past profession." He tilted his head. "You should've been straight with me about still being married."

She shook her head. "What are you talking about? Who said I was still married?"

"Your husband."

"What?" Time seemed to stop. "When?" She raised her hand as her mind raced. "Ryan, please ... start at the beginning. You spoke to Nick?"

Ryan explained the phone call. "I wasn't sure I believed him at first, so I texted you, a day later. I got a message back saying you were sorry but not to contact you again."

Pain shot through her head. "I can't believe he did that. We were together at the hospital, and there were times I left my purse with him, but..."

A trace of starch left Ryan's shoulders. "Are you telling me you're not married to him?"

"No. Not anymore. We've been divorced for a few months."

He shook his head. "Why would he do something like that?"

"Because he wanted us to get back together. He was hounding me about it, the entire time we were at the hospital with Ty."

"How is your son?" Ryan asked, and this time there was a definite softening in his tone.

"He's good. He's mending at school. I offered to let him come home, but he didn't want to leave campus."

"Kids are resilient. They bounce back a lot faster than we do."

Jane nodded, and found the courage to ask, "Why did you call me?"

Ryan scowled. "Maya let it slip that you'd come to the restaurant before you flew home. I finally pried the conversation out of her. She was nasty to you, and that woman you saw me with wasn't a client. It was Gretchen's sister. I was keeping her company while she waited for Gretch. That's all it was. I called because I needed to tell you that Maya was wrong. About everything."

"She wasn't wrong about your actions that weekend. After hearing Maya explain your formula I realized that I wasn't special at all. Not to you. Maybe you should've kept the fee."

Ryan cocked his head. "Are you finished?"

She shrugged, then nodded.

"Good," he said softly, "because if you can stop talking for a minute, I'll explain." He laced his fingers with hers and guided her to an empty bench.

She resisted a moment before sitting.

Ryan sank down beside her. "At first, yes. We met at a bar where I met most of my clients, but that's it."

"Really? What about the tour the next day?"

"I've taken clients to some of those places. I've also done it for out-of-town friends. I'm proud of my city, and I like to show it off." His voice was silky and warm. "But I never took a client to see my grandparents' house. I never shared my favorite strudel. And I certainly never took any of them to meet my family."

She wanted desperately to believe him, but she had to be sure. "And the next day?" As the question left her lips, the image of their bodies between the sheets flashed into her mind.

"That was all real to me. Every incredible moment of it. I thought it was real to you, too. I never would've pursued you if I hadn't believed you felt the same way. I was too far gone."

"Too far gone?" she whispered.

"Into you. I waited for you the whole day, hoping you were going to walk through the doors at Vine."

"Then why didn't you tell me how you felt before you left?" Jane asked.

"I wanted to be fair and give you some time to think. I wanted to give you a graceful out, if you needed to take it. I wanted you to come to me without any regrets or reservations."

"And I did! But Maya—"

"I know. And I'm sorrier than I can say about that whole misunderstanding."

She shrugged. "You didn't seem too broken up about it when I saw you at Rio Iguana with that blonde."

His eyes widened. "Hold on. That *was* you? I only saw the back of your head as you left, but I could've sworn it was you. I smelled your perfume. I went after you, but you'd already left. The woman I was with was a liquor distributor. She was trying to sell me a new line of tequilas, and she wanted me to see how the Rio Iguana crowd loved the product."

Jane searched his eyes.

He lowered his voice. "I wanted to see you again. I wanted another chance to get things right between us."

Her heart was melting. "I'm sorry I wasn't there to get your call or your text." She shivered. "I still can't believe Nick had the nerve to do that to me. To us."

They sat side by side without another word spoken. Sounds of Ryan's family at Vine faded into the background as Jane tried to make sense of it all. She leaned toward him, just a little, letting her shoulder brush against his. "So where does all that leave us?"

A slow smile crossed his face. "Wherever we want to take it. Come with me." He stood and pulled her up.

"Where are we going?"

"Someplace that's not here. Preferably someplace that has large quantities of tequila."

Ryan led Jane through a series of dimly lit pathways.

"Seriously. Where *are* we going?" Jane asked again as she stared at the darkness ahead.

"Trust me. It's worth the hike." Ryan squeezed her hand, and she heard music playing in the distance.

Jane peeked around Ryan's broad shoulders and spotted a grouping of trees decorated with twinkling white lights. "What is this place?"

"The best-kept secret in San Antonio. Locals come here to get away from the tourists."

They stepped onto a patio filled with wooden picnic tables. A few food trucks lined the street beyond the casual seating area. A band played a bluesy beat, not far from where they stood. Ryan guided her to an empty table.

A woman Jane estimated to be about her age approached them. "Haven't seen you around, Ryan. Good to see you back here. What can I get you?"

"Tequila. Two shots now and a couple on standby."

"Take a seat," Ryan offered. "The bench gets a whole lot more comfortable after a couple of shots."

Jane laughed. Slipping her legs over the bench, she sat down, closer to Ryan than she'd intended. A spark ran through her as the outside of her thigh touched his leg. In a silent statement, his palm came to rest near her knee, just as four shot glasses filled with golden liquid, accompanied by a saltshaker and a plate of lime wedges, were placed on the wooden slats of the table.

"You two look like you could use those standbys now," the waitress said, and winked.

Jane surveyed the spread before her. "I'm not much of a shot drinker. What is all this?"

Ryan's sexy grin warmed her in all the right places. "Never done tequila shots?"

Jane shook her head. "I guess that makes me a shot virgin."

"In that case, this is going to be even more fun." He took her palm in his hand and traced a circle on the sensitive spot of skin between the base of her thumb and index finger. "First, lick your hand right here."

Jane raised her eyebrows. "You want me to lick my hand?"

"Unless you'd like me to do it for you."

The heat in her belly moved lower, and she pressed her thighs together. As seductive as that sounded, she needed to keep a level head. "I think I can manage." When she raised her hand to her mouth and gave the area a lick, she could have sworn she heard Ryan let out a low groan. "Now what, Tequila Master?"

"I like the sound of that. Sprinkle a little salt where you licked." He demonstrated on his own hand, and Jane followed suit. "Now, hold a lime wedge in the same hand and pick up a shot glass."

She did as he directed.

"Ready?"

"No. But I'm not going to let that stop me."

"Okay. Do what I do." Ryan raised his fist to his mouth, so that the tip of his tongue touched the sprinkle of salt on his skin.

As Jane watched him lick the white specks, an image of his tongue's ministrations on the inside of her thigh flashed through her head. *Whoa.* She raised her fist to follow his lead, and smiled when his gaze traveled to her own tongue. Then he lifted his shot to hers. The glasses touched with a soft clink as their fingers brushed for a moment. "Cheers," they said in unison.

"Try to drink it down in one gulp."

Jane touched the glass to her lips and emptied the contents into her mouth. Tipping her head back, she directed the tequila in the right direction, and she swallowed. A numbing burn meandered down her throat.

"Now bite into the lime, to cut the sting."

She sank her teeth into the green fruit wedge, and bursts of citrus exploded on her tongue, tempering the flame smoldering in her mouth. "Wow."

"Are you up for another?" Ryan challenged.

Jane could feel the stress of the past weeks melting away as the effects from the shot coursed through her veins. She rolled her shoulders. "Let's go for it," she said boldly, then held up an index finger. "With one variation."

Jane reached for Ryan's hand and coaxed it into a loose fist, then brought it to her mouth. Her tongue darted out, and she licked his skin, tasting the residual salt from the first shot.

His groan rumbled through her. "My turn." Intertwining his fingers with hers, he touched his lips to each of her fingertips before drawing a wet circle in the crease of her hand, at the base of her thumb.

Jane swallowed hard as heat flooded her lower belly.

Ryan hooked his arm through hers and sprinkled salt onto the moistened spots on both of their hands. Next, he handed her a shot and wedge of lime.

"Cheers," They clinked glasses again. "One, two, three."

The second shot went down, smoother than the first.

"Oh that's good," Jane gasped. A breeze swept through her hair, and she closed her eyes, allowing the effects of the tequila to race through her body.

"What are you thinking?"

She took a deep breath. "I'm thinking there's not a single place I'd rather be right now than right here." She opened her eyes and turned to him. "With you."

Ryan swung one long leg from under the table and straddled the bench. Wrapping his arms around her, he pulled her back against his chest, just as the band started a new set.

Jane closed her eyes again and swayed to the beat of the music.

"Dance with me." His whispered words tickled her ear.

She smiled. "I don't dance," she said, and continued to sway.

"You're doing pretty well, right now. All you need to do is stand up." She felt his breath move to the nape of her neck, tickling the strands of her hair.

"I can't dance," she repeated, and stopped moving to the music.

"Who told you that?" Ryan asked.

"My ex-husband." Jane thought back to the weddings and dinner parties she'd attended with Nick. He would take her onto the dance floor for one token slow dance, then sit out the rest. Jane had always loved music, and enjoyed bopping around her kitchen while she cooked to top forty songs. But Nick had nothing but snide comments for her dancing ability.

Ryan wasn't giving up that easily. "They say dancing is like making love with your clothes on. I'll admit I haven't seen you dance, but I can vouch for the second activity, and if what they say is true, then you're a spectacular dancer, *Querida*."

She couldn't help the smile that spread across her face. "How about another shot?"

"Dance first."

Jane squinted at the band and pointed to the empty dance floor in dismay. "There's no one else up there. I'll make a fool of myself."

"It's a safe bet that everybody here has already had a lot more than two tequila shots. They probably won't even notice we're there."

The beat of the music reverberated in her chest. "I'm sure you dance really well."

"They'd revoke my Spanish heritage card if I didn't," Ryan said, and laughed. "Come on, one dance. Please?"

"Okay, but promise me you'll let me stop if I make a fool of myself."

"Deal." He stood, helped her disentangle herself from the picnic table bench, and guided her to the dance floor. Between the dim lights and the lasting effects of liquid encouragement, she found she wasn't afraid to wrap her arms around Ryan. In fact, she kind of loved it, especially when his hands encircled her waist and pulled her against his rock-hard body.

They swayed with the beat of the music, and she focused carefully on where she placed her feet.

"Relax and feel the music," Ryan murmured into her ear.

"I don't want to step on your toes."

"I'll live, even if you do. Close your eyes and rest your head here." He patted a spot on his chest, just below his shoulder.

"This is nice." Her fingers slid up the back of his neck and played with the fine hairs at his nape. Shivers ran through her as his fingertips traced up and down her spine, then came to rest at the base of her backside.

Then the song ended, and Jane bit back a sigh of disappointment. The band began to play an up-tempo song, and her insecurities returned. "Ryan, I can't—"

But his hands moved to her hips and guided her movements.

Tossing aside her fear of stomping on his feet, she let Ryan's hands and the music take over.

It was a magic combination, one that Jane wished could go on forever. But Ryan suddenly took her hand and twirled her once before pulling her in for a dip, just as the song ended.

Applause filled her ears as Ryan set her back on her feet. Grinning, he said, "I think we've cleared up that 'I can't dance' thing. Take a bow, *Querida*."

The singer waved his hand toward Ryan and Jane. "Give it up for this spectacular couple."

Ryan picked up two water bottles on their way back to their table.

"You two are just too cute together," their waitress exclaimed as they returned to their table. "These are on the house." And she placed two more tequila shots in front of them.

As soon as they downed those shots, the waitress brought more as the locals stopped to say hello to Ryan and meet Jane.

Jane lost count of how many new San Antonio friends she'd made on the night she learned that she loved to dance. She also lost count of the quantity of golden liquid that passed through her lips and down her throat. But she knew she didn't have to worry. Ryan was with her, and that made everything all right.

In fact, it made everything perfect.

Chapter Sixteen

Jane tried to blink, but her eyelids felt like sandpaper as she squinted at the clock on the bed table. It was, she realized, an unfamiliar bed table, with an equally unfamiliar lamp and clock. Next to the clock sat three ibuprofen and a note leaning against a water bottle.

Jane rubbed her eyes, trying to chase the sleep from her brain. *Where the hell am I?* She plucked the note with her thumb and forefinger and turned it over.

Swallow the pills and drink the entire bottle of water before you attempt to get out of bed.

I'll be right back. ~R

Of course. It all came back to her. Little Isabel. Ryan. Tequila. Dancing. Tequila. Kissing. More tequila...

Damn. Jane scanned her surroundings. Was this Ryan's place? She had no recollection of how she'd gotten there or what had happened after they arrived.

She lifted the sheet from her body, and saw that she wore only her panties and what she assumed was one of Ryan's t-shirts. Did she... Had he... Her mind raced, searching for clues, but she was still unenlightened when she heard a door open.

"Honey, I'm home!" Ryan's cheerful voice called from what sounded like the lower level of the house. His footsteps sounded on the stairs, before he peeked through the half-open door. "Oh good, you're awake. Take the ibuprofen right away. It'll make you feel better."

Jane rubbed her forehead. "Why did I drink so much?"

"Blame the tequila." He strode to the bedside table and handed her the water bottle. "Drink this. It'll make you feel better, too."

She tipped the opening to her lips and washed down the pills with a few sips of cold water. It cleared her head enough for her to continue her train of thought. "We didn't—uh, you know. Did we?"

Ryan sat at the foot of the bed, and a smile played across his lips. "I have rules against taking advantage of drunk women."

"But you undressed me."

His gaze moved down her body. "Yes."

"And you took off my bra."

"It looked terribly uncomfortable. I don't know how women can stand to wear those things."

Their gazes locked for a moment while Jane debated whether or not to believe him.

His look didn't waver. Instead it seemed to travel under her skin, making itself at home. Taking root…

She needed to change the subject to something less intimate than how she had ended up in a strange bed, wearing not much more than half of her underwear. She glanced around the bedroom. "This is your house?"

Ryan nodded. "This is it. And I live alone, if that's your next question."

Jane closed her eyes and leaned the back of her head carefully against the headboard, which made the ache in her temples subside just a little. "How drunk was I? Did I dance again?"

Ryan chuckled. "No. No more dancing, but lots more tequila. I didn't realize how much the shots were affecting you until it was too late. I didn't want you to be alone to deal with the consequences when you woke up, so I brought you back here."

"Did I say anything embarrassing?"

"Actually, you're quite an amusing yet lightweight drunk."

Jane rubbed her temples. "Do I even want to know? Wait. No. I don't think I do."

"I'll give you the condensed version. You said you wanted to show me how much you liked me, and then you passed out."

Jane took a few more swigs from her water bottle. "Which is why I usually don't drink anything stronger than wine. So, I *did* embarrass myself."

Ryan winked. "Actually, I kind of liked it."

"Sounds like you could've gotten lucky pretty easily, last night."

"Like I said, I would never use a woman's lack of a clear head against her for my own enjoyment. That's not the kind of sex I want with you."

Jane tilted her head. "Meaning?"

Ryan shrugged. "There are different types of sex, just like there are different types of relationships. On the one hand, there's your casual, just-for-fun variety. On the other hand, there's your mind-blowing, make-a-real-connection sex. Most couples never travel past the first kind. You and I, on the other hand, were lucky enough to start at the second phase. And I'm not a fan of going backwards."

"Mind-blowing, huh?" In truth, it had been, for her. But that wasn't the reason for her question, although she was pleasantly shocked that he thought so, too.

"It's rare to connect with someone on a level of honesty and trust, but that's what I felt with you. Right from the beginning, we had a connection. I wasn't about to screw that up before finding out if you'd felt it, too … and if you feel it, now."

Jane nodded. "It's the reason I went back to Vine, the morning after we'd been together—because I felt it. Being with you was like nothing I'd ever experienced, even after eighteen years with my husband. Intimacy is complex. A person can be there without actually … being there." She thought back to the various scenarios she'd made up in her head, over the years, while having sex with Nick. And yet she'd thought she had a perfectly idyllic life, until she put some distance and time between them.

"I know exactly what you're talking about," Ryan said, looking bleak.

Jane didn't ask, but she was sure he was thinking about some of the clients from his escort days. She smiled at him. "It was different with you. I didn't feel judged. So many times, I built a wall with Nick. It was easier to hide behind that protective barrier than to pick apart the reason why I was unhappy."

He gave her an assessing look, and she braced herself to hear what he would say about her revelation, but the words that came out of his mouth were, "I think you need something to eat." Ryan strode to his closet and pulled out a plush burgundy robe. He draped it over the comforter that covered her legs. "Help yourself to anything in the bathroom. I put a fresh toothbrush on the counter. When you feel like it, come down for some breakfast," he said, and left the room.

Jane didn't feel like eating, but she supposed it was the best way to soak up the indulgences of the night before. She peeled back the comforter and sheet from her legs, and swung her feet over the edge of the bed. The stone floor tiles felt cool against the soles of her feet. She slipped her arms into Ryan's robe. His scent tickled her nose, and she inhaled deeply, savoring his distinct smell. She padded to the bathroom and attempted to wash the remnants of the night before from her face and brushed her teeth. She felt slightly more human as she stepped from the bedroom and a new aroma wafted into the hallway. Her mouth watered as she followed the sound of crackling bacon and eggs.

She ventured downstairs and found Ryan in his small, well-appointed kitchen. From the doorway, she took the opportunity to appreciate the planes and dips of his back through his white t-shirt as he busied himself at the stove. His biceps moved and flexed as he chopped vegetables and scraped them into a frying pan.

Ryan stopped and turned to face her. "Hope you like old-fashioned omelet and bacon. I ran to the market and picked up the basics."

"I thought you chefs always had a fully stocked kitchen, like on that food channel."

"If I did, most of it would go to waste. I'm hardly ever here. In fact, you're my first houseguest since I moved in."

Jane sat on one of the two stools in front of the kitchen island. "Oh, come on. You must be one of San Antonio's most eligible bachelors. I'm sure there are women here all the time."

He reached into an overhead cabinet, and she caught a glimpse of golden skin under his shirt. He pulled down two plates and placed them on the counter next to the stove. "Nope." He plated the contents of the frying pan and added two strips of bacon to each before sliding the delicious-looking breakfast under her nose. "Coffee?"

"Please."

He carried the second plate, along with a coffee carafe, to the other side of the counter and sat down. "Breakfast is my favorite meal." He poured her a mug of steaming coffee. "Cheers."

"Don't remind me." Jane groaned, thinking about how many times she said that word the night before.

They ate in comfortable silence. Apparently bacon and eggs was the best combination for her hangover. She felt almost like herself by the time Ryan poured her a second cup of coffee.

She squinted at the digital clock display on his microwave and chuckled.

"Laughing is a good sign. Means your headache must be gone."

"It is. And so is my flight home. It just took off and I couldn't care less," she assured him with a smile. "I'll call the airline and see if I can go standby on a flight, later today or tomorrow." She glanced around his kitchen, hoping to spot her purse.

"Your purse is upstairs with your clothes," he said, seemingly reading her mind. He pulled her into his arms. "Don't leave yet."

She melted into his chest. "I don't really have anything going on that I have to rush back for." It was the truth. She had originally considered staying in San Antonio for a few more days, to work at her client's office, but had decided against it because it hurt her to be so geographically close to Ryan and yet not see him.

He cupped her cheeks and lifted her face to meet his gaze. "I'd like it if you would stay for a couple days. Here with me."

She wanted it, too, and yet a million reasons why it was a bad idea flooded her brain. "But—"

The pad of his thumb coasted over her lips. "Don't. You may think you have more reasons to leave than to stay, but let's not think about them now. For today, let's not try to figure it all out. Let's just be."

Jane smiled. There was nothing she wanted more.

Ryan moved closer and filled the air around her. For that moment in time, she was his. His lips grazed hers softly at first, and she met every kiss, as need bubbled up within her body. Her fingers found the back of his neck and raked through his hair, which managed to be coarse yet so soft. He nudged her off of the stool and drew her to stand between his legs before reaching to loosen the sash at her waist.

As the robe puddled at her feet, he lifted the t-shirt above her midriff. His palms cupped her breasts and played with her nipples. She moaned as he pulled the over-sized shirt over her head.

Ryan stroked her shoulders and broke their kiss. His gaze drifted down to her breasts. "You're magnificent." His fingers traced a line up her neck to her swollen lips. "So incredibly sexy."

A sensual confidence coursed through her veins as she stood before Ryan. Her naughty vixen was not only alive and well, but was almost naked in a young sexy god's home. Empowered, she pulled his shirt from the waist of his pants and slid her palms over the planes of his abs. He groaned as her fingers traveled south to the closure of his pants. She made quick work of the button and zipper, and slipped her hand inside. And her unpracticed vixen knew all the right moves, judging by Ryan's choppy breath.

"Jane." His thumb and forefinger encircled her wrist.

She stopped and raised her eyebrows. "Something wrong, cowboy?"

"The only thing wrong is you'll make me finish before we even get started. I'm taking you upstairs so I can take care of you properly." Before she knew it, his arm was under her knees, and her body was in the air.

"You shouldn't lift me," she giggled. No one had ever confused Jane for one of those bone-thin girls.

"I believe I just did, with ease," Ryan boasted and carried her upstairs to his bedroom, where he laid her gently on the bed. Opening the drawer of his nightstand, he pulled out a box of condoms and placed them beside the lamp.

"A whole box?" she asked with a smile.

"With luck, they'll last the morning," he teased, and hooked his fingers under the waistband of her panties. His tongue trailed a warm trail down the inside of her thigh as he swept the fabric from her legs. Naked and bare with every physical imperfection exposed, she froze for a moment. But he nudged her thighs with his face and Jane slowly melted into a deep sigh as his mouth reached its target. She tilted her hips upward as he licked and stroked her into an unstoppable wave of delicious abandon. Jane closed her eyes and her world exploded into a sea of glitter as she screamed his name.

****

A long, lovely time later, Jane nuzzled her head in the crook of Ryan's solid shoulder, listening to his rhythmic breathing as her head rose and fell with his chest. They'd been in bed since returning from gathering her things and checking out of her hotel. She'd lost count of how many times she'd climaxed. Until Ryan, Jane had never loved sex. Now she couldn't get enough. Ryan was like a fine wine that she couldn't stop drinking, no matter how much he made her head spin. She chuckled and traced the line of one of Ryan's ribs.

"What are you laughing at?" he asked sleepily. His fingertips grazed the small of her back.

"I thought you were asleep," she whispered.

"Just resting. I have to go to the restaurant soon. I'll try to get home early."

Jane raised her head to look him in the eye. "Don't worry about me. Really." Guilt rose in her chest. Even though she'd agreed to spend a few days at his place, she didn't want to get in the way of his routine or his business.

"I'll send dinner over for you."

"Don't bother. Why don't you drop me off in town so I can rent a car for the rest of my trip? That way, I won't be such a nuisance."

He turned on his side so they faced each other. "You're not a nuisance. Besides, I like the thought that you're stuck here in my house, especially in my bed."

"Like a kept woman."

"Mmm, I like the sound of that, too." Ryan kissed her, then kissed her again before rising with a groan and heading to the bathroom.

Jane pulled the sheet around herself, listening to the shower and imagining the water dripping from Ryan's soapy body. She took comfort from the sounds of another person going about their daily life. It was one of the things she missed, now that she was single. Her apartment felt so quiet and lonely, and she'd come up with reasons to go to the shopping mall or grocery store, just for the human contact.

Ryan strode back from the bathroom in nothing but a towel. Water from his hair dripped down his back as he surveyed his closet for something to wear. Jane enjoyed watching him move around his room as he chose black slacks and t-shirt.

"You look sexy in black," she told him. His dark hair and golden skin added to the allure, and his blue eyes blazed even brighter against his dark ensemble.

He picked up her purse from his dresser and sat down next to her on the edge of the bed. "Do me a favor and jot down your account information. I'm going to take care of the oversight today."

"It's really not a big deal."

"No. It's a huge deal, and I don't want anything to come between us."

Jane nodded. "Okay." She ripped a slip of paper from a small pad of paper she carried and copied her account information from an app on her phone. "Here you go."

He kissed her softly on the lips. "I'll be back as soon as I can." In the meantime, I'll send Victor over with one of our specials and a bottle of wine."

"Thank you." She would've declined his offer of dinner, but he'd been truthful when he talked about not having anything to eat in the house. In typical bachelor fashion, other than the remaining uncooked eggs and bacon from breakfast, his refrigerator contained nothing but a bottle of ketchup and four bottles of beer. And she had to admit, after spending the day in bed with Ryan, she'd worked up an appetite.

Jane used her time alone in Ryan's house to indulge in a long shower, then ran a load of laundry. She'd only packed for a two-day trip, and she'd run out of clean clothes. She spotted a pair of sweatpants and a San Antonio Spurs t-shirt in a pile of Ryan's clean clothes folded in a laundry basket. She pulled on the sweatpants and rolled the waistband so the pant legs wouldn't drag, then slipped the shirt over her head hurriedly when she heard the doorbell ring.

She hadn't expected Ryan to send dinner over so early, but her own clothes were still on spin cycle, so she had no choice but to answer the door as she was, looking like a Ryan Ziegler groupie. She partially hid behind the door as she opened it. "Sorry, I'm doing some laundry and ran out of—"

"You answering the door in my Spurs shirt is almost as sexy as answering the door in nothing at all," came the husky reply from the porch.

"Ryan?" Jane pulled the door open the rest of the way. "What are you doing back?"

He held out two large brown bags. "I decided to be your delivery boy and double as your dinner companion."

"Don't you have to get back to the restaurant? I mean, it's only—"

Ryan pulled her against his body. "I got to the restaurant and realized I had a capable staff at Vine and an extremely hot woman alone at my house. There was something wrong with that picture. So here I am. And here you are, in my Spurs shirt." His breath blew warm against her lips as he spoke.

"I'm glad you did." She rose up on her tiptoes to meet his kiss.

"Let's eat while it's still hot." He wrapped his arm around Jane and led her to his small dining room.

She stopped and smiled at him. "I have a surprise for you, too. Go upstairs for a few minutes and don't come down until I say so."

He grinned. "A surprise?"

"Yup. Go. Before the food gets cold."

Ryan nodded and headed upstairs. Jane ran through the kitchen and pulled open the sliding glass door. She'd gone outside earlier and found his table on its side, along with four matching chairs stacked neatly together. She had swept the outdoor patio and cleaned the dining set before placing it in the middle of the patio, with the plan of surprising Ryan with breakfast outside the next morning. The patio was dark now, but she recalled the hurricane candles and a string of Christmas lights she'd seen in his laundry room.

With just a few minutes of work, Jane turned the patio into a scene straight from a Nancy Meyers movie. The final touches were placemats and wine glasses. She unloaded the bags and plated the beautiful meal of filet mignon and baked potato.

"Dinner is served," Jane called, and Ryan practically ran down the stairs.

"Good, because I think my stomach was beginning to eat itself." He looked into the kitchen and dining room. "Where exactly *is* dinner?"

"Follow me, Mr. Ziegler." She led him to the slider and opened the door. "I hope you don't mind. I set up the furniture on your patio."

Ryan stepped outside. "I can't believe you did all this." His gaze darted from the table to the twinkle lights she'd strung along the low tree branches. "I was going to get rid of this set, but you've managed to make it look like a million bucks."

"It just needed to be cleaned up a little."

He turned to Jane. "This is the nicest thing anyone has ever done for me."

Jane waved her hand at him. "Come on now. All I did was hose it down and dry it with paper towels. You need more paper towels, by the way."

"That's not what I mean. It's the whole thing." He pulled her into his arms. "You have this uncanny way of showing up and turning my life upside down, making it better and more beautiful than it ever was before."

"Like a sparkly snow globe?"

"Better than a sparkly snow globe." He smiled down at her. "I'm never going to let you leave. You know that?"

She searched his eyes. In truth, she'd have to leave soon, and they both knew it. But, for that moment, Jane refused to think of anything beyond a night of twinkle lights, candles, great food and drink, and an extra helping of Ryan Ziegler for dessert.

Chapter Seventeen

Ryan reached for her before opening his eyes. Over a few short days, he'd fallen hard for this woman who'd landed in his life, and he wasn't about to let her go.

Right now, however, her side of the bed was cold. He sat up and glanced toward the bathroom. No Jane.

He pulled on a pair of sweatpants and ventured downstairs in search of her. He began to panic when he didn't find her bouncing around the kitchen, making breakfast. Then his heartbeat steadied as he heard music coming from the direction of the sliding glass door, which she'd left partially open.

In the span of a couple days, the patio had become her favorite area of his home. She'd talked him into taking her to a garden center, where they bought several wooden planters and potted flowers. On the way back, they'd picked up an outside speaker. Ryan watched as Jane's foot tapped against the empty chair, keeping the beat of a Top Forty song playing in the background while she worked on her laptop. He leaned his shoulder against the doorjamb and appreciated her for a moment. He had to admit, she'd become a fixture in his home. Having her near him was as easy as breathing.

Her phone buzzed on the table next to her, interrupting the peaceful scene. He saw Jane glance at the display and frown before sliding her thumb over the screen. Ryan had come to recognize the faint worry line that appeared on her forehead.

"Hi, Paul. Yes, I know. I just needed a few mental health days to clear my head. I understand. I'll be back in the office tomorrow. … Yes … see you then."

Ryan pulled open the slider and locked gazes with her. "You wouldn't have to deal with that if you had your own business."

Her eyes looked as sad as they'd been when he first met her. "I also wouldn't be guaranteed the much-needed paycheck." She dropped her phone back onto the table. "I guess you heard."

He nodded.

"I'll take the last flight out tonight."

"I knew I couldn't keep you here forever," he said. "But when will you be back in town?"

Jane stood. "Ryan. Don't—"

He narrowed his eyes. "Don't what?"

"Don't do this. I live in New York. You live here. That won't change."

He shook his head. "I'm not asking for that to change, at least for now. We can still have a relationship, even if it's long-distance."

"That won't work," she said quietly.

"Why not?" he demanded.

She looked away. "It wouldn't be fair to you."

"The way I see it, you're not being fair to me by not giving this a chance."

"Don't you see? I'm a forty-year-old divorcee with a kid in college. I come with baggage you don't need. You're—" She shrugged. "Well, how old are you anyway?"

"Thirty-two, but I don't see—"

"Thirty-two. You don't need to be tied down to someone like me at thirty-two. You have women like Tilly fawning over you daily."

Ryan took a step forward. "First, you're not forty. You're thirty-nine. You can't claim forty until December." He took another step. "Second, the fact that you're divorced and have a kid has nothing to do with us.

I don't see that as baggage, and if you do, I'll gladly help you with your bags." It only took him one more step to stand a few scant inches from Jane. "I want you, and I want to be tied down to you. God, that sounds sexy. I want to make this work." He tipped his forehead to hers. "Will you try?"

She was quiet for a minute, clearly thinking. Then she said, "Okay, but on two conditions: there can't be any lies between us. I've been lied to, and I can't go through that again."

"I've never once lied to you, and I don't intend to start. What's the second condition?"

"I don't want to hear any talk about commitment or long-term plans. Let's just see where this goes, without labeling our relationship."

"No lies, no labels, and no long-term plans. Those are all your demands?"

Jane nodded.

"Good, because I have a few of my own."

Jane folded her arms. "I'm listening."

"No putting yourself down with 'baggage' talk. And I have one exception to your 'no long-term plans' rule. I'm coming to New York for your birthday, and we're spending the weekend in the city. I'll make all the plans. You just need to show up." He thought it was great that her birthday fell two weeks before Christmas Day. But Jane, clearly, had been less thrilled. She'd told him that her birthday was always overshadowed by the holidays.

Now, a sweet grin teased at her lips. "You want to celebrate my birthday with me?"

He wrapped her in his arms and tipped her chin up so that she gazed into his eyes. "Your birthday, Christmas, hell, I want to celebrate National Doughnut

Day with you, as long as you keep looking at me that way."

"I don't know what I ever did to deserve you," she whispered.

But he knew, beyond a shadow of a doubt, that he was the lucky one.

Chapter Eighteen

Ryan stood with the limo drivers at the airport, holding a piece of white cardboard. He turned it over for a second, to make sure it wasn't upside down. JANE. He smiled as he thought about how Isabel had carefully created the sign, using pink and purple markers.

He'd stood in this exact spot, holding this exact sign, four times since the day they had struck their deal. It had become their ritual. Much to Ryan's pleasure, her San Antonio clients were not fans of virtual meetings, and they had requested her attendance at each of their strategy meetings. Jane's national marketing campaign catapulted the company's results to an all-time high, and they were now making plans to expand their product line. She spent every other week in San Antonio, arriving Friday evening and staying through the following weekend.

A group of passengers headed Ryan's way, and he craned his neck, trying to find Jane in the crowd. He first spotted her dark hair with its golden highlights, loving the way it bounced along her shoulders. His gaze moved to her face as she first laid eyes on him, and her expression of delight took his breath away.

Dodging her fellow passengers, she ran into his arms.

"Hey there, Beautiful. Need a ride?"

"I missed you!"

He hugged her tight and closed his eyes, breathing deep, taking her inside him. Each time she returned, it was like Christmas day. "I missed you more," he said, taking her bag and coat. "Getting cold in New York?"

"Yeah, freezing! And it's only November."

"Well, your oasis awaits at Casa Ziegler. You'll love this week's project." Ryan surprised Jane each week with a new addition to his patio. They'd already replaced the furniture and added a sitting area with an all-weather sofa.

Jane clapped her hands together, beaming. "I can't wait!"

He watched as she inhaled when they left the airport.

"I love the warm air and not having to wear a coat. I'm beginning to like this place more and more. It's almost like home," she said, walking with him to the parking lot.

He squeezed her hand. She didn't know it, but she had become his home. Jane seemed to have wrapped herself around his heart, and she was never far from his thoughts. Just like the flame from his new fireplace, she licked at his skin and electrified his soul. She gave him purpose and happiness. "It *is* your home."

He grinned as Jane tried to coax the surprise out of him during the short ride to his house. "I'll give you a hint," he said at last. "It'll come in handy during chilly winter nights."

"Long underwear?" she teased.

"Guess again."

"A fire pit?" Her eyes crinkled at the corners as she smiled.

"Closer," Ryan said as he pulled into his driveway. She reached for the passenger door handle, but he grabbed her other hand. "Hold on. This one's special. Stay here a moment."

Normally, she'd run to the backyard to see what he had done. This time, he made her agree to stay in the car while he ran to the patio and lit a flame under the kindling he'd left in the opening of the fireplace. Soon a blaze of light fanned over the pavers of the patio. He uncorked the wine bottle and poured two glasses of her favorite red. "Perfect," he said, and strode back to the car. "Ready?"

"You're killing me, Ry," she complained in mock-distress as he helped her from the car.

Instead of replying, he twirled her around, tied a bandana over her eyes, and led her to the patio.

The pop and crack of the fire welcomed them to their oasis. He positioned Jane in front of the fire, placed a glass in her hand, and pulled the fabric from her eyes. "Ta-da."

Her mouth dropped open, and he saw a reflection of the flames dance in her eyes. "Ryan, it's beautiful!" She placed the wine glass on the table and approached the tall fireplace. "This design is exquisite." She traced the painted-vine pattern with her fingertips.

He'd commissioned a local artist to paint two different flowering vines on either side of the opening. Standing alongside her, he explained, "The vines represent you and me." He pointed to the left side. "This one is purple wisteria. It looks and smells beautiful, but it's a very deceptive plant. It may appear delicate, but it can withstand adversity. That's you." He shifted his gaze to the right. "This other one is yellow jasmine. It turns a deep bronze in the sun, and its long leaves provide support and protection."

"You." She blinked back tears as she flattened her palm on the cool brick façade.

"They each grow tall and proud on their own, but look what happens when they intertwine in the middle." He followed the line of the jasmine vine until it met the wisteria. Bursts of golden yellow mixed with various sprays in hues of purple.

"They're beautiful together," Jane said, and turned toward Ryan. Heat from the fire radiated from her skin.

"Just like us." He pulled her in, capturing her warmth. The scent of smoke clung to her hair, and he knew he'd never again inhale the smell of wood burning outdoors without thinking of her.

Ryan slanted his mouth over hers and stepped backward until his calves hit the front of the cushioned sofa. Then he pulled her down, and she straddled his lap, her skirt bunched high on her legs. Kissing her, he reached down and trailed his fingers slowly up the soft flesh of her inner thigh toward her heated sex.

Jane filled his mouth with a deep moan.

"I want you so much," she said, reaching between their bodies. She palmed his hardness with one hand while unbuttoning his waistband with the other.

He grasped her shoulders and broke their kiss, his gaze moving from her swollen lips to her passion-hooded eyes. "It kills me to say this, but I need to go inside for a second. I don't have any protection on me."

Jane clamped her knees around his hips. "It's okay. I can't get pregnant."

"You're sure?" he asked.

"I've never been more sure. I don't want anything between us."

Ryan quickly helped Jane with his pants just enough to free himself before pushing the lace of her panties to one side. He sank into her ready flesh, and they moaned in tandem. Jane moved above him, rising up before taking him completely in, repeating her movement over and over again, increasing the pace until they both shattered into oblivion.

I'm home, Ryan thought helplessly as she sank down onto him, limp with the pleasure they had just shared. *You are my home.*

"I love you," he whispered into her ear.

Jane pulled back and searched his face, as if testing his sincerity. Then she swallowed hard, and tipped her forehead to his. "I love you, too," she admitted. "When I first met you I thought you smelled like fire and midnight. Now, I know you do."

They spent the rest of the night in front of the fire. Ryan whipped up spaghetti and meatballs, which they ate under the twinkle lights in the trees. He took a sip of wine and watched her twirl a forkful of pasta and pop it in her mouth.

As if sensing his scrutiny, she glanced up at him and smiled as she swallowed. "Why are you staring at me?"

"May I ask you something?"

"Shoot," she said, and leaned back in her chair.

"What did you mean when you said you couldn't get pregnant?" He had wondered why Jane only had one child.

"After Tyler was born, I had some issues, and the doctor said there was very little chance I'd ever get pregnant again. Nick and I tried for years, but nothing ever came of it. Now that I'm forty—excuse me, thirty-nine, I'm sure that 'very little chance' has been whittled down to zero." She tilted her head. "Does it bother you?"

Ryan shook his head. "No."

She folded her arms. "No lies, remember?"

Ryan took a deep breath, knowing he was treading on dangerous ground. "I'm just surprised you never mentioned it before."

"I'm not sure how it's relevant."

"It's relevant because I love you and I want a future with you. I'd like to think there aren't any secrets between us."

"Secrets? Not being able to get pregnant isn't a secret. It's a fact, and one that has nothing to do with our relationship. My baby-making days are over." She stood, and the chair legs slid along the patio pavers, echoing over the soft music. "This is what I was talking about. You and I are at different stages of our lives. You want a family. I've already had mine." She picked up her plate. "And now you go and … and love me, which means if we have a future together, you'll never have children. Damn it, Ryan. This is getting complicated."

She only had time to take one step toward the kitchen before he stopped her. He snaked a hand around her waist and took the dish from her with the other. "Hold on. This is very simple. You are my family. Babies or no babies, I want you, and everything that comes along with you."

She swallowed a sob. "You say that now, but—"

"No buts. You are my home." He spun her around so she faced him, and her body melted against his.

"What do you want?" she asked in the barest of whispers.

"You. Only you. Nothing else matters," he assured her, and knew that he had never spoken truer words.

Chapter Nineteen

Black Friday had taken on a new meaning. Ryan stayed in San Antonio since Vine was open to serve Thanksgiving dinner to the holiday tourists, and she'd spent a quiet Thanksgiving with Tyler and her mother in the city. There was something else missing other than Ryan, and it had eluded her for exactly twelve days. She plucked her phone from the bedside table and scrolled to Charlotte's number.

"Hello?" Charlotte's sleepy voice slurred at the other end of the phone.

"I'm late," Jane replied, pressing the phone to her ear … then hesitated. She could've sworn she heard a voice in the background. A distinctly male voice. "I'm sorry. You're not alone. Call me back later." Jane's finger was poised above the phone's touch screen.

"Oh, no you don't. There's a reason you called me at seven in the morning. And since I can't picture you waiting in line for a hot Black Friday deal, you can't possibly be late for anything at this ungodly hour, I'm assuming we're not talking about time here."

Breathe, Jane reminded herself sharply. *Just breathe.* "No. We're not. What am I going to do, Char?"

"Have you taken a test yet?"

"No, but I have one. I'm just too chicken to take it." She glared at the box on her nightstand. She'd purchased the pregnancy test kit the night before, still hoping she'd wake up with her period.

No such luck.

"Do it now, while I'm on the phone. If you don't, you'll stress about it all day. I know you," Charlotte said, sounding very calm and a little amused.

Well, she was right. Left to her own devices, Jane knew that she would find a million reasons not to take the test.

"But what if it's positive?"

"If it's positive, you'll have a baby in nine months, Jane. Do I have to teach you everything?" Jane could almost see her friend's smile through the phone.

"You know what I mean. What will I do? I'm too old to have a baby. And, jeez, how will I tell Ryan? *What* will I tell Ryan?"

"First of all, you're not too old to have a baby. Women have babies in their late thirties and early forties all the time. As for Ryan, I don't know him, but judging by what you've told me about him, I'd think he'd be ecstatic."

"But I told him I couldn't get pregnant." She pinched her nose with her thumb and forefinger.

"Well then, what a surprise for both of you. Come on, Jane. The suspense is killing me. Pee on the stick already."

"All right. Hold on a sec." Jane laid the phone next to the box and pulled the lid open. With the directions in one hand and the plastic stick in the other, she walked slowly to the bathroom. She followed the instructions to the letter, then washed her hands before returning to the phone. She poked the speaker button. "Still there?"

"Yup. What does it say?"

"Nothing yet." Jane's hand shook as she placed the stick on her nightstand and stared. "It takes a minute." A faint line appeared and grew darker. "One line." She looked at the box. One line not pregnant, two lines pregnant. "I guess I'm not—" But her gaze fixed on the stick as another faint line appeared, darkening with each beat of her racing heart. "Holy shit, Char. I'm going to have a baby."

"Holy shit is right. Um, congratulations?"

Jane's mind raced. *A baby. A baby. I'm having a baby.* In spite of her fear, a smile spread across her face, and she cupped her palm protectively over her belly. It'd been almost twenty years since she'd carried a life inside of her. At one point she'd wanted it so badly, and now it was finally happening.

It was a blessing, and she absolutely refused to think of it any other way.

"How am I going to tell him?"

"In my experience, the Band-Aid approach works best. Rip it off fast and as soon as possible. When's the next time you'll see him?"

"Not until he comes to New York for my birthday."

"Well, little does he know he's the one who'll be in for a surprise." Char's tone softened. "Meanwhile, let me know if there's anything I can do."

"There is something. You can promise not to tell a soul. I have to keep this absolutely quiet until I've told Ryan. No baby talk, and no baby jokes, deal?"

"My lips are sealed. And, speaking of lips, I have a sexy pair waiting for me in bed. Catch you later, momma."

Jane powered down her phone. She needed uninterrupted time to think. Right now, she was in no shape to talk to anyone, especially Ryan. She had two weeks to get used to the idea, and to figure out how best to break the news.

Chapter Twenty

"Happy Birthday, Ma!" Tyler's voice carried through the phone. "Hey, sing Happy Birthday to my mom!" he shouted, which was followed by an off-key rendition of "Happy Birthday" sung by what sounded like a room full of people. She laughed when she heard "Happy Birthday, Tyler's mom," drawing out the last "m" like it was a syllable of its own.

"Thank you, Ty," Jane said when the song ended. "That was sweet. Where are you, anyway? How are exams going?" She'd hoped he was studying.

"They're going well. I'm at the dining hall. What are you doing for your birthday?" Tyler asked.

"Remember I told you I was spending the weekend in Manhattan?"

"Right, with Ryan?" Jane sensed tension in his voice.

"Yes. You'll meet him at Christmas. You'd really like him, Tyler." She mentally slapped herself for not arranging for Tyler to meet Ryan earlier. She pictured how awkward the meeting will be now that she was pregnant. *Nice to meet you, Ryan. I hear you're my mom's baby daddy.* What would Tyler think of her having a baby at her age? A rush of worried thoughts took over her brain.

"I guess I'll find out soon. Hey, I gotta go. Love you."

"I love you, too, Ty. See you soon," Jane said as she headed to the elevator on her office floor. Her phone buzzed again as she strode across the lobby to the revolving door leading to the sidewalk. She glanced at her phone and smiled at the display. Jane had set a picture taken of Jane and Ryan at Vine as Ryan's contact. It was a cheesy shot of them raising their wine glasses at dinner one night, but Jane loved it. She swiped her finger across the screen. "Hi there."

"Just landed and wanted to hear your voice," he said huskily.

Ryan's words caressed Jane's frayed nerves. She smiled as she pictured him walking through the terminal. Stepping out of her office building, she used her free hand to wrap a scarf around her neck. "I hope you brought your coat. You're not in San Antonio anymore."

"I have it, and I can't wait to warm you up. Or will you warm me up?"

"How about we warm each other up?"

He lowered his voice. "I like the sound of that." His deep voice made her body hum. She wasn't sure if the pregnancy was causing her hormones to shift into overdrive, or if it was the fact that it'd been three weeks since they'd seen each other that had the heat pooling in her belly.

It was probably a little of both.

"I'm on my way now. Meet you in the lobby."

A summer's worth of butterflies fluttered in her stomach as she hopped into a cab. As much as Jane was looking forward to her weekend with Ryan, her stomach tied itself into knots every time she thought about the news she'd unleash on him that night.

When the cab turned onto Fifth Avenue, she forgot the well-rehearsed speech she'd planned to deliver. Her ride came to a stop in front of a luxury hotel. Ryan had obviously spared no expense on their weekend getaway, beginning with their stay at one of the most luxurious hotels in the city.

Jane's suitcase was whisked away as a doorman in a top hat directed her through the glass doors. She scanned the lobby, her heart beating like a jackhammer in her chest.

How would he react when she told him? What if he was angry? What if he accused her of tricking him? That would be a punch in the gut to her, but she'd survive. She owed it to her unborn baby to stay calm, whatever Ryan said.

Jane paced the lobby, waiting for him.

Maybe this wasn't a good idea, after all. Doubts swam through her mind, and the pounding in her chest moved to a new position, right above her eyes. A fog clouded her head, and a dizzy spell took over her body. She felt her knees begin to buckle … and then she was being caught by someone warm and strong who smelled delicious, just like…

"Ryan." She blinked, focused with difficulty on his face.

"What happened, *Querida*?" he demanded, his voice thick with concern. "You looked like you were about to faint." His brows seemed stitched together in concern, and he hadn't loosened his grip on her one bit.

"I'm okay. I didn't eat breakfast today. I'll feel better after I eat something."

He eased her into the nearest chair. "Stay here. Don't move. I'll grab you some water."

Jane leaned back and loosened her coat. The temperature in the lobby seemed to have spiked twenty degrees.

Ryan rushed back with two bottles of water. "Here." He twisted the cap off and handed her one of the bottles. "Little sips."

"Really, I'm okay." She held the bottle to her cheek before taking a drink. When she lowered the bottle, Ryan slipped her coat from her shoulders, and she smiled her thanks. "I'm much better. Really. Don't worry."

Concern still etched lines around his eyes. "Keep drinking. If you feel steady enough to be alone for a minute, I'll get us checked in so you can lie down."

"That sounds perfect," Jane assured him, and watched him stride to the registration desk, turning his worried gaze in her direction every few seconds.

Soon, with card access keys in hand, he returned. "Twelfth floor. Elevators are that way," he said, pointing. "Want me to carry you?"

Jane's gaze ticked up to meet his, and she smiled. "I can walk just fine," she assured him, but she wobbled slightly as she stood up.

Ryan's arm snaked around her back, steadying her as they walked to the bank of elevators and rode upward. But Jane felt her energy return as he opened the door to their suite.

"It's beautiful!" She walked to the large windows of the living room. "And check out this view. You can see the Park from here."

Their luggage arrived. Ryan tipped the bellman and closed the door. Then he joined her at the window, wrapping his arms around her and pulling her back to rest against his chest. His breath blew warm as he kissed the top of her head. "So, want to tell me what's going on?"

She turned in his arms and gazed into his eyes, which were filled with concern. What expression would those eyes hold, after she told him? Would they be filled with contempt instead of worry? She searched his face, and a lump formed in her throat as her pulse quickened. She needed more time.

Jane offered him a feeble smile. "You mean down in the lobby? I told you, I haven't eaten anything today. Besides, I still had my coat on, and the lobby was hot, wasn't it?"

His stare bored into her. "People don't faint easily, *Querida*. Besides, I've heard something in your voice, these past few weeks on the phone. Something's going on. We said we wouldn't keep anything from each other, remember? It was one of *your* demands."

"I believe my demand was that we wouldn't lie to each other." But, in effect, that was exactly what she was doing. Keeping something that important from him was the same as lying. But then she remembered Charlotte's advice: the Band-Aid approach. "No, I'm sorry. You're right." She took a deep breath. "Ryan, I'm pregnant."

He blinked. "You're… But you said … how can that be? Are you okay?"

She nodded. "Everything's fine. I've been to my doctor, and I asked her the same thing. I couldn't believe it. I'd tried for years to get pregnant again, and it seemed as if it just wasn't meant to be."

"So what did your doctor say?"

"Her exact words were 'Miracles happen.' But, Ryan, I want you to know that I truly believed I couldn't get pregnant. I don't want you to think I was trying to trap you into anything."

"Trap me? Why do you think I'd ever feel that way?" He shook his head. "Who do you think I am?" When she didn't reply, he pulled away and turned to face the window.

Jane looked at the back of his head. "I'm just giving you an out here. I can do this on my own if I have to." She moved to the sofa and flopped onto the cushions.

"Why would you think I need an out?"

She couldn't tell from his tone whether he was hurt or angry.

"Because this wasn't supposed to be forever," she explained. "We weren't supposed to be in a relationship."

He whipped around and moved to the chair next to the sofa where she sat. Grasping both ends of the upholstered chair-back, he leaned toward her. "But who made up those rules, Jane? *You*. You did." His nostrils flared. "Let's get this out in the open now. I don't know why you've constantly shut me out of anything long-term, but it has to stop, right now. A baby is long-term."

She swallowed hard. "I don't want to get hurt again. I promised myself that I wouldn't let anyone else hurt me the way Nick did." It was the first time she'd voiced her greatest fear.

Ryan stiffened. "You're comparing me to that ass of an ex-husband of yours? What makes you think I'd ever do that to you?" He walked around the chair and sat down, pinning her with his gaze.

Jane sighed. Why couldn't he see what was so self-evident to her? "Well, on one side of the equation we have you. You're young, sexy, and amazing. I see how women look at you—and that's just when we're together. I'm sure you're hit on all the time at Vine. And on the other side of the equation we have me. I'm going to be a forty-year-old new mom. How un-sexy is that?"

His features softened. "It's the sexiest thing I can imagine," he said and reached for her hand.

But she pulled away. "You say that now, but in a few months, or years, you may wish you were with someone younger."

He tilted his head. "I could say the same thing about you. How do I know *you* won't look for someone younger? Maybe I'll get too old for you." He shot her a crooked smile.

"You're making fun of me."

He slid next to her on the sofa. "No. I'm just trying to show you how silly your worries are. Jane, I love you. I think I fell in love with you before we even met. The moment I saw your picture, I felt a connection with you, so much that it scared me." He nudged her gently with his shoulder. "The main reason I stopped escorting was I couldn't tell the difference between what was real and what wasn't, so I stopped caring. It impacted my whole life. I even pulled away from my family and friends. But you've taught me what's real. What you and I have is real." He beamed. "I can't picture my life without you, and now with a baby. A baby! That's what's real."

His smile lit up her heart. "Why are you so perfect?"

He chuckled. "I'm far from perfect, but I'll always be there for you and our baby. I promise you that."

It was all she needed to hear. A tear escaped her eye. Then another. "I'm so scared." Until that point, she'd treated her pregnancy like a task to attend to. She'd made doctor appointments, taken her prenatal vitamins, eaten nutritious meals, and given up coffee. It was easy to focus on all of the things she had to do, because it kept her busy, which kept her from having to deal with the rest. Now that she'd dropped the bundle in Ryan's lap too, the emotional hurricane hit her, full force. "I never expected to have another baby. I thought that part of my life was over. What are people going to think?"

"This is between us. Who cares what people think?"

"I don't know how Tyler will react. And your sister certainly won't be pleased. She voiced her feelings about us to me, loud and clear."

"From what you've told me about Tyler, I think he'll handle it well. He seems like an easygoing kid. I can't wait to meet him. As far as Maya, she'll deal with it. And Isabel will be thrilled," Ryan said with a smile.

"I'm already spending Christmas in New York, and that'll give me a chance to get to know Tyler. And you'll be in San Antonio for New Year. Perfect!" He gave her a searching look. "Does anybody else know?"

"Just Charlotte," Jane admitted. "She was on the phone with me when I took the test."

"Well, I'm glad you had her for moral support, but I wish I could've been there for you." He gathered her into his arms. "We have a lot to talk about."

Jane took a deep breath and blew it out slowly. "We have time to figure it all out. Nearly nine months. For now, let's just enjoy the weekend, like we planned."

"What about your mother?"

"My mother... Oh crap. My mother. I forgot about the reservations." They had made dinner plans for the following evening, to introduce her mother to Ryan. Jane shook her head. "We'll have to tell her. I'm convinced that the woman has telepathic super powers."

Ryan chuckled. "If you're not ready, I'm sure we can keep it quiet."

"Impossible. She can read people like a book. Me especially." Jane rolled her eyes. "Oh, this is going to be great. 'Hey, Mom, meet my boyfriend. Oh, and guess what? I'm knocked up.' It's like a bad reality show."

But Ryan looked unruffled. "No matter how bad the ratings may get, they can't cancel us. Other people don't get a vote. Right now, there are only three people who matter."

"Three?"

"You, me, and our baby."

Chapter Twenty-One

"Are you sure you're okay to walk? We've had a busy day," Ryan said as he helped Jane with her coat, happy to see that the stress of the previous day had melted from her face. He'd ordered room service for breakfast and had tried to insist they spend the day in the suite. But Jane had scoffed, telling him it was her birthday, so she got to plan the agenda.

It had been a magical day. He loved seeing how her eyes lit up as she shared her favorite part of the holiday season in New York: window-shopping on Fifth Avenue. In addition to touring the beautiful window displays at Saks, Barney's, and Bergdorf Goodman, he'd talked her into some actual shopping, too.

"I feel great," she was assuring him now, retrieving her clutch from the table. "It's only a couple of blocks. The cab should be dropping my mother off soon, so we should hurry."

"There will be no hurrying for you, *Querida*. Your mom can wait a few minutes."

Jane raised her eyebrows as she applied her lip balm. "You don't know my mother. She's not used to being kept waiting. Oh well. At least you'll get brownie points for taking her to her favorite restaurant. She adores the place."

Together, they crossed the street and entered Central Park. The white stone building shone like a beacon as it sat nestled in a patch of trees and shrubs. "There," Jane said, pointing. "She's just getting out of the cab."

Ryan focused on the stately woman, whose almost-white hair was pulled back into a low bun. She was taller than he'd expected.

"Mom," Jane called and waved.

The woman's face lit up at the sight of her daughter. "Happy birthday, darling!" she said as she hugged Jane.

Ryan knew instantly that he needed to land—and remain on—the good side of Beverly Connolly. Her gaze was already flicking over to him, assessing him closely.

"Mom, I'd like you to meet Ryan Ziegler."

The older woman offered her hand. "Beverly Connolly. It's nice to finally meet the man who's been taking up so much of my daughter's time," she said, her voice slow and distinct. Ryan had the feeling that when Beverly talked, people listened.

He took her hand and kissed the top of her knuckles. "The pleasure is mine. I hope I haven't stolen any of your time with Jane."

"I'm happy if my daughter is happy," she said with a slight rise in her brow. "Shall we sit?"

They followed the maître d' to a table overlooking the garden. "I think this calls for champagne. A bottle of my favorite, please," she requested.

"Right away, Madam."

A waiter returned with the bottle and three champagne flutes.

"None for me, thank you. Water is fine," Jane said when he placed the glass to her right.

"No champagne on your birthday?" Beverly's gaze moved in her direction before lifting her glass. "Well then, to a beautiful night with a beautiful couple."

"Cheers," Ryan said, clinking his glass with Beverly and Jane.

Beverly took a long sip and closed her eyes as she swallowed. Then, carefully placing her glass on the tablecloth, she folded her hands. "You could cut the tension in here with a steak knife. What's going on?"

Ryan couldn't help but smile at Jane. "Your daughter told me how astute you are, Mrs. Connolly."

"It's Beverly, dear." She turned to her daughter. "Out with it, Jane."

Jane reached for Ryan's hand. "I don't know how to say this … so I'll just say it. I'm pregnant."

Beverly's gaze bounced from Jane to Ryan and back to Jane before she reached for her glass. She took a longer sip than the first, and held the glass between her fingers in silence for a moment before speaking. "Not much surprises me at my age, but I have to say, I'm very much surprised."

"I know, Mom. No one is more surprised than me."

"Tell me, darling, are you happy about it?"

Jane squeezed Ryan's hand. "Very much. It wasn't planned, but it was something I've wanted for a long time and I never thought it would happen again. I consider it a blessing."

"Then I'm happy, too. And I have questions. Lots of questions. For now, though, let's celebrate and enjoy the news of our new family member," she said, staring at Ryan.

He wasn't sure if she meant the baby or him.

The mood lightened from that point on. "Is this your first trip to New York?" Beverly asked.

Ryan shook his head. "I was here before I bought my restaurant. It was a research trip, to find out what made the best restaurants great. And what better place to find the best restaurants than New York?"

"And what did you discover? What makes a great restaurant?"

"Food, of course, but it's more than that. It's the energy and buzz of the atmosphere. When things are working well in a restaurant, it's like magic. You can feel it the moment you walk in."

She nodded slowly, and he was pleased that she seemed to like his answer.

Orders were placed and meals were eaten, along with great conversation and laughter. Beverly Connolly was like no one Ryan had ever met, but he liked her from the start. What he liked most about Jane's mother was that she didn't seem to care whether she was liked, as long as she was respected.

"Excuse me a moment," Jane said, and turned to Ryan, her eyes offering a silent apology. He stood, held her chair, and waited while she left the table.

Beverly patted the armrest of Jane's chair. "Sit next to me for a moment, Ryan."

He angled the chair so he faced the older woman. "I know this is a lot to take in, but I want you to know that I—"

"I know you love my daughter. I can see it in your eyes when you look at her. That's not my concern. I know it's fashionable to have untraditional relationships nowadays, but that's all a crock of shit, as far as I'm concerned. What are your intentions for my daughter and this child?"

"You don't beat around the bush, do you?"

"There's not enough time for a good beating. Judging by the look on my daughter's face, she was scared to death about leaving you here with me alone. She'll be back soon."

Ryan looked her in the eye. "I want to marry Jane, Beverly. I wanted to marry her even before I found out about the baby. I had already planned to propose to her this weekend." He patted his jacket and pulled a small box from his pocket. "I even have the ring." He flipped open the top, revealing a square-cut diamond solitaire.

Beverly reached for Ryan's hand and pulled the ring closer. "It's beautiful. You have fine taste." She released his hand and pointed to his chest. "You can tell a lot about a man by his taste in jewelry. Why haven't you asked her yet? I'm sure you've had the opportunity."

"I wanted to do this the right way, and speak with you before I asked her."

"I see."

"But now I'm afraid she's going to think I want to marry her just because of the baby. You and I both know she's not going to go for that."

She patted his hand. "That may indeed happen, but don't give up. She'll come around."

"I'll never give up on her or our baby."

"You're a good man, Ryan. Now put that away. Here she comes."

He slipped the box back into his pocket as the lights cast Jane's shadow across the table. "Are you two having some sort of powwow without me?"

"I'm just getting to know our dinner companion better. Come and sit. I have a surprise coming."

Their waiter appeared, carrying a chocolate cake on a silver platter, bearing a single lit candle. The other wait staff soon joined and began to sing "Happy Birthday".

As Jane blew out the candle to a round of applause, it seemed to Ryan that she had never looked more beautiful.

When their time together finally drew to a close, Ryan and Jane walked Beverly to the waiting cab.

The valet opened the cab door for Beverly. "Thank you for a lovely evening, Ryan." She gave him a light hug before cupping his cheek in her palm and offering him a slight nod.

"It was wonderful to meet you, Beverly. I hope to see you again soon."

"Take care of your bundle, Jane. Remember, love has a way of working itself out. Don't fret so much. Just let it be," Beverly ordered, and hugged her daughter.

"Okay, Mom. I'll call you soon."

They watched the taillights of the cab as it turned toward the park exit.

Clop, clop, clop.

Ryan's ears perked as the sound came closer. "What's that?" he asked innocently.

Jane turned toward the sound of the hooves and pointed to the horse and buggy meandering its way up the restaurant's driveway. It came to a stop just short of where they stood, and Jane stepped forward to pet the horse's nose. "How sweet. Someone ordered a carriage ride."

The driver swung his legs over the carriage and jumped to the ground. "Are you the Zeigler party?"

"Yes, sir," Ryan said, and winked at Jane.

"Me? This is for me?" Jane asked, her voice becoming practically a squeal in her excitement. "I've always wanted to take a carriage ride through the park. How did you know?"

"Just a guess," he said, leaving out the fact that Charlotte had called him, a few weeks earlier, and given him the tip, all the while swearing him to secrecy.

"I'm Max," the driver said, "and this is Daisy. We'll be your hosts for a stroll through the park. Your carriage awaits."

Jane clapped like a little girl and hopped aboard. Ryan followed her into the seating area of the carriage. A neat pile of pillows and blankets was perched on the padded bench. Ryan wedged a pillow behind Jane's back before unfolding the throw blanket and spreading it over her legs.

"The hot chocolate is there in the basket, just like you asked." The driver pointed to a wicker basket on the floor of the carriage that contained two travel mugs.

"Thank you, Max." He pulled one from the basket, twisted the top and handed it to Jane. "I figured hot chocolate was a good substitute for that champagne you had to pass up."

Jane took a sip. "A girl could get used to this treatment, Mr. Zeigler. This is hands-down the best birthday I've ever had."

He slipped his arm around her, and she rested her head on his shoulder as the carriage began its descent into the park. The slow rhythm of Daisy's hooves and the gentle rocking of the carriage calmed his nerves enough to make his decision. He'd had every intention of proposing tonight. It had been his plan for weeks. But his decision had wavered after Jane's reaction to telling him about the baby. However, Beverly's words at the restaurant had set him back to his original course. He only hoped like hell that he wasn't about to ruin the best birthday Jane had ever had.

Ryan scanned the path ahead, and spotted a place where it widened under a tree lit with small white lights, which reminded him of their patio oasis. "Max, would you stop up there near that tree?"

"Of course, Mr. Zeigler."

Jane gave him a curious look as he took a swig of hot chocolate. He wished he'd also had a shot of whiskey.

"Whoa, Daisy," Max called and brought the carriage to an easy stop. Jumping down, he walked forward to attend to the horse.

"What's going on?" Jane asked, then drew an audible breath as Ryan slid from the bench and got down on one knee in front of her. "Oh, Ryan, you're not going to do what I think you are, are you?"

He couldn't read her half-smile. All he could do was hope for the best. There was no turning back. He pulled the box from his jacket and fumbled with the top.

"Jane, I love you with all my heart, and my only wish is for you to be my wife." He flipped open the box and she gasped.

Her gaze bounced from the ring to him, and she began to shake her head slowly, back and forth. "Is this about the baby? Because, if it is—"

"Jane, look. Look at the box. I bought this ring more than a month ago, at a jewelry store in San Antonio." He pointed to the print on the small box. "I've been planning this for weeks. It has nothing to do with the baby. I was already planning to propose."

Jane squinted at the ring box. "You wanted to marry me, even when you thought I couldn't have kids? You'd have given up having children, just to marry me?"

"Honestly, I'd hoped we might try to adopt a child one day, but yes, absolutely, I wanted to marry you, with or without kids. Jane, my knee is frozen to the floor. Would you please say you'll marry me, so I can get up?"

Her lower lip trembled. "Yes. Yes, I'll marry you," she said, and threw her arms around him.

Ryan stood up, taking her with him, lifting her body against his chest. He kissed the tears from her cheeks, then brushed his lips over hers. "You've made me the happiest man in New York." He set her down and turned to the path below. "She said yes, Max! Did you hear that? She said yes!"

Max climbed aboard. "Of course she did. No one ever says no on my carriage. Daisy brings good luck."

"We'll take all the good luck we can get," Ryan said.

Ryan heard laughter and a few congratulatory cheers from passersby. Setting Jane down and sitting beside her, he plucked the ring from its case. "Give me your hand," he said taking her left hand in his, and slipping the ring on her finger.

"It fits perfectly. How did you know my size?" When he just smiled, she nodded. "Charlotte," they said in unison.

Jane held her hand away from her face and stared at the diamond. "It's so beautiful. My mother always says you can tell a lot about a man by his taste in jewelry."

"I know. She told me," Ryan said, and grinned.

"So, now we have two bombshells to drop on our loved ones during the holidays," Jane said, smiling.

"So we do." Ryan picked up the mugs of hot chocolate and handed one to Jane, then tipped the edge of his mug against hers with a little clang. "Happy Birthday, *Querida*. And get ready for a Merry Christmas."

Chapter Twenty-Two

Jane slid the scalloped potatoes into the oven as the doorbell rang. "Coming," she called in a sing-song voice, then pulled her oven mitts off and dashed to the front door. Tyler was late, as usual, but she couldn't wait to see his goofy smile, and she still hoped he would arrive before Ryan returned with Beverly.

She smiled recalling Ryan taking the phone from her hand when she'd been in the middle of arguing with her mother about her mode of transportation. Beverly's fierce independence had her set on taking a cab to and from Jane's apartment, because she didn't want Jane driving. Jane almost regretted telling her mother about the baby so early in the pregnancy, and yet she couldn't imagine keeping that kind of news from her mother. As she tried to explain it was perfectly healthy for pregnant women to drive, Ryan solved the problem by announcing he'd drive in and pick Beverly up. Her mother seemed pleased with the new plan, because she'd stopped protesting immediately, although she'd continued to wax on about how driving could cause stress to an unborn baby.

It was going to be a long pregnancy.

She pulled the door open, ready to wrap Tyler in a hug, and instead her eyes widened in shocked surprise. "Nick?" She couldn't have been more surprised if Santa Claus himself appeared on her doorstep in his red suit and hat.

"Merry Christmas," Nick said sheepishly, and held out a bouquet of flowers she was sure he'd picked up at one of the gas stations near the bridge.

Jane didn't budge from her spot on the door's threshold. "What are you doing here?"

"Tyler invited me. Didn't he tell you?" When she still didn't move, he sighed. "Aw, come on. Give me a break, Jane. No one should be alone on Christmas, right?"

She blew out a long-suffering breath, just as the kitchen timer sounded from inside. "Okay," she said, shaking her head in disbelief of her rotten luck. "Fine. There's plenty of food."

"It'll be like old times," he said as he stepped into the small entry.

"I promise you it won't be anything like old times, Nick." She huffed out a sarcastic laugh. He had no idea what he was in for that evening. She almost felt bad for him. Almost.

Nick followed her into the kitchen. "Nice place," he said, looking around. Then she saw his gaze shift to her small Christmas tree. Over the years, she'd saved all of Tyler's handmade ornaments, hanging them on the tree each Christmas, and this year was no exception. "A lot of memories there," Nick said softly, then coughed and said, "You always do a nice job of decorating for the holidays."

"Thanks. You can hang your coat over there." She pointed to the closet door.

On his way back from the coat closet, he slowed down at her small dining alcove to scan the place settings on the table. "Is Charlotte coming?"

"Nope, Char's in Aruba with her new friend," Jane said. Lucky Charlotte. Jane would give her eyeteeth to be lounging on a tropical beach, instead of breaking the news she'd have to break.

"Of course she is. So, you gonna tell me who the extra setting is for, since you clearly weren't expecting me, or should I just keep guessing?"

His tone grated at her last nerve. She set the knife on the cutting board and twirled around. "Ryan. It's for Ryan."

Nick cleared his throat. "Ryan? The guy from your business trip? Tyler didn't mention he was going to be here."

"I imagine Tyler didn't mention it because he didn't actually invite you, did he? Jeez, Nick. Why do you feel like you have an invitation to just waltz into my life whenever you please?"

He huffed out a breath. "You want me to leave so your little boy toy won't be offended," he spat and started toward the closet.

"Wait." Jane pinched the bridge of her nose between her thumb and index finger, and closed her eyes. Nick had to hear the news sometime, and the present moment was as good as any. "Stay. Sit down for a second. I have something to tell you, before everyone gets here."

Nick furrowed his brows, but he pulled a stool from under the kitchen island. Then, with another huff, he rested his folded arms on the counter. "What is it?"

She studied his condescending expression, wondering why she'd stayed with him as long as she had. She'd been wrapped in a cocoon of the life of Nick Keegan for so long, she'd truly had no idea what she was missing until she finally broke free. "Ryan and I are engaged."

Nick's eyes and mouth flew open, and Jane had to stifle a laugh, because he bore an uncanny resemblance to a striped bass. She held up her palm and remembered Charlotte's advice: the Band-Aid approach. "Before you say anything, that's not all. I'm also pregnant."

An insolent laugh erupted from Nick's throat. "You're kidding me, right? This whole thing is some kind of warped joke. Remember, this is Christmas, not April Fool's Day."

Jane straightened her spine and folded her arms. "It's no joke."

Nick stood so fast, the stool made a loud scraping noise on the tiled floor. "Wow, Jane. How fucking stupid could you be?" He threw up his hands. "Can't you see it? He's going to leave you broke and with a kid to take care of." He narrowed his eyes. "You're forty years old. What do you think a guy like that wants from you?"

A seething heat rolled up Jane's neck to her cheeks as a flurry of emotions hit her, each one feeling like a blow to her stomach. Anger, hurt, and disappointment all vied for her attention.

She was trying to formulate a coherent reply when the door slammed and two sets of footsteps started down the hallway. Ryan appeared with Beverly's hand tucked in the crook of his elbow. His gaze sought Jane's before he turned to help Beverly with her coat.

"Nick, dear," Beverly said. "What a surprise— although not an altogether pleasant one, by the looks of things. Still, on the bright side, now I have a date!" she said, as her gaze toggled between Nick and Jane.

Nick walked over to Beverly and hugged her. "You're looking well as always, Bev." He turned toward Ryan and extended his hand. "I'm Nick, Jane's hus—ex-husband. You must be Ryan."

Jane watched the muscles in Ryan's jaw clench. "Yes. As you may recall, you and I spoke on the phone, a couple months ago," Ryan said, meeting Nick's palm with his own, and raising one eyebrow.

"Right. About that … it was a misunderstanding. I apologize."

"Misunderstanding? No, I believe I understood you completely." Ryan's voice was calm and even as he moved to Jane's side and slipped his hand around her waist. "I also overheard the questions you were firing at my fiancée when I came in. I don't need to explain my intentions to you, Nick, but let's get something straight. If you ever speak to Jane that way again, least of all in her own home, you won't be using your mouth for anything else for quite a long time afterward. Are we clear?"

Nick nodded once, and Jane caught the nervous bob of his Adam's apple as his gaze followed Ryan's fingers stroking up and down her side.

"Tyler's on his way in," Ryan said, "so if your presence is going to ruin the holiday for Jane, I suggest you leave now. If you choose to stay, I expect you to treat her with respect."

Jane turned to Ryan. "Tyler's here?"

"Outside." His hand trailed up her back, and he lightly kneaded her neck with his fingers before his lips touched hers. "He had to park on one of the side streets. He'll be here in a second. Are you okay?"

She nodded and turned her gaze to Nick. "Tyler doesn't know about any of our news yet, Nick. I want him to hear it from me."

"Understood." Nick backed out into the hall. "I'll go see if he needs any help." He grabbed his coat and shuffled to the door.

As the door closed, Jane asked, "You met Tyler?"

Ryan nodded. "He gave me his parking spot when he saw Beverly. He's a good kid. You sure you're okay?" He grazed her cheek with the back of his hand.

"I'll be fine. Nick just gets me so mad. He showed up out of the blue, claiming Tyler had invited him. I should've sent him away, but I felt sorry for him, alone at the holidays. And he is Tyler's father." She managed a smile. "Besides, I figured I'd have to tell him, sooner or later. It wouldn't be fair to ask Tyler to keep the news from his father. I just regret that you had to hear his venom."

"What he said about me doesn't bother me. He's just jealous. But it took every ounce of self-control I had, not to throw him through the wall for what he said to you. As far as I'm concerned, he's used up his one free pass. Next time, I won't be so nice." Ryan kissed her again. "Now, go sit down with your mom. I'm serving dinner."

A minute later, Tyler bounded into the apartment and gave Jane a bear hug. "Sorry I'm late. Lots of traffic." He hugged Jane and Beverly then turned to Nick. "I didn't know you were going to be here, Dad," he said giving him a hug.

"It's quite a surprise," Jane said surveying her son. She could've sworn he'd grown taller since the last time she saw him. Or possibly it was the way he carried himself, with confidence and maturity. She cupped his cheeks in her hands. "I'm so happy you're here. Grab something to drink and tell me what's going on at school."

Jane and Ryan shared stolen glances as she listened to Tyler's stories about school, while Ryan kept busy in the kitchen. He rearranged the table to fit their extra guest, who seemed to be following Ryan's directions to the letter. Nick was so quiet, Jane almost forgot he was there.

"Dinner is served," Ryan announced at last. Taking Jane's hand, he led her to the head of the table, his actions an unspoken but unmistakable statement.

Between Tyler's humor and the amazing food, the mood lightened. Soon, everyone was eating, drinking and being merry.

"Wow, Ma. Either you really outdid yourself or I've eaten too many bad meals on campus. This dinner is delicious."

"Probably a little of both. But I can't take all the credit. Ryan did most of the cooking."

"Mom told me you own a restaurant in San Antonio," Tyler said.

Ryan nodded. "It's called Vine, and it's a restaurant and wine bar on the River Walk."

"I hear the River Walk gets pretty rowdy," Nick said.

"That's one reason I chose the location as the perfect venue for my restaurant. Vine's quiet atmosphere gives people a calm alternative to some of the more rambunctious spots."

"Is that where you two met?" Tyler asked, looking from Ryan to Jane.

Jane glanced at Ryan, and the circumstances of their introduction flashed through her mind.

But Ryan answered calmly. "Yes. Your mom stopped in for dinner, one night. It was late. I think she had just arrived in San Antonio." He squeezed her hand under the table.

Tyler laughed. "I can just picture my mom, shying away from the party spots."

"Oh, come on," Jane teased. "I can party with the best of them." She looked around the table. "How about dessert?" she asked, and stood, reaching to gather the dinner plates.

"Leave them, Ma," Tyler urged. "I'll clean up."

"This was wonderful, but I'm beginning to feel tired," Beverly said. "Nick, you're heading back to the city. I'm sure you wouldn't mind going a little out of your way to drop an old broad home on Christmas."

"I wouldn't mind at all," Nick said, and smiled at Beverly. "I'll get your coat," he said, and left the table.

"Thanks, Mom," Jane mouthed. Slipping into the kitchen, she packed two slices of Ryan's pecan pie, and brought them out as Beverly and Nick said their good-byes.

Tyler put his arm around Jane's shoulder as they watched Nick's car drive away. "You know I didn't invite him, right?"

Jane smiled at her son. "I know."

"And it didn't turn out as bad as I thought it'd be, having Dad here with Ryan."

Jane laughed, thankful that Tyler hadn't arrived in time to witness the first Nick versus Ryan showdown.

Tyler pointed his thumb over his shoulder. "By the way, he's a good dude. I'm glad you found somebody. Now I don't have to worry about you so much." He gave her his best toothy smile.

"Isn't it my job to worry about you?" she asked. "Let's get some dessert. Ryan and I have something to tell you."

They headed back inside, where Ryan was setting out pies. "I didn't realize how much food we had!" Jane exclaimed, surveying the four pies and platters of leftover food.

"It'll come in handy when you're gone next week. When do you leave for San Antonio?" Tyler asked.

"Ryan's leaving tomorrow, to get back to the restaurant. I'll fly out Wednesday, to spend New Year's with his family. You sure you don't want to join me?"

"Nah, some of my friends are going into Times Square. Dad said we could crash at his place."

Jane nodded, hoping Nick would live up to his word. "You can always come back here."

Tyler cut a huge slice of apple pie and topped it off with two scoops of vanilla ice cream. "You said you have something to talk about?" Tyler asked between bites.

Jane took a deep breath. "Ryan and I are getting married."

Tyler's gaze moved from Jane to Ryan and back to Jane. "Sorry but it's a little fast, isn't it?"

"Not really. I know you just met him, but Ryan and I have known each other for a while now." She turned to Ryan for the strength to get through the next part. "We're also having a baby."

"Whoa. I wasn't expecting that." Tyler set his plate down. "Wow, Ma. A baby? Wow." He narrowed his eyes. "Are you okay? I mean, you're older now."

Jane shook her head, smiling in spite of herself. "Thanks for pointing that out, Ty. To answer your question, I will need to take it easy, especially toward the end, but the baby and I are doing just fine. I'm due in July."

Tyler gnawed at his bottom lip, the way he always did when he was thinking hard about something. "So, where will you live?"

"I'll live primarily at Ryan's house in San Antonio."

"*Our* house," Ryan corrected with a smile.

"Our house. There's plenty of room there. There's a bedroom for you there, too. Plus, I'm going to keep this place for when I'm in New York for work." The issue of Jane keeping her job was the only topic Ryan and she had disagreed on. He'd urged her to quit and stay home, but Jane didn't feel ready to give up her career.

Tyler nodded and extended his hand to Ryan. "Welcome to the family. You don't want me to call you 'dad' or anything, do you? Because that would be weird."

Ryan shook his hand and chuckled. "Ryan will do. And thanks."

Tyler took a deep breath. "If this is what you want, I'm happy for you. I don't get why you want to change poop diapers, though."

"Hey, I changed your poop diapers and I survived, just barely," Jane teased.

Tyler shrugged. "I'm going to grab another slice of pie."

Tyler headed to the kitchen, and Ryan wrapped his arms around Jane, pulling her against his chest. It was her favorite place to be. "Well, there. Your family is done. Mine's next," he said, and kissed the top of her head.

"That should be fun," Jane said, thinking, *if fun means having a root canal without Novocain.*

"Who knows? Maybe Maya will surprise us," Ryan said.

"Maybe," Jane said.

Chapter Twenty-Three

Jane's frequent trips to San Antonio usually began with a belly full of butterflies as she almost sprinted through the airport terminal into Ryan's arms. This time her stomach was tied in ugly knots.

Nevertheless, it seemed that she was the only person in a "bah-humbug" mood. Happy passengers in Christmas sweaters, lugging bags of gifts, bustled around her as she walked, searching for her first glimpse of Ryan and his sign. She smiled when she spotted the sign, but it wasn't cradled in Ryan's tanned, masculine hands. Instead, the sign was held about two feet lower than usual, and it was bouncing up and down.

"Isabel!" Jane ran to the little girl and gave her a hug. "What are you doing here? Where's Uncle Ryan?"

"He's right over there. I told him I wanted to be your pickup person today."

A wave of calm washed over Jane when she spied Ryan beaming at her from his perch nearby. His expression told her that everything was going to be okay. Taking Isabel's hand, she walked the final distance to him.

"Hello, *Querida*."

"Hi." Jane rose on her tiptoes and kissed him lightly on the lips.

"Eww," Isabel squealed. "I'm never gonna kiss a boy."

Ryan knelt to Isabel's level. "You'd better not, or I'll have to beat him up."

Isabel covered her mouth and giggled.

"Ready to take Miss Jane to the new Italian ice place we found?"

"Let's go!" Isabel's left hand retained its grip on Jane as she slipped her right hand into Ryan's.

Jane's gaze swept from Isabel, who was busy singing a song about ice cream, to Ryan.

He flashed her a wink. "I thought you might need a little taste of what's to come."

Isabel swung their arms as the threesome strolled to the baggage carousel. Jane and Ryan would soon have their own child to hold hands with and take out for ices. For Jane, that thought made the event she would soon endure a little easier to swallow.

They collected her bag and headed through the glass doors to the parking lot. Jane took a deep breath, savoring the warmth that hung in the air, a sharp contrast to New York's late December weather. "It's the perfect day for an Italian ice in San Antonio," Ryan said to Isabel as he helped her into the car.

Jane folded her coat and laid it on the seat next to Isabel.

"Why did you bring a coat?" Isabel asked.

Jane smiled, explaining, "I won't need it here, but I needed it where I just came from."

"Where's that?"

"New York City. It's cold there now."

"Momma said people from New York aren't very nice," Isabel said with a frown.

Jane looked at Ryan. "I suppose that's true of some of them."

"Just like not all of the people in San Antonio are nice," Ryan added. "But the great thing about New York is, there are so many people there that you can just ignore the mean ones." He steered the car out of the parking lot.

"I think Miss Jane is nice."

"So do I, Iz. So do I."

****

Ryan's reflection appeared behind Jane as she checked out her flowing dress in the full-length mirror.

"You look beautiful," he assured her, his smoky voice caressing all the warm places on her body.

"The boho look is the perfect camouflage for my little tummy." She'd already changed several times while waiting for him to return from the restaurant.

Vine was booked solid for New Year's Eve, and Ryan had been there all day, to ensure that his staff could handle the rest of the night without him. Now he reached around her and slid his palm over her ribs. The heat of his hand smoothed its way over her stomach and came to rest low on her belly. "I can't wait to feel our baby move inside you."

She turned in his arms and trailed her fingertips from the sleeve of his shirt up to his collar. As she played with the ends of his hair, his mouth slanted over hers, and pregnancy hormones exploded into a sea of heat and want.

Ryan groaned. "We'd better go, before we end up back in bed," he whispered.

Jane matched his groan. Spending the evening in bed sounded infinitely better than being at his sister's house, where the entire Rosales clan would watch her, and judge her, and whisper to each other in Spanish, leaving her to wonder what they were saying. But it would be a relief to have everything out in the open, even if it meant exposing herself to unwanted attention and possible ridicule.

"I won't let anything happen to you, *Querida*," he said kissing her lightly.

With his strong arms wrapped around her in strength and love, Jane found the courage to nod. "Let's go do this."

****

Ryan shifted his car into Park as Jane surveyed the house. She hadn't been to Maya's since the weekend

187

she met Ryan. At least, judging by the cars parked on the street, there weren't as many guests as there had been during her last party.

Ryan seemed to read her mind. "Maya limits the New Year's Eve guest list to immediate family. This is the first one I've been to in a few years."

"Well then, I should earn at least a few brownie points for getting you here, right?"

"She was happy when I told her we were coming," Ryan said, smiling down at her as he opened her car door.

Jane could translate that easily enough: Maya was overjoyed *he* would be there. Her? Not so much.

She took his hand, and he helped her from the car. "Do we have a plan?"

"The perfect one. They love to watch the New York City festivities on television so we'll tell everyone just before the ball drops at Times Square."

"I like the way you think, Mr. Zeigler. Hit them with the news, then move the focus from us to the New York countdown. Clever."

"With any luck, we'll be out of there to celebrate the stroke of midnight in our own way."

Jane grinned up at him, then stole a kiss before he opened the front door. "I love the sound of that." If things got uncomfortable, they could be out of there in just a couple of hours.

Isabel met them inside. "Momma's letting me stay up to watch the ball drop, this year!"

"That's fantastic, Iz." Ryan looked around. "Where is your mom anyway?"

"In the kitchen with Tia Rose and Tilly."

Jane raised her eyebrows. "You told her I was coming, right?"

A muscle in Ryan's jaw clenched, and he nodded. "Of course. She's unbelievable." He squeezed her hand, and they headed toward the kitchen.

"Reyo!" Maya caroled as soon as he appeared. "There you are. We were wondering when you'd get here." She pulled him against her tiny frame for a hug.

"And you remember Jane."

Jane managed a smile, with Ryan's hand on her back providing the support she needed to deal with Maya's icy gaze.

"How could I forget?" Maya gave her a once-over. "What an interesting dress."

Ryan turned Jane to face his aunt, and leaned down to kiss the older woman's cheek. "*Feliz Año Nuevo, Tia.* I'd like to introduce you to Jane."

"*Mucho gusto, Señora Rosales*," Jane said carefully. She'd asked Ryan to teach her a few Spanish phrases so she could begin to communicate with his non-English-speaking relatives.

The gesture seemed to impress his aunt. She gave Jane a warm smile and nodded her head as Uncle Pascal strode into the kitchen.

"Ah, *Señorita*. It's wonderful to see you again." He took hold of her hand and kissed her knuckles making her feel welcome. "You met *mi esposa,* Rosa?"

"*Sí.*" Jane smiled warmly at the elderly couple who spoke in soft voices to each other.

"Rosa is shy about speaking English, but she says you're *bonita* … very pretty."

"*Muchas gracias*," Jane responded as she eyed Tilly shimmy up to Ryan. Where Jane's dress was long and flowing, Tilly's skimpy outfit clung to every dip and curve. Who needed to watch the crystal-encrusted ball in Times Square when Tilly could bend over and flash her own perky attributes?

"Hi, Ryan. I'm glad you could make it this year," she purred.

"Thanks," he said, and turned back to Maya. "May I speak to you outside for a second?" he asked, and pointed to the sliding glass door leading to the deck.

"Only for a second. I have a party to attend to."

Ryan gave Jane's shoulder a reassuring squeeze before he followed his sister to the deck.

Left behind, Jane scanned the counters filled with food and desserts. "Everything looks delicious," she said, although she doubted whether her nervous stomach would allow her to try a thing. Instead, she bought some time by dropping ice cubes into a plastic cup, one by one.

The glass door finally slid open again as she twisted the cap off of a bottle of club soda. A moment later, Ryan took the bottle from her hand and poured the clear bubbly liquid into her cup.

"Everything okay?" Jane asked.

"Couldn't be better."

She held the cup to her mouth and stole a glance at the open door leading to the deck. "Where's your sister?" she whispered.

"She … needed a minute. Let's go say hello to everyone else." Ryan guided Jane into the large family room, saying softly, "I had to put a stop to her. I told her everything, at least the summarized version. Hope you don't mind."

Jane's heart skipped a beat. "How'd she take it?"

Ryan chuckled. "I wish you could've seen the look on her face. Priceless."

"You two certainly enjoy tormenting each other."

Isabel ran up and grabbed her free hand. "Play cards with us, Miss Jane," Isabel pleaded, and led her to a group of kids sitting in a circle. "Know how to play Go Fish?"

"I'm a Go Fish champ." Jane sat on a sofa in front of the coffee table surrounded by a half dozen children who appeared to be close to Isabel's age or older.

Isabel climbed into Jane's lap. "We'll play as a team." Isabel beamed then focused on the cards they were dealt. She held them to her chest as the boy next to them leaned closer. "No fair, Daniel. You're peeking."

"No, I'm not." And the boy flashed Jane a crooked grin resembling Ryan's smile. Seemed as though charm flowed through the Rosales bloodlines.

Isabel glanced up at Jane. "They try to trick me because I'm the youngest, but I know what they're doing."

Jane gave her a squeeze. "Okay let's see what we have."

Isabel shielded her hand from Daniel and showed the cards to Jane.

"Do you have any sevens?" Daniel asked.

Isabel glared at him. "Did you see my cards?" She plucked the seven of hearts from her hand and picked up a new card.

"Nope," he said and placed his pair on the table.

"It's our turn," Isabel whispered to Jane. "Do you have any tens?"

As a girl sitting cross-legged on the other side of the table passed Isabel her card, Jane made note of the serenity that settled upon her while watching them play. She pictured how her own child would fit into the tight-knit Rosales family quilt. Would they accept him or her or would the child be the proverbial black sheep of the family?

A shadow fell over her cards, and she smiled at the sound of Ryan's voice as he asked, "Well? Is she as good as she claims, Iz?"

Isabel giggled and shook her head. "Not really."

"Then you won't mind if I steal her for a little while, will you?"

Isabel slid off her lap as Jane accepted his outstretched hands and he pulled her to a standing position. They made their rounds through the house meeting Ryan's relatives and listening to family stories. She even managed to eat a few bites.

"Your family is never-ending."

"It does feel that way sometimes." He checked the television screen for the time. "The ball drops in fifteen minutes. Are you ready?"

She bit her lip. "How about if I hide in the bathroom while you do the honors?"

"Not a chance. I already took care of the tough one. You've won over everyone else. This will be a piece of cake." He grabbed the remote from the table and turned down the volume of the television.

"Everyone," he said, his voice pitched to cut through the ambient noise of the party, "may I have your attention?"

The chatter died down to a low murmur.

"Thanks. I'm glad we're all together to celebrate the New Year, because I want you to share some special news with us." Ryan's hand snaked around Jane's waist, and she felt the weight of the stares of a roomful of Rosales family members. "This beautiful woman has agreed to be my wife. Jane and I are getting married!"

Applause erupted, and a sea of smiles flashed her way.

Ryan raised his hand. "Hold on, hold on. There's more." He beamed. "We're also going to have a baby." He gazed into her eyes, and Jane knew beyond a doubt, in that moment, how very much he wanted their baby.

A stunned silence swept over the room. Then Uncle Pascal shouted something in Spanish, and everyone laughed and clapped.

"What did he say?" Jane murmured.

"He said, 'Leave it to Reyo to top his own news.' I think they approve."

Jane scanned the room of happy faces, and her gaze snagged on the only scowl in the group. Maya was leaning against the wall at the back of the room, her arms folded at her chest. She glared at Jane, then turned and trudged back to the kitchen.

"I should talk to her," Jane said reluctantly, and started toward the kitchen.

Ryan caught her arm. "That's a discussion for another day, *Querida*."

"I'd like to clear the air. We're going to be family after all."

He shook his head. "Leave it alone for now. Let's enjoy the celebration with the family."

Pascal slapped Ryan on the back, interrupting their conversation. "I have to take some credit for this," he said with a pleased smile. "I knew you two had something special which is why I took you to Marriage Island." He turned his attention to Jane. "Do you remember?"

"How can I forget?" she replied, remembering the night she'd met Ryan.

Someone raised the volume on the television again, and the crowd began to chant the countdown in time with the numbers flashing on the screen.

"20 ... 19 ... 18 ... 17..."

Ryan pulled her against his chest. "We did it. We told both our families, and we're still standing."

"13 ... 12 ... 11 ... 10..."

Jane's gaze flicked toward the kitchen. "So far, yes. But we don't know what she's planning in there," she teased.

"7 … 6 … 5…"

"How about we get out of here before we find out the hard way?"

Jane nodded.

"2 … 1 … Happy New Year!"

Ryan hooked his thumb under her chin and pressed his lips to hers. "Happy New Year, *Querida*."

"Happy New Year." She kissed him, but she couldn't help feeling a little dazed as she imagined all the changes the coming year would bring.

****

A few minutes later, Isabel intercepted Jane as she headed for the front door to meet Ryan. "Miss Jane, are you leaving already?"

"Uncle Ryan needs to check in at the restaurant, but I'll see you again real soon." She bent and held out her arms for a hug.

"Is it true you're going to have a baby?" Isabel's eyes were wide.

Jane nodded. "It's true."

"And you're going to get married to Uncle Ryan?" Isabel sang.

Jane laughed. "That's true, too."

"I'm going to wear a pretty dress to your wedding and put flowers in my hair, just like you had when we first met."

Jane was touched that the little girl remembered such a small detail. "That sounds absolutely lovely. Happy New Year, Isabel."

"Happy New Year, Aunt Jane," Isabel said, and gave her a big hug.

Jane's eyes welled up with tears at Isabel's replacement of "Miss" with "Aunt". She waved good-bye to Isabel and stepped outside with Ryan, letting out a relieved breath when he pulled the door closed behind them.

"Ready to celebrate your first San Antonio New Year's Eve?" he asked as he helped her into the car, and she nodded, grateful that the hard part of the evening was over.

They headed toward the bright lights of downtown San Antonio. Ryan parked as close as he could, but they still had to weave through throngs of people wearing light-up glasses and hats, laughing and blowing whistles.

Slowly, she and Ryan made their way toward Vine. Strands of colored lights hung from the light posts, trees, and restaurant terraces for as far as she could see. "Wow! San Antonio certainly goes all out for New Year's Eve."

By the time Jane spotted Vine, Gretchen was already waving at them from the hostess stand next to the patio.

"I didn't think you'd be back," Gretchen shouted over the noise. "What's the matter? Don't you trust us?"

"I'm off duty. We're here for the best table on the River Walk to watch the fireworks." Ryan surveyed the filled tables. "How are things going?"

"Off duty, my ass," Gretchen retorted, and laughed. "We've been filled to capacity all night, and we're selling a ton of alcohol. Now let me see what I can do about a table for the two of you."

Gretchen had the waiters pull a small table and two chairs from the back to the patio. A tablecloth and candle completed the romantic New Year's Eve setting. Jane and Ryan sat down just as the first boom of fireworks sounded above their heads, followed by a stream of sparkling lights.

Jane gasped. "It's beautiful." The crowd started chanting the countdown. "This is for real, now."

"Things are about to get *very* real. Are you ready for it?" Ryan asked, and kissed her hand.

She watched the waves of color light up the sky. Then, lacing her fingers through his, she pulled his hand to her cheek and closed her eyes. The warmth of his skin gave her strength to face the onslaught of changes that would be thrust upon them soon. "As long as you're by my side," Jane said, "I'm ready for anything."

Chapter Twenty-Four

Wedding plans and New York's cold, dank weather kept Jane in San Antonio for a good portion of the winter, and Ryan couldn't have been more pleased. He was far less happy about how her workload multiplied with the success of her biggest client's new campaign. She was increasingly in demand at work, which was a curse, as far as he was concerned.

Jane, however, considered it a blessing. It enabled her to negotiate more flexibility in her schedule, as well as a generous increase in her salary, although it came at a price that was immediately evident to Ryan. A never-ending onslaught of e-mails, phone calls, and texts left little room in Jane's life for anything other than her clients and their projects. The line between work and her off time became ever more blurred. Ryan tried to be supportive, telling himself that she would eventually draw a line in the sand and push back some of the work. Still, as the weeks wore on, she seemed to choose work over him more times than not, and his patience wore thin.

In an effort to break her work-athon schedule, he proposed a deal with Jane for Valentine's Day weekend. She agreed to shut off her phone and stay away from her laptop, doing no work for the entire weekend, while he, in turn, promised to take her on a scouting tour for wedding locations, followed by a special dinner at Vine.

Ryan woke early on Valentine's Day and decided to up the ante. He prepared Jane's favorite breakfast and, instead of serving it on the patio, decided to surprise her with breakfast in bed. He crept upstairs with a tray piled high with coffee, juice, and her favorite cinnamon French toast. Nudging the door open with his hip, his gaze moved to the bed where he'd expected to find her sleeping soundly … and stopped abruptly, causing the glass to rattle on the tray.

At the sound, Jane looked up from the laptop that was propped on her legs. Her eyes widened in surprise, and she pointed to the screen. "Just checking my e-mail for a second." She closed her laptop, placed it on the bedside table and eyed the tray. "What do you have there?"

Ryan swallowed the lump of anger in his throat, and strode to the dresser, sliding the tray onto its surface. "I thought we agreed not to work, today."

"We did. I just needed to check something."

He took a deep breath. "Lately, there always seems to be something you need to 'check'. You're putting in way more hours than they have any right to expect from you."

She shook her head. "It's not that simple. If I don't keep up, they'll think I can't handle the extra accounts."

He moved to her side of the bed and sat on the edge. "And that's a bad thing why?"

Stress etched lines at the corners of her eyes. "I'm finally getting somewhere with my career. I can't drop the ball now."

"Damn it, Jane. Is this how it's going to be? You working all the time?" The words fell from his mouth, and he instantly regretted his tone.

Jane blinked back tears. "We've talked about this. I've already told you I'll cut back."

"Yes, you've told me—but you haven't done it. In fact, you've taken on more. The baby's coming in a few months. What's going to happen then?" He didn't mention that their wedding was only a few weeks away, or that he'd planned on surprising her with a trip to Mexico for their honeymoon.

"I'm taking time off after the baby is born. You're making me feel like an uncaring monster." A tear fell from her eye and traced a wet line down her cheek, melting his heart.

"Come here." He pulled her into his arms. "I'm sorry. I didn't mean it to come out that way. It's just that I'm worried, and I'm having a hard time understanding why you're working so much. I make enough to provide for both of us *and* the baby. You don't have to work at all, if you don't want to. And you certainly don't have to be constantly attached to that." He pointed at the offending laptop. He never thought he'd be capable of hating an inanimate object, but he was beginning to loathe her laptop.

He and Jane had been over the subject all too many times before. He wanted her to be a stay-at-home mother, but she was adamant about keeping her career. The subject was a growing source of contention between them.

Unfortunately, it was an easy issue for Maya to also pick at, as well. He'd done his best to avoid his sister since New Year's Eve. Her words still hurt him, and he certainly didn't want to throw Jane into Maya's line of fire. It still burned when he remembered his sister's response after he told her about the baby, on the deck that night.

I'm sure she's going to go on working after the baby is born. You know why, Reyo? So she can make her own money and leave you whenever life gets hard. It's probably what she did to her first husband.

Ryan couldn't help but divulge the secret Joe had asked him to keep from Maya that night. He had been so hurt by Maya's words, he told her how he'd lent Joe money multiple times to help her family. From the look on his sister's face, she'd had no idea they were having financial problems. The truth was finally out.

Even though Ryan wouldn't entertain Maya's remarks about Jane, they had left him wondering why Jane had her heart so set on continuing her career after the baby.

Jane nuzzled her head into his neck and intertwined her fingers with his. They remained silent for a while, and the only sound was the rhythmic in-and-out whisper of their breath.

"I know you don't want me to work after the baby," Jane said at last. "But I think I can make it all balance. Just have a little faith in me," she urged, her head still tucked near his shoulder.

Ryan leaned back and tipped her face up to meet his gaze, wiping her tears away with the pad of his thumb before coasting it over her bottom lip, leaving a damp trail. He leaned down and brushed his mouth over hers, tasting the salt from her tears. "I put all my faith in you, *Querida*. You're my home, my family, my love. I want nothing more than for you to be happy." He gave her a gentle squeeze, then released her and straightened. "Right now, though, you need to eat your breakfast, before it gets cold."

****

The French toast was delicious, but too soon it was transformed by guilt into a leaden lump in her stomach. She believed Ryan when he said that he wanted nothing more than for her to be happy, and she wanted the same for him, but she couldn't bring herself to say the words. They would sound silly to him—or, worse, insulting—because they both knew that she had the power to make him happy by saying just two words: *I quit*.

Those words would make her a failure, and she refused to fail. After all, she already had one strike against her, as far as Ryan's family was concerned. With the exception of Maya, the rest of the family acted as though they liked her, but they stole glances at her when they thought she wasn't looking, and they spoke together in hushed voices. She didn't know a lot of Spanish, but it didn't take a foreign language major to understand the word she'd overheard: *divorciada.*

Sometimes, she wondered whether she was the right person for Ryan. She loved him so much, it had made her heart hurt, but she knew how much the rift between Ryan and Maya affected him. She hated to be the source of acrimony between Ryan and his sister, and she wondered whether he would eventually come to resent her for having driven a wedge between him and the Rosales family. Maybe Ryan would have been better off with cute little Tilly.

Still, as Ryan would say, that was all spilt wine now, because she had a new life growing inside her body, one Ryan and she created together.

"What are you thinking about?" he asked as he played with a lock of her hair.

"How lucky I am to have you, and what a great father you'll be."

"I know when that brain of yours is in overdrive. You have a lot more than that on your mind. Want to talk about it?"

It was almost scary how well he'd come to know her. She wanted so much to tell him the thoughts and fears she kept buried inside. Sometimes, she felt like a shaken bottle of seltzer water on the verge of exploding.

But now was not the time. Instead, she closed her eyes, letting her head rise and fall with his chest. "Can we just stay like this all day?" She ran her fingers over the bulge of his bicep. "Stay in bed with you all day? Now that would make me happy."

Just as he lifted the tray from her lap, the baby gave her a swift kick. Jane jumped and cupped her stomach with her hands.

"Are you okay?" Ryan asked.

"Give me your hand." She pulled up her shirt, flattened his palm on her growing bulge, and guided his hand to the location of the kick. "Right there. Let's see if it'll happen again."

Ryan froze like a statue, tense and attentive.

"You can breathe," she said with a giggle.

"I don't want to miss it." After a few moments the baby obliged with another jab. Ryan gasped. "Was that it? Did I just feel a kick?"

"Mmm-hmm." Jane grinned. "I think the baby's thanking you for breakfast." A flutter of kicks to the exact spot of Ryan's hand confirmed her statement.

"It's the most incredible thing I've ever felt. That's our baby in there."

When Jane glanced up and saw that his eyes were dancing in amazement, a warm glow of happiness spread through her. Despite everything, she *had* managed to make him happy.

Carefully, Ryan slid under the covers and curled up behind her, cupping his hand around her belly. "What does it feel like when the baby moves inside you?"

She smiled. "At first, you're not even sure it's the baby. It feels like little bubbles trying to escape."

Ryan chuckled. "In other words, you're not sure whether it's the baby or gas?"

She nodded. "Pretty much. Then, after a while, you're sure it's the baby. You come to know the pattern. When the baby moves and stretches, it's like being caressed from the inside. It's almost like when we're making love, and you push all the way inside me and pull out just a little, then push full inside me again."

His breath blew hot on her shoulder, and she felt his erection against her backside. "I can't hurt the baby, can I?"

"As long as you don't put your full weight on my stomach, the baby's perfectly safe. I promise." She caressed her hand over his hip.

Ryan whipped off his clothes in record time. With infinite care, he pulled her panties off and pushed inside her from behind. He cupped her breast, while he trailed damp kisses up her neck. When he reached her ear, he whispered to her in Spanish while his hand trailed down her belly to the spot that set her body on fire.

"Please don't stop," Jane said breathlessly. The directive applied to the magical way he stroked her to a spiraling oblivion, but her words meant so much more. *Don't stop being there for me. Don't stop loving me. Just don't ever stop being mine.*

He thrust deeper, but not as far inside as usual. She knew he was holding back because of the baby. "I love you," she said between moans as her climax carried her over the edge.

Afterwards, they lay together, catching their breath. "No one ever told me how hot pregnancy sex was," he murmured in her ear.

"Mmm, well, you're in the club now. But, speaking of pregnancy, I have to pee. Then we should probably get dressed and tackle at least one location on Gretchen's list, don't you think?" She kissed him and slid her legs over the side of the bed.

"I'd rather stay here with you, but you're probably right. She's expecting a decision on the wedding venue when we're there for dinner tonight," Ryan said.

Jane was glad that Ryan had asked Gretchen to help them with their wedding plans. After much debate, they'd decided it would be best to have a small wedding, with a handful of relatives and friends. Charlotte, Tyler, and her mother would be Jane's only guests, and Ryan had pared his list down to a few key people as well. She knew it hurt him to leave Maya off the guest list, but he refused to allow his sister to ruin their wedding.

Since the wedding would be so small, Ryan had asked Gretchen to suggest a few locations in town for their ceremony, confident that the weather in March would be perfect for an outside wedding.

They showered and were on the road within the hour.

"Do you have Gretchen's list? Where are we headed first?"

He handed her a folded piece of paper. "She thinks we'll like the first one best."

Jane unfolded the paper and glanced at the short list. "The Japanese Tea Garden? Never heard of it."

"I haven't been there in years. It was an old quarry that was developed into gardens. It's a popular spot for weddings around here," he explained as they merged onto the highway.

Soon, they turned into the park's long driveway, and followed signs to the gardens. Jane loved the peaceful vibe as soon as she stepped out of the car. "Gretchen's right. This place is great," she said as she took Ryan's hand.

They strolled along the walkways that snaked around colorful gardens, stone bridges and koi ponds. Then Jane spotted a large, open-air gazebo on a hill that peeked over a thick brush of bushes and trees. "That would be a great place for the ceremony. Let's check it out," she said, and headed toward the winding stone stairs leading up the hill.

They were halfway up the steps when her belly suddenly tightened. "Oh!" She stopped and placed both hands on her stomach.

"What is it?" Ryan asked. "Are you okay?"

The twinge passed, and she rubbed her belly. "Must be a little indigestion. I'm okay." She slid her hand into Ryan's again, and started up the next set of stairs.

"Wait." He held her hand, preventing her from going farther. "I don't think we should do this today," Ryan said, and wrapped his arm around her shoulder.

She shrugged from his grasp. "Don't be silly. We're already here. Let's go see what it looks—" Then a spasm stole her breath away. Jane grabbed her belly and doubled over. "Ryan!" She could barely bite out his name through the searing pain.

"I'm here, *Querida*." He eased her down on the step. "Where's your bottle of water?"

She clamped her eyes closed. The pain was almost too much to bear. "Purse," she said between clenched teeth.

He pulled the water bottle from her bag and unscrewed the cap. "Take a sip," he urged, and held the opening of the bottle to her lips.

Jane took a small swig of water, and was able to draw a few deep breaths, but then her stomach tightened again. Tears of pain and fear stung her eyes. "Contractions. I'm having contractions." She felt as if someone had turned the thermostat up as far as it could go. The air turned thick, and she had to fight to take a breath. Her hair stuck to her cheeks as she rocked on the step.

The bottle fell to the ground and rolled down the steps as she felt her body rise, supported by Ryan's arms.

Her surroundings turned into a blurry mix of colors, the way her windshield looked before she flipped on the wipers during a rainstorm. Ryan's graveled voice murmured something in Spanish in her ear. She didn't understand a word of what he said, but it calmed her into a hot, dizzy state of surrender, secure in the knowledge that Ryan would take care of her and the baby.

"Stay with me, *Querida*. Please, stay with me," she heard, as the buzzing in her ear grew louder and louder.

And then ... nothing.

Chapter Twenty-Five

Jane squinted into a sea of lights and whitewashed walls.

For a second, she thought she had died, but her eyelids scratched her eyeballs like sandpaper, and she had a nasty taste in her mouth. If she was in Heaven, it was definitely a letdown. She reached to the side, groping for something to help her pull herself up.

"Just relax, *Querida*. You're going to be okay," a deep voice rumbled.

"Ryan?" His voice calmed her instantly, and she relaxed, trying to focus. "Where am I?" she asked, as memories started coming back. The gardens. The pain. The baby. "The baby." She blinked, her vision still blurry, and reached for her stomach.

"The baby's okay. You're in the Emergency Room. Just rest. The doctor will be in soon to explain what happened," Ryan said, and stroked her hand, which rested on her belly.

Jane took a deep breath and turned toward his voice. "What happened? Did I do something wrong?" Her thoughts went to the fight they'd had about her working so much. She blinked again, and his face finally came into focus. "If I caused something to happen to our baby, I couldn't forgive myself."

"Shh, shh. You didn't do anything wrong. Don't worry yourself." His smile reassured her slightly.

A nurse appeared at the curtain. "Good. She's awake. I'll send the doctor in."

The curtain whipped to the side, and a young woman in scrubs, who didn't look much older than Tyler, strode into the tiny room. "Hi, Ms. Keegan. I'm Doctor Parker, the obstetrics resident. How are you feeling?"

"Like I just ran a marathon." Her legs were like jelly, and her arms felt too heavy to lift. "How's the baby?" she asked, searching the young doctor's face.

"The baby's heartbeat is steady and strong, and your cervix shows no sign of dilation. You're out of the woods, for now."

"For now? What does that mean?"

"The reason you passed out today is because you have a condition called preeclampsia. You have high blood pressure. We're going to admit you so you can be monitored here until we're sure you're stable enough to go home. After that, you'll have to stay on complete bed rest until the baby is born." The doctor rattled off her prognosis as if she was reading from a textbook.

Jane's gaze moved from the doctor to Ryan, then to her belly. She tried to picture the baby curled up in her womb. "Preeclampsia? How did that happen? I've never had high blood pressure."

"It just happens in some women ... and the chances of preeclampsia increase with the mother's age."

Dimly, Jane remembered her own doctor telling her the same thing, and how she had dismissed the possibility, telling herself that it was something that might happen to other women, but not to her.

"It comes out of the blue. There are really no warning signs. There was no way you could've known."

Jane nodded slowly, digesting the news of her condition. "Is 'complete bed rest' what it sounds like?"

"Yes. You'll need to stay in a reclined position, preferably on your left side, at all times. You can get up to use the bathroom and go to doctor's appointments, but that's about it. No stairs, no driving, and no more than a few minutes at a time on your feet. The goal is to prolong your pregnancy as long as it's safe for you and the baby, hopefully until the baby is developed enough to thrive outside the womb," Dr. Parker explained.

It all sounded so simple, but Jane knew it wouldn't be. She'd have to stay in bed for the next four months. Four whole months.

She glanced at Ryan. "I'm sorry," she said.

"What do you have to be sorry about?" he asked, and tucked a lock of her hair behind her ear.

"This is going to be a huge burden on you. It's not like I have any friends or family here. And—"

"Whoa. You're getting ahead of yourself, Jane. First, you and our baby are not and will never be a burden to me. We'll work it out. And, before we know it, the baby will be here."

"We'll get you transferred upstairs today, and then your own doctor can take over and decide when it's safe for you to go home. Do you have any questions?" Dr. Parker asked.

Jane shook her head, and admitted, "I can't help blaming myself for this. What if I caused this by traveling too much, or overworking, or eating Chinese food? There's MSG in Chinese food, you know." She bit her lip and considered other ways she might have brought on her high blood pressure.

Ryan laughed. "Why must you always wear the weight of the world on your shoulders? You didn't do this. It just happened. And, like everything else, we will get through it."

Jane was moved to a private room in the obstetrics wing so she could be monitored. She was poked and prodded by doctors, nurses, and technicians almost hourly. After two days she finally convinced Ryan to go home.

"Are you sure you'll be okay?"

She surveyed the dark circles under his eyes and his overgrown beard. "You need to get some rest."

"But I think you need me more," Ryan said, as Jane's doctor entered the room.

"Listen to her," Doctor Murcia said. "Go home and get some rest while she's in the hospital. You'll have plenty of time to take care of her when she's back home."

Ryan nodded and rubbed his face with his palm. "I can see I'm outnumbered here. I'll go get some sleep. But I'll be back around six," Ryan promised, and kissed Jane good-bye.

"You have a good man there," Doctor Murcia pointed out after Ryan left.

Jane smiled. "I do. Too good, sometimes. I'm afraid of what all this will do to him."

The doctor folded her arms. "Seems to me he played a part in how this baby got in there, so now he has an equal responsibility in the care of you and your baby."

"This baby was a complete surprise to both of us. I just hope he's ready."

"Sometimes, the surprises can be the most rewarding. Now, speaking of surprises, I want to be sure you still don't want to know the sex of the baby," Dr. Murcia said as she scanned the laptop screen.

"Nothing's changed with that," Jane said, but she eyed the screen in Dr. Murcia's hand. "It's written down, right there in my records. Isn't it?"

Dr. Murcia nodded. "It's on the sonogram report. I'll make a note here not to tell you." The doctor's nails tapped along the keyboard.

"Thank you." Jane bit her lip to prevent herself from asking. She was personally in favor of knowing whether the baby was a boy or a girl, but Ryan had requested they wait until the birth to find out. She supposed the least she could do was keep her promise.

"Dr. Murcia? Tell me honestly, is the baby okay? I mean really okay?" Her "advanced maternal age", as the doctor liked to say, had been a concern of Jane's from the moment she saw the two lines on the pregnancy test. Her new condition only increased that worry factor.

Dr. Murcia's fingers tapped the laptop. Her eyes narrowed as she seemed to find something of interest on the screen. "The baby is a little small for twenty weeks, but all of the other test results look good. The heartbeat is strong, too. We'll keep a sharp eye on you. You really must stay off your feet and watch your diet. But to answer your question, yes, the baby is really okay."

"Thank you." Jane breathed a sigh of relief.

"I'll release you in the next day or so. Other than Ryan, do you have more support at home?"

"I'm pretty new to the area, so I don't have many friends here, but my mother and a good friend from New York have offered to help out," Jane replied, but she knew it wouldn't be quite that simple. As nice as it would be to see her mother, they had decided it would be best for her to wait until after the baby was born. Since her mother didn't drive and had a few medical issues herself, she wouldn't be much help while Jane was on bed rest. But Jane was looking forward to Charlotte's visit. Her friend had agreed to fly down as soon as Jane was out of the hospital.

"What about Ryan's family? You're going to need help for quite a while."

"We're working on it. Ryan's setting up a bedroom in a spare room off the kitchen for me, so I won't have to climb stairs. We'll figure it all out," she said, hoping it was true. But the fact was that they had no idea what they'd do after Charlotte left, beyond Ryan's promise to make frequent trips home from the restaurant each day. "What about work?"

"As long as it's work that you can do from your bed, and it's not going to stress you out, feel free to continue working. It'll help take your mind off worrying about the baby and give you something to do." Dr. Murcia tilted her head. "You don't look thrilled. Isn't that the answer you wanted?"

"Honestly, I don't know. I've been thinking about cutting back on work," Jane admitted, "but I haven't been sure when to do it."

"I don't know of a more perfect reason than this," Dr. Murcia said, and patted her belly.

****

Jane woke with a smile.

After Dr. Murcia had given Jane and Ryan detailed instructions on Jane's diet and activity restrictions, she had finally cleared Jane to go home.

The door to her hospital room swung open, and two balloons tied to an enormous bouquet of flowers bobbed into the room. Jane wondered why Ryan brought flowers to the hospital when she would be leaving later that day … until she saw the smiling face of the person carrying the gift.

"Charlotte!" Jane exclaimed, so excited that she wanted to bounce out of bed and give her friend a big hug.

"Stay right there, girl. I'm coming to you."

"I thought you weren't coming until next week," Jane said.

"She wanted to surprise you."

Jane's gaze flew to the door as she hugged Charlotte. There stood Ryan, leaning against the wall with a playful smile on his face. "We figured you needed some fun after all this."

Jane's heart warmed. "I'm so happy you're here."

Charlotte looked great, as usual. Her blonde, chin-length hair contrasted with the red t-shirt and jacket she wore. Jane chuckled.

"What's so funny?" Charlotte asked.

"I'm thinking how wonderful you look, and how my hair isn't brushed."

"Darlin', you can pull off the messy-hair-no-makeup-in-the-hospital look like nobody's business. Now, how about we bust you out of here so we can get the bed rest party started?" Charlotte demanded, rubbing her hands together.

"You make it sound way more exciting than it will be. I promise you'll be bored to tears within days," Jane said.

"Hey, if we can have fun at your boring company parties you used to drag me to, we can have fun on bed rest. Let's get you home."

Ryan drove the car up to the hospital entrance, and Charlotte pushed Jane's wheelchair to meet him, despite Jane's insistence that she was able to walk.

"Remember what the doctor said. No more than is absolutely necessary," Ryan said, shaking his finger at her.

She rolled her eyes and let him fuss over her. It was going to be a long four months.

Minutes later, they pulled onto the highway, where he proceeded to drive more slowly than she thought was possible.

"Hey, Ry, I think Uncle Pascal just passed us," Jane joked.

"There are some bumps on this road. I want to make sure you're not jostled around too much."

"Dude, she's not a Faberge Egg," Charlotte called from the backseat.

"Oh, shut up back there," Ryan called back with a smile.

Pulling into the driveway of their home was like snuggling into a favorite blanket. Her mood brightened instantly as she set foot inside the house. "I wish I was able to go upstairs and stay in our bed." Jane looked longingly at the flight of stairs.

"I know, but wait 'til you see what we did." Ryan guided her into the spare bedroom off the kitchen. They'd planned for it to be Tyler's room when he visited, and had postponed decorating it. The only thing in it had been a twin bed and a few mismatched pieces of furniture. But when Ryan led Jane inside, with the exception of its size, the room was almost an exact replica of their master bedroom.

Her eyes widened. "You brought everything down here?"

"Everything except the bed. Our king wouldn't fit in here, so I bought a queen. It was just delivered yesterday. It was Charlotte's idea."

"I love it. I've gotta say, I was really dreading spending the next four months in this room. But now it's not so bad!"

"That's not all. If you're up to it, I want to show you something else."

She nodded and wrapped her arm around his waist as he led her to the patio.

Jane gasped when she looked through the sliding glass door. "Is that what I think it is?" She slid open the door, her gaze riveted on a canopied outdoor daybed. She'd seen one in an airline catalog, and had commented to Ryan that it would be perfect for their patio, but hadn't given it another thought.

Carefully, Jane sat on the edge and scooted to the top, where a sea of colorful pillows was splayed under the gauzy canopy. She patted the cushion. "Come on in, both of you. There's plenty of room."

Ryan stretched out next to her, and Charlotte settled, cross-legged, at the foot of the bed.

Charlotte shook her head. "You two are the cutest couple I know. You make me sick," she said, and winked.

"I'm definitely outnumbered by the two of you," Ryan said, sitting up again. "How about I go fix us something to eat while you catch up?" He leaned over and kissed Jane lightly on the lips. "I'm glad you're home."

"Me, too." Her gaze traveled to Ryan's backside as he disappeared into the house. Unfortunately, sex was also on her restriction list.

"Seriously, girl, he's too good to be true."

Jane smiled. "Almost. If I could get him to lay off about me working so much, he'd be absolutely perfect."

"He's just worried about you. Besides, I thought you were supposed to slow down."

"I did. My boss reassigned everything, other than my two main accounts, but they still take a lot of time. You know how clients are—not much different from babies. They're always in need of attention."

"Yes, but you'll have your own baby soon, who will also need your attention. What are you going to do then?"

"I don't know, Char." Jane was still up to her ears in work. She'd been having enough trouble, keeping up on a daily basis. Now, thanks to her unexpected hospitalization, she'd lost several days and inherited a long list of restrictions. In truth, she was increasingly convinced that she wouldn't be able to keep up the pace after the baby was born.

"Maybe you should consider quitting and taking a year or two off. You can always go back to it. Sounds like

Ryan's doing well with the restaurant. I'm sure you two can swing it, financially."

Jane sighed. "Money's not the issue. I've just worked so hard to get to this point. I'll feel like a failure if I quit now."

"You're far from a failure, my friend." She flopped down on the bed next to Jane and batted her eyes. "You're my hero."

Jane swatted her friend. "Enough about my life. Tell me about yours! How are things with…" Jane wracked her brain, trying to recall the name of Charlotte's flavor of the month.

"Jacques."

"Jacques? You're with a French guy now? What happened to…" She snapped her fingers. "Doug. That was it. What happened to Doug?"

"Doug's yesterday's news. I met Jacques a few weeks ago, in the park. He's in New York for work. He asked me for directions, we started talking, and I offered to show him around. We've been practically inseparable ever since." Charlotte lowered her voice. "What they say about Frenchmen is true. They're amazing lovers. Seriously, that man can have my panties off and heading for my second orgasm in nine seconds flat."

"That long, huh?"

"He may be the one."

Jane blinked, startled. "Really? You never say that. What happened to your stable of interchangeable, discardable men?"

"Actually, Jacques is quickly becoming indispensable."

"Charlotte Snow! You're not falling in love, are you? I thought love was a no-no in Snow's Dating Rulebook." Feigning surprise, Jane raised her hand to her mouth.

"Oh, don't get all carried away with yourself, Miss Happily Ever After. It'll take more than a few abso-fucking-lutely amazing orgasms for me to entertain the 'L' word. Let's just say … it's going really well."

Jane clapped her hands. "I'm so happy for you, Char, and I feel horrible about taking you away from him."

Charlotte patted Jane's leg. "If he's worth anything, he'll be there when I return. You need me now."

"And I'm eternally grateful. Do me a favor, okay? Don't discount the possibility of falling in love."

Charlotte waved her hand. "Meh. Falling in love is for nice people like you. I'm too jaded to get all lovey-dovey."

"Love comes in all shapes and forms. Don't be surprised if it creeps up and bites you on your perfectly toned ass."

Charlotte pointed her manicured index finger at Jane. "That would be fantastic on a greeting card! There you go. I just found a new career for you." She smiled. "Do you really think my ass is perfect?"

Chapter Twenty-Six

Charlotte's weeklong visit flew by, and the house seemed quiet without the company of her best friend. Too quiet. Silence accentuated the long span of time during which Jane would have absolutely nothing to do but lie around while the baby cooked.

"I know how much you'll miss her." Ryan sat on the bed beside Jane and squeezed her hand. "Believe me, I offered her part-ownership of Vine to stay."

"I know. She told me." Jane laughed. Charlotte had promised to return in a few weeks, but Jane didn't want to take her away from her work and, more importantly, Jacques. Charlotte wouldn't admit it, but Jane knew love when she saw it, and her friend had fallen in deep. It was just a matter of time before Char realized it. "I'll be fine." Jane reassured Ryan. "I called the number for that pregnancy concierge service that Dr. Murcia's office told us about. They're going to send over a couple of bed rest specialists for us to interview, this week." She wasn't crazy about having strangers in her home, but she couldn't justify having Ryan run back and forth from the restaurant to see her multiple times a day, either.

"Funny you should mention that, because another option just came up," Ryan said, with a hopeful smile.

"Really? What is it? I'm open to anything, at this point."

"Well, actually, it's not a what, it's a who." He took a deep breath. "Maya has offered to help."

Jane was shocked. "Maya offered to help *me*?"

"I mentioned that we were looking into a service, and I asked her if she'd heard of any. She said there was no reason to have strangers in our home. She said she'd come over each day and help you with whatever you need, while Isabel's at school."

Jane tried to choose her words with care. "Maya and I haven't spoken to each other since New Year's Eve. Frankly, I'm astonished that she offered." A sudden suspicion struck her, and she narrowed her eyes. "You didn't ask her, did you?"

Ryan raised his hands. "Nope. I've been avoiding her lately, but she's constantly calling to check up on you. Then she offered to help. I had nothing to do with it, I promise."

"I'd have sworn I'd be the last person she'd offer to help."

He shrugged. "Family is unconditional. As Uncle Pascal says, *Familia es la familia*. Family is family." He shot her a worried look. "Are you okay with it? Will you let her try?"

"Sure, as long as she doesn't try to poison me," Jane teased, then sobered. "Ryan, you don't think she'd actually try to do something to me, do you?"

Ryan chuckled. "Of course not. In fact, I think something good may come of all this. I'll invite her to come over tomorrow, and you two can talk."

****

"Hello?" Maya called from the front door.

Knowing that Ryan had given Maya a key to their house, Jane had been forewarned that she would let herself in.

"I'm in the bedroom off the kitchen, Maya," she called in a tone two octaves higher than her regular voice. If she was ever going to get on Maya's good side, this seemed like the best time to do it. Determined, Jane plastered a smile on her face and waited for Maya to enter the bedroom. And waited. And waited some more. Her ears perked at the sound of kitchen cabinets and drawers opening and closing. Next, she heard the refrigerator and freezer doors open, then close after a minute or two.

Finally, Maya strolled into sight in the open doorway of the bedroom, writing in a spiral-bound notebook. "I took a quick inventory of what you have on hand, and I'm making a list of what you need. Reyo told me your diet restrictions, and I started a menu, if you'd like to take a look at it." She pulled a folded white sheet of paper from the notebook and held it out, from her spot at the bedroom door.

Jane blinked. "Um, that's okay. I don't need to see it. I'm sure I'll like anything you make."

Maya nodded once. "Good. I'll plan on making extra when I cook for my family. Of course, I won't add salt to yours, or any other ingredients that are on the restriction list. Other than food, what else do you need me to do?" she asked, with a neutral expression that seemed to look right through Jane.

"Um, well, I'm not supposed to get up without someone around, so I'll need to time my bathroom breaks around your visits. Ryan helps me in the morning, so I don't need any assistance bathing or anything like that," she explained hurriedly. "Maybe just a fresh pitcher of ice water. I'm supposed to drink a lot of water." Which, unfortunately, made her pee. Which she wasn't supposed to do without someone around. It was a vicious cycle of frustration.

Maya sauntered to the bed table and lifted the empty pitcher. "Do you need to get up to use the bathroom?" she asked Jane, as if she was addressing an annoying child.

"Yes, but I can manage it on my own, thank you." Jane slowly slid to the side of the bed and lowered her feet to the floor, as the nurses had taught her, then held onto the bedpost as she stood. She could swear that she felt the heat of Maya's stare as she shuffled to the bathroom and closed the door. Jane took care of her business and twisted the hot water faucet, letting the steamy water flow over her hands. She stared at her reflection in the mirror. Part of her wanted nothing more than to have it out with her future sister-in-law, but she knew it would kill Ryan. She swallowed her pride and decided to take a different approach with Maya: she'd kill her with kindness.

Jane came out of the bathroom just as Maya placed the refilled pitcher of ice and water on the bedside table. A fresh glass with a straw sat beside it. But as soon as Jane was safely resettled in bed, she left the room without a word.

A few minutes later, Maya returned, carrying a plate of grilled chicken wrapped in a homemade pita. Jane's mouth watered. Even though Maya clearly wasn't interested in chitchat, at least it was becoming apparent that Jane would be well fed.

"It smells wonderful. It's really nice of you to help me," Jane offered, another over-the-top smile.

"You're welcome. But let's get one thing straight. I'm doing this for Reyo and the family. If you don't need anything else from me right now, I'll clean up the kitchen and go." She glanced at her watch. "I'll be back in a couple of hours, before I pick Isabel up from school."

Chapter Twenty-Seven

Weeks passed, and no day differed much from the first. Maya stopped in twice a day to deliver delicious food and help Jane with her necessities. Jane tried to be as nice as possible, even though her patience was coming to an end.

The squeak of the front door opening woke Jane from a nap. She rubbed her stomach as the baby gave her a swift kick in the side. In a way, she was grateful for the discomfort. It meant the baby was doing well.

Beyond the bedroom door, she could hear Maya shuffling around the kitchen as usual, clanging dishes, opening and closing cabinet doors. After a few minutes, when her footsteps came closer, Jane sat up in bed. Propping herself with pillows, she ran a hasty brush through her hair in an attempt to look halfway human. She couldn't even remember the last time she'd applied makeup.

Maya appeared in the doorway, carrying a tray, but Jane noticed that she also had an overnight envelope wedged under her arm. "I hope you don't mind tortilla soup again," Maya said, setting the tray on the bed table.

"I love your tortilla soup," Jane said, rubbing her belly. "So does the baby."

Maya nodded toward Jane's stomach. "That baby is a quarter Latina. It'd better like tortilla soup." She handed Jane the envelope. "Here. This was on the doorstep."

Jane peered at the return address. It had to be the client ad proofs she'd been waiting for. She tore open the envelope and pulled out the mockups.

"Sure. Work before feeding the baby," Maya muttered as she strode to the door.

It was the last straw. "I've had a lot of time to try to figure out why you hate me so much," Jane said, shoving the papers back into the envelope.

Maya turned around and opened her mouth to speak.

Jane raised her hand. "Actually, I've come up with three possibilities. One, I'm not Latina. Two, I'm divorced. And three, I have a career outside the home. Which one is it, Maya? Because I really want to know."

Maya's eyes grew in rage. "You want to know? It's all three, plus you're an outspoken bitch. Why didn't you just stay in New York? I'm sure you could've found a man-whore up there who could've scratched your itch. But no, you had to sink your hooks into my brother, and now look what you've done?" Her hand waved over Jane's belly.

"You think this was some type of master plan? You think I wanted this to happen?"

"You love the fact Ryan is jumping through hoops for you. He's working his ass off for you, and you throw it in his face with your work. You don't trust him to take care of you? Is he not good enough for you, Jane?"

"You have it wrong. I love and trust Ryan more than anything, but you can't believe that. In your eyes I'm not the ideal person for him because I'm different. But your mother and father came from opposite ends of the culture spectrum, and they had a wonderful marriage. You and Ryan are a product of that marriage, so aren't you being hypocritical?"

"You're confusing heritage with culture. My mother and father came from different heritages, but culturally they were very similar. Family came first, always. Marriages were forever, not until you got sick of the other person. Husbands and wives worked out their differences. Divorce was not an option, and a woman's place was in the home. Period."

Jane let Maya's words sink in. "I see. And I assume you subscribe to those same ideals."

"Our whole family does. I thought Reyo did, too, until I learned about his stint as a gigolo."

"He was an escort."

Maya let out a snort. "Same thing." She pointed at the tray. "You should eat."

Jane picked up the bowl and swallowed a few spoonfuls before returning it to the tray, thinking carefully about what to say next. "Ryan started escorting for good reasons. It got him the means to live his dream. You should respect that about him."

Maya's eyes bored into Jane as she moved closer. "Respect? Don't you dare tell me about respect. Not when you obviously had no respect for your marriage or for Ryan. If you did you wouldn't need to work. I know what's best for him, and it's definitely not you. You're going to chew him up and spit him out just like you did to your first husband."

Jane narrowed her eyes. "You don't know what you're talking about. My husband was a cheater. That's why I left."

Maya paused. "He cheated on you?"

"Get out of my house," Ryan's booming voice sounded from the doorway. His eyes were wide with a fury of anger. "I've let your comments slide for weeks because I thought you were making an attempt to accept Jane. But you'll never change, Maya. Never."

"Reyo, I—"

He held up a palm. "I don't want to hear it. Get out. Now."

Maya's gaze moved from Ryan to Jane before she lowered her head and shuffled to the door. Ryan stepped aside to let her pass.

Jane heard the front door open and close as Ryan sat on the edge of the bed. "You shouldn't have thrown her out. I think I was getting somewhere with her."

He shook his head. "She's too pigheaded and set in her ways. I can't subject you to that any longer. It's not good for you or the baby."

Jane studied his face. She'd never seen him look so tired. "Lie with me." Ryan stepped out of his shoes, and Jane made room for him on the bed. He slipped in next to her and wrapped one arm around her shoulder. His free hand rubbed her bulging belly. The baby shifted under his touch.

"I have all that I need right here. This is my family." His lips touched hers as her fingers trailed up his arm and tangled in his hair. His tender kiss becomes more urgent as his tongue parted the seam of her mouth. Jane sighed and deepened the kiss pulling him closer, draining him of his sadness, filling him with love.

Chapter Twenty-Eight

As if Jane and Maya's blowout wasn't enough, his streak of bad luck continued. It had started when he'd learned that his order for a specific vintage from Napa had been delayed. The wine was for a special order placed by a California tech company that had reserved Vine's private room for the coming evening. Ryan knew all too well that the party contained a bunch of corporate bigwigs from Silicon Valley who would only drink wine from their own state, and that the CEO favored a certain vintage. So he had spent a good chunk of his morning hitting four area liquor stores, paying retail, just to fulfill their request. Then his best server called in sick, and he'd discovered that the butcher had cut his order of porterhouse steaks too thin. He'd stopped home to check on Jane on his way back to Vine, to find his sister verbally attacking his bed-ridden future wife. He was convinced Maya had no heart in that little body.

Ryan pulled into his parking spot, grabbed his phone from his pocket, and tapped the speed dial button for Vine.

Gretchen answered after the first ring.

"Send one of the busboys out to the lot with a hand truck. I have a couple cases of that Napa wine for the private party."

"Oh, good! Glad you found some. I tracked down the truck, and they're still in Austin. Not sure they'll get here in time, and the white'll need to be chilled. Hey, Cole, grab the hand truck from the back and take it to Ryan in the lot. He'll be right there, Ry." She paused before continuing, in a whisper, "Hey, there's someone here to see you."

"Who?"

"Hold on a second. I'm going into the office." After a few moments, he heard the click of the door. "Okay. She came in and asked for you. I told her you'd stepped out and I didn't know when you'd be back, but she said she'd wait for you. Didn't want to tell me her name. Just said that you two were old friends."

Old friends? Ryan figured it was probably a former classmate. "What does she look like?" he asked, hoping a description would jog his memory.

"Attractive, but hard looking lady. In her forties, I'd guess. Blonde dye job. Long blood-red nails. She's sitting at the bar, drinking her fancy martini, looking bored," Gretchen said with a chuckle.

But Ryan wasn't laughing. He had an uneasy hunch that the blonde visitor wasn't an old schoolmate. "How'd she order her martini?" he asked, with a sinking sense that he already knew.

"I took her order. Dry with a twist."

Camille.

Ryan closed his eyes. His day had now officially turned from "bad" to "good" to "I don't need this shit". He groaned as he heard the hand truck's tires bumping along the pavement of the parking lot.

Ryan popped the trunk and pointed to the boxes, then slumped into the front seat of his car again, blowing out a shaky breath.

"You know who she is?" Gretchen asked.

"Yeah, I have a pretty good idea."

"Want me to get rid of her, Ry? I can chase her out, if you want."

"Nah. Let her know I'll be there in a few minutes." There was no point in making her leave before he got there. He was sure she'd just wait outside for him. When Camille LeVan had her mind set on something, she usually found a way to get it.

"Got any more boxes to unload, boss?" Cole called from behind the car.

Ryan lowered the phone from his ear. "No, that's it. Head back, and put the white in the chiller right away. We need to cool those bottles down before the party gets here," he told Cole, before wedging the phone back between his ear and shoulder. "Gretch, did we get the new meat delivery?"

"Yup, and the steaks are beautiful. Oh, and Carly offered to come in on her day off to serve the party. Crisis averted. I have it covered."

Ryan smiled into the phone. "You always do."

"So, you gonna to tell me about the Blonde Bitch?" she asked playfully.

"Nope, and you probably wouldn't believe me if I did." He tapped the "End" button and leaned his skull against the leather headrest, recalling the last time he'd seen Cam.

What the hell did she want, today of all days?

There was only one way to find out. Ryan stepped out of his car and trudged toward Vine.

He thought about slipping into the restaurant from the back, so he could get a look at her before she noticed him, but he decided it was better to meet her head on.

He marched through the front door like he owned the place, because he did. He chatted with Gretchen for a few minutes, intentionally keeping his gaze trained away from Camille as she tried to catch his attention. Then Ryan wrapped up his conversation with Gretchen and strode to the empty stool next to Camille.

"Hello, Ryan," she said. "You look well."

He stared straight ahead, his gaze fixed on a beer tap. "I asked you never to come here." Ryan clenched his jaw. He'd taken great care to shield his staff from any awareness of his prior career, and he had no intention of letting Camille blow the lid off his past now. "Follow me." He pushed the stool out and marched to his office.

The clicking of her heeled sandals followed close behind.

He held the door for her, then shut it with purpose after they were both inside his office. Ryan took a deep breath, steadying his nerves before turning to her. "You have a lot of nerve coming here after stealing from me."

Camille laughed and strode to the lone window in the office. "Stealing from you? Now that's a serious claim."

"What would you call taking a client's money even after the date was canceled then deducting your fee from the money you owed me? Sounds like stealing to me."

Camille spun around. "You told me to keep my fee."

"Yeah. *After* you returned hers. That's low, even for you, Cam."

She met his gaze, and something in her face changed. Her normal razor sharp stare softened, and lines formed between her brows. She slumped into the chair next to his desk. "I'll be honest—"

"That'll be a first," he muttered.

She ignored his comment and continued. "I purposely kept the fee because I thought you'd come after me for it. It was the only way to get you to contact me. You stopped taking my calls and ignored my texts."

"I needed out. I told you that many times, but you somehow reeled me back every single time. I had to make a clean break and cut ties."

"The client never contacted me for the refund."

"She got her money back."

The tough exterior was back complete with an evil grin. "Ryan Zeigler to the rescue. You take it upon yourself to save the world. You bail your brother-in-law out every time he gets in over his head, you helped little Janie whatever her name is, you even tried to reform me once, but that didn't last long. You gave up on me."

Ryan recalled suggesting Camille purchase one of the restaurant spaces that had opened on the River Walk. His idea was for a toned down and cleaned up version of the male revue club in town. The River Walk was a magnet for bachelorette parties and ladies' weekends. A restaurant catering to women would've done well in the area, and Camille had the resources and manpower to pull it off. "I didn't give up on you. I simply made a suggestion, and you chose not to take it."

"That's not what I'm talking about. You gave up on us."

"Damn it, Cam. There was no us, and you know it. I was one of your possessions that you tried to control with money."

"That's not true, Ryan. It was more than that. We had something special."

He'd thought so at the time until she'd ripped his heart out of his chest. He choked out a sarcastic laugh. "You have a warped sense of reality. It's always been about you and only you. It's the Camille LeVan show all the way."

"You make me sound like some kind of an ice queen."

"Don't get me wrong, Cam. You can be real warm when you want something. Like when you recruited me into The Cowboys. Then you gave the same treatment to young Zackary on your office couch. You certainly know the meaning of a warm welcome. Is he your newest second in command?"

"Get serious, Ryan. Zack could hardly find his way out the front door. He can't replace you." Her gaze trailed down his body. "He doesn't hold a candle to you." She stepped closer.

"What do you want?" he bit out.

Camille stopped a few inches from him and shot him a cocky grin. "The question is: what do you want, Ryan?"

"Nothing from you."

"Your mouth is telling me one thing, but your body is screaming something else entirely." She cupped his cheek and the pad of her finger traced his jaw and slid down his neck.

He turned his head. "You couldn't be more wrong."

Her finger touched his lips as the door flew open.

"Reyo, I'm—" Maya stood frozen in her tracks, her gaze ping-ponging between Camille and Ryan. "When Gretchen said you were busy, I never imagined you were doing this."

"It's not what it looks like." He shrugged away from Camille's grasp.

Maya glared at Camille before turning her attention back to Ryan. "Then what exactly is it?"

"It's a business matter."

"Maybe in your world, but not in mine. You better get your priorities straight, Reyo. You're about to become a father. Jane deserves better than this." Her hand waved at Camille like she was shooing a fly before she stormed out of the office and slammed the door.

"Shit," he muttered. Ryan strode to his desk and slumped into the chair and rubbed his eyes. "Just leave, please."

Camille ignored his request and took a seat on the other side of his desk. "Do you want to know why I came here?"

Ryan shrugged.

"I sold everything and bought a club in Las Vegas. I hoped there was a chance you were ready for a change and wanted to go into partnership with me. But I see that's not going to happen. You've changed. Getting out of the business was a good thing for you." She paused. "You're going to be a father?"

He smiled. "Yeah."

Camille nodded slowly. "I'll send you what I owe you, including the client's fee you refunded her. I know you don't believe me, but it wasn't about the money." She stood and folded her arms across her chest, hugging herself as if the room had grown too cold for comfort. "Good-bye, Ryan." She headed for the door.

"Cam?"

She stopped but didn't turn around.

"You have great business sense, but there's one thing you don't understand—people can't be bought."

Her shoulders slumped slightly as she reached for the door and walked out of his life forever.

Ryan watched her leave, reflecting on their conversation. When he was wrapped up in the world of Camille LeVan, he'd been convinced that he'd fallen in love with her. After seeing her again he realized he hadn't had a clue what love really was, until he'd met the woman who nestled herself so deep in his heart.

Chapter Twenty-Nine

The click of the lock followed by the squeak of the front door woke Jane from her nap. "Ryan?" she called sleepily.

"It's Maya. May I come in?"

Maya? "Um ... sure." Jane leaned forward and propped her pillows against the headboard as Maya appeared in the doorway.

"Here, let me." She shuffled to Jane's side and fluffed a pillow. "Sit up a little."

Jane leaned forward and Maya slid the pillow behind her back. "Thank you."

"May I sit?" Maya nodded to the edge of the bed.

Jane tilted her head. "Sure. Is there anything wrong?"

Maya took a deep breath. "Nothing's wrong. I've been thinking about our conversation earlier."

Jane raised her eyebrows. "You mean our argument?"

Maya nodded. "I jumped to conclusions about you, and it was unfair. I think it's time to clear this thing up between the two of us. It's gone on long enough. I apologize for the way I've treated you, Jane."

"Okay, who are you and what did you do with my future sister-in-law?" Jane smirked.

"I'm serious."

"Just like that? I don't understand."

"Before Ryan walked in on us earlier you'd said your husband cheated on you. It made me realize I was wrong about you. I'd assumed you were the cause of breaking up your marriage," Maya explained.

Jane shot her a tight grin. "God, Maya. I wanted my marriage to last forever. When I married Nick, I swore it *was* going to be forever. I was totally in love with him. We had our son, Tyler, and I stayed home and raised him while my husband worked. Those years at home with Tyler were some of the happiest times of my life." Jane smiled as she remembered Tyler as a little boy. "To this day, my son and I have a bond like no other. He's such a good kid, and he's growing up to be a fine adult."

Maya met Jane's gaze. "Reyo told me about Tyler. I look forward to meeting him."

"I didn't go back to work until Tyler was in high school. Nick didn't care whether I worked or not, but I did. I was bored, and Tyler didn't need me as much, so I started working again. I'm glad I did, because it gave me something to fall back on when my world came crashing down." She took a steadying breath and rubbed her belly. "My husband had an affair. A long affair. He didn't tell me about it until it was over. I was oblivious, and the only reason he came clean was because he thought the woman was going to tell me, and he wanted me to hear it from him."

"You don't have to tell me all this," Maya said quietly.

"It's okay. I want you to know." Jane continued. "He apologized up and down. Swore it wouldn't happen again. He said he wanted to stay married to me … and I agreed. I tried to pretend the affair had never happened. I went through all the motions of what had been my idyllic life, thinking I could get past it." She sighed. "That worked, more or less, for a while, but then I realized what I was sacrificing—my self-respect. Divorcing my husband wasn't a decision I made lightly, and it was the hardest choice I ever made, but I'm glad now that I did it. I'm also glad I had a good job, so that I was able to support myself. I wasn't looking for a replacement husband when I met your brother. In fact, I'd pretty much resigned myself to spending the rest of my life without a partner. But Ryan and I just … happened. And the baby just happened, too. And I wouldn't trade either one of them for anything. I won't apologize for being divorced, or for having a career, or for my heritage, but I will swear to you that I love Ryan with all my heart, and that I want to be his wife for the rest of my life."

Maya shook her head. "I had no idea what you went through."

"There's no way you could have known. It was a horrible time in my life, and I've never gone into that much detail about it with anyone, before—not even with Ryan."

Maya slid off the bed and began to pace the floor. "I admire you," Maya said at last.

Jane smiled wryly. "In the space of a day, you've gone from hating me to admiring me? Why?"

"Because you had the strength and courage to leave. It's something I didn't have." A single tear escaped onto her cheek, and she wiped it away with her sleeve.

"Maya?" Jane said softly, searching her face for answers.

"Soon after Isabel was born, I found out Joe was being unfaithful," Maya confessed in a voice that barely rose above a whisper.

"I'm so sorry," Jane said, stunned.

"I confronted him, and he didn't deny it. I thought about leaving him. I was so angry." She pushed out a frustrated breath. "But what was I going to do? I had a baby. I could have moved in with family, but then I would always be *that* girl. The one who failed. The one who couldn't keep her husband happy. So I stayed with him, to avoid the shame."

Jane nodded, as tears gathered and fell from her own eyes. "I know how you felt. Other women know how you felt. It may have seemed to you that you were all alone, at the time, but there are women going through that same pain, every single day."

Maya's shoulders slumped. "Ryan told me he'd been lending Joe money. I had no idea. Joe doesn't tell me anything. Sometimes, I wonder if he's still running around behind my back. Every time he's late, or smells really good, or even when he acts really nice to me, I wonder if it's because he's having another affair. I'll always have doubts. If he did it once, what's to stop him from doing it again? The drinking, too. He said he stopped and I hope he did, but I just don't trust him. Will I ever be able to trust him again?" Lack of trust was the reason Jane had finally left Nick. "I can't answer that. But I know one thing—you did what you believed was right for you and little Isabel." She thought about stopping there, but conscience drove her to add, "Still, situations change, Maya. What was right for you then may not be right for you in the future."

"You say that, but if I left him now, what would I do? I don't have any skills."

"Something tells me you can do whatever you put your mind to. Don't let a fear of the unknown make you settle for a life of unhappiness. I've done it both ways. Your happiness is worth fighting for," Jane said, and wiped each eye with her finger.

Maya nodded. "And so is yours. Oh gosh, you're crying, too. I didn't mean to upset you like this." Maya darted into the bathroom and returned with a wad of tissues. She handed some to Jane, keeping the rest for herself.

Jane waved the tissues casually. "Pregnancy hormones. Everything makes me cry."

Maya sat on the edge of the bed next to Jane. "While we're being honest here, I guess I have something else to confess. I'm a little jealous of you."

"Jealous? Of me?"

"*Un poco*. Just a little," Maya said, holding her index finger and thumb close together. "You're an independent woman. You're not afraid to go out there and get what you want."

Jane laughed out loud. "I'm glad that's how I appear because, more times than not, I'm scared. So I'll let you in on a secret." She pointed at Maya. "I'm jealous of you, too."

Maya scoffed. "Why?"

"Because you command such respect in this family. You may be pint-sized, but you have everyone running around, trying to please you, especially the Rosales men. Ryan says, 'She may be tiny, but she carries a big stick.' You are the family matriarch. And what an incredible family you have! All of you are there for each other, through thick and thin. You can count on each other. I never had a big family. Other than my mother, I didn't have anyone but my husband and son. But I don't worry about that with this baby, because he or she will have such a safety net of love and support within the family. This baby will never feel alone."

Maya smiled. "She, *mi amiga*. The baby is a little girl."

Jane gasped and shook her head. "How could you possibly know that?"

"I just do. And she will be loved and cherished by this family. *Your* family. I don't want you to feel like an outsider anymore, Jane. You're as much a Rosales as I am." Leaning forward, she drew Jane into an embrace. "I'm sorry I treated you badly."

Jane hugged her back. "You were just trying to protect what's yours."

"Yes. But Reyo is yours, now. I don't have to worry about him anymore."

"Are you two talking about me in here?"

Jane looked over Maya's shoulder and spotted Ryan standing in the doorway.

"We have. I was just telling Jane how lucky you are to have her and how you'd do nothing to sacrifice the bond you both share." Maya held Ryan's gaze. "Am I right, brother?"

"You've never been more right," Ryan said in almost a whisper.

"I feel like I'm missing something here," Jane said staring at Ryan.

"Maya and I had a misunderstanding, but everything's okay. Actually, it's better than okay because the family feud is finally over."

Maya stood and wiped her eyes. "Family feud? Really, Reyo, must you be so dramatic? There was no feud. My future sister-in-law and I just needed some time to get to know each other better." She squeezed Jane's shoulder and kissed her lightly on the cheek. "Thank you," she whispered, then strode to the doorway and pointed at Ryan. "You make sure she feeds my niece," Maya said, and left.

Ryan looked over his shoulder as he moved to the bedside. "Niece?"

"Maya thinks the baby's a girl."

"Then it's a girl. Maya's never wrong. She has a sixth sense about these things."

"Then you and I had better start working on girl names."

"I hope our daughter looks just like you," he said, and kissed her.

"Now that Maya likes me do you think she'll give me the recipe for her tortilla soup?" Jane asked hopefully.

"Don't press your luck."

"I didn't think you'd be home until late. What made you come home?"

"*Te eché de menos, Querida.* I missed you."

"Mmm, you know how hot I get when you speak Spanish to me," she said as he came to her side and brushed his lips over hers. "But I thought you had a big party coming in tonight."

"I do, but I wanted to talk to you about something that happened today because we agreed we'd always be honest with one another."

Jane blinked. "Anything wrong?"

"Camille came to Vine today."

Jane paused, trying to place the name. "Camille from The Cowboys? Did she want you to return as one of her studs?"

"Something like that. She came on to me, and for a brief moment the past came flooding back and I remembered what I once felt for her. But it made me realize what we have and how desperately I love you." He tucked a lock of hair behind her ear and trailed a row of lazy kisses up her neck, his hot breath on her skin lighting a fire deep in her heart. There was something downright magical about the two of them.

"After she left, there was nothing more important to me than having a romantic dinner with the soon-to-be mother of my baby, on our lovely patio, in front of a crackling fire. So I left the party in Gretchen's capable hands, had Chef George whip us up a couple of the salmon specials, and here I am." He kissed her again. "Give me a few minutes to get everything ready, and I'll come in to get you," he promised, and headed for the kitchen.

"Ry?" Jane called after him.

He turned in the bedroom doorway, and the way he caressed her with his eyes melted her insides.

"I love you."

"*Te amo*," he said.

She threw her hands in the air. "There you go, making me all hot and bothered again!"

Ryan grinned. "I'll be right back. Don't go anywhere."

"Like that's an option," she joked.

He returned after a few minutes. "You ready?"

She sat up and swung her legs over the edge of the bed. "Oh!"

"What's wrong?" He hurried to her side.

Jane gasped and rubbed her belly. "I'm fine," she panted, then said more firmly, "Just a weird pain. It's gone now. I think the baby was stretching. Dr. Murcia said I'd start feeling more aggressive movements as the baby grows bigger."

"I'm calling her."

Jane grabbed his arm. "No, no. Don't. Really. I feel fine. In fact, I'm really hungry, and I need a change of scenery."

"You sure?" He searched her eyes.

"Absolutely."

Supporting much of her weight, Ryan guided Jane to the patio, then propped pillows around her body the way she liked before setting a plate next to her on the daybed. He pointed to the dish. "No salt added. Just a few spices." Breaking off a small piece with his fork, he pierced it with the tines and lifted the morsel to her lips.

Jane lifted her index finger after she swallowed. *"El salmon es delicioso,"* she said slowly, and lifted her eyebrows, as if awaiting his critique.

"You've been practicing," he said, and kissed her finger.

"I started an online Spanish tutorial. I'd like to be able to communicate with your family members who don't speak English. Also, I've been thinking about something. I think we should raise the baby with both languages. She should be bilingual."

"She?" he teased, smiling.

"Yes, Maya's not the only one who thinks this baby's a girl."

"Whenever I think I love you so much that I can't possibly love you any more, you do something that makes my heart overflow."

She tilted her head. "Then I guess this is a good time to tell you that I resigned today."

His eyes widened. "You did? This doesn't have anything to do with Maya, does it?"

Jane shook her head. "She just helped me realize I was holding onto my job for the wrong reasons. I thought by leaving my job I'd become too reliant on you, and lose the me I've fought so hard to find. But *you're* the reason I'm happy and complete, not the job. And talking to Maya made me remember what a precious time Tyler's childhood was to me. I want the luxury of being a full-time mommy to our baby. I can always go back to my career when I'm ready."

He searched her gaze. "You're a wonderful mom, with or without your job, but I'm happy you resigned. Now, I can have you all to myself," he said, cupping her cheek.

"Just for a little while longer. Then you'll have to share me," Jane said, and cradled her belly with her hands.

Carefully, he slid his arm around Jane and pulled her closer. "How did I ever get lucky enough to have you in my arms forever?" he whispered in her ear.

Chapter Thirty

Jane almost missed hearing the knock on the door over the murmur of the daytime television show she'd switched on to keep her company. Wondering if she was imagining things, she turned down the volume.

Knock, knock, knock.

Jane hadn't expected any other visitors, that day. Maya had stopped by earlier, and Ryan wasn't due home until the afternoon. *It's probably just a delivery person*, she told herself. *They'll leave when no one answers the door.*

She heard the scrap of metal as the key turned in the door and froze in a panic.

"Hello? Jane?"

She reached for her phone, not recognizing the deep voice.

"Jane? Are you here?"

She cocked her head. *No. It can't be...* "Nick?" she called.

Footsteps clomped closer. "Where are you?"

"Through the kitchen. The last door on the right," she said dropping her phone on the table and placing her hand on her chest calming her nerves.

The sound of footsteps grew louder until a shadow darkened the floor at her doorway.

"Jeez, Nick. You scared the crap out of me!"

"Don't you know you shouldn't place a spare key under your mat? It's the first place an intruder looks," he said with a smirk.

"Obviously. What do I owe the pleasure of your breaking and entering my home? You certainly have a knack for showing up when you're least expected," Jane said as Nick's face came into view.

He shrugged with an air of nonchalance. "I was in town, so I thought I'd drop by."

Jane stared at her ex-husband. "You're in *town*? You thought you'd drop *by*?"

He held his palm out. "May I?"

Grudgingly, she nodded. "You've come all this way, so you may as well come a few steps farther."

Nick strode to her side and kissed her cheek. "How ya feeling?"

"Like a turkey left in the oven too long." She knew she looked like a mess. She hadn't seen a lipstick in months and couldn't recall the last time she'd had a haircut.

He smiled. "You look great."

"That's the second round of bullshit you've tossed my way since you got here. Why don't you just tell me why you're in San Antonio and standing in my bedroom?"

"Tyler told me what you're going through, and I felt sorry for you. Then I started feeling bad for the things that happened between us, and the way I treated you afterwards. I guess I just wanted to say I'm sorry."

She shot him a suspicious glance. "Really? You came all the way from New York to cleanse your soul? You could've called."

Nick held his hands up. "Okay, okay. Full disclosure, I'm on my way to a golf trip in Arizona. Turns out I had a long layover in San Antonio, so on a whim I asked Ty for your address, rented a car, and here I am."

"Ah. At least that makes more sense, and it's definitely less creepy."

He grimaced. "Ouch." Crossing his arms, he smiled down at her. "So, how's everything going?" he asked, his gaze moving to the blanket-covered bulge of her belly.

"The baby's doing well. I'm just hanging around here until she's fully cooked." Jane rubbed her stomach.

"She?" Nick asked.

"We don't know for sure, but Ryan's sister insists it's a girl. I got used to saying 'she' instead of 'it'. I haven't had much to do, over these past few weeks, so the baby and I have gotten to know each other pretty well. She even likes my singing."

"That's true love," Nick said, and winked. His gaze shifted to the pile of paper on her bedside table. "Have you been working while you're on bed rest?"

"Only to transition my accounts to another account manager. I quit my job," Jane said with a smile.

Nick raised his eyebrows. "Quit? I thought you loved your job. Tyler said you were able to work from here in San Antonio."

"True and true. It was going fine, but I've had a lot of time to think, and I realized how fast time goes by, and how precious it is. I want to spend time with my family." She smiled down at her belly. "Who knows? I may go back to it, one day." She shrugged. "Or I may not."

"Looks like you have it all figured out."

"Hardly. I keep having this dream that I'm juggling a bunch of balls, trying so hard to keep them all in the air. Then I miss one, and it drops to the floor with a loud thud. Everything's quiet for a moment, and then all the balls come crashing down." She laughed. "See what pregnancy hormones and too much daytime television do to a person? Hey, would you mind filling that pitcher with ice and water while I hit the bathroom?"

"Sure. Need any help getting up?"

"Nope. I can do it. But you could cut me up an apple."

Jane eased out of bed as Nick left the bedroom. She shuffled toward the bathroom when a sharp pain caught her off-guard, seeming to slice through her lower belly. She grabbed for the edge of the small table outside of the bathroom, the closest thing in reach. But she slipped, the table wobbled, and Jane tumbled to the floor as the lamp slid across the table's surface and landed with a crash.

Nick rushed back to her side, his shoes crunching on the broken glass. "Jane!"

She lay in shock for a moment. Then another wave slashed through her core. "No, no, no…" She shook her head and cupped her hardening belly in her hands.

Glass pierced her forearm.

Nick pulled a blanket from the bed. "Breathe, Jane. In and out," he said as he wedged the blanket under her head. "I'm gonna get you some help." He started to rise, but she stopped him with a death grip on his forearm.

"Don't leave me," she gasped, a mixture of tears and sweat stinging her eyes.

"I need to call for an ambulance."

"It's too soon. The baby's not ready," she cried as her thoughts raced in a million different directions. She knew she needed help, but fear stopped her breath. For an instant, she thought that everything might be all right if she just curled up on the floor and froze in place, not breathing, not moving. Then a sensation of warmth traveled through her panties to her thighs. She reached between her legs and touched a rush of wetness that was forming a puddle on the floor.

"The baby seems to have other plans, sweetheart. We have to get you to the hospital. Now." Again, Nick tried to stand, but she held him even tighter.

"I can't do this." Terror sliced through her as she pushed out a shaky breath. "I can't lose this baby."

He wiggled his hand free from her grasp and cupped her cheek in his palm. "Listen to me, Jane. You are the strongest person I know. You'll get through this."

"But what if … what if I don't? What if I can't?" Desperation rolled through her body, prickling her skin with fear. "What if I've failed this baby? What if I've failed Ryan?" She choked down a sob as tears flowed down her face. She shook her head. "I can't live with that. I don't know what I'll do."

Nick chuckled and smoothed her hair. "Look, I've caused you a lot of pain, but you stayed strong through all of it. I expected you to crumble, but you never did. Instead, you stuck by me. You stayed strong and tried to make it work, even though I'd been a world-class asshole. I kick myself every single day for what I did to you and what I lost in the process. You deserve everything good in life. You deserve a good man like Ryan, and you deserve this baby. The baby will be fine. *You* will be fine, because you have the strength to do anything you set your mind to. But we have to get you to the hospital. Okay?"

She searched his face, absorbing his words while she reasserted control over her senses. The fear receded slightly, and she was back. She nodded. "Yes."

He wrapped one arm around her back, slid the other under her knees, and lifted her off the ground. Then his gaze landed on the puddle. "We're not waiting for an ambulance. I'm taking you to the hospital now. We'll call your doctor and Ryan in the car." Stopping next to the bed, he bent just far enough to grab her cell phone.

Jane braced herself as another wave passed through her insides. It felt as if her vital organs were passing through a food processor. She grabbed Nick's arm as he carried her outside and headed toward his rental car. "I'm calling my doctor. You call Ryan," she bit out through clenched teeth, swallowing the new surge of fear that tried to crawl up her throat. She had to be strong for Ryan and the baby, but she knew her limits. If she called Ryan, she'd melt into an incoherent puddle of tears, right there in Nick's rental car.

He eased her into the passenger seat, ran around to climb in on the driver's side, and started the engine, then pulled out his cell phone, his gaze flicking to her. "What's his number?"

She barked out Ryan's number and poked the speed dial button to the emergency number of her doctor's office.

She heard Ryan answer through Nick's phone as they backed out of the driveway and started down the street. "Ryan, this is Nick Keegan. Jane's in labor. We're on the way to the hospital," Nick said. Ryan's voice took on an angry tone, but she couldn't understand a word of what he said to Nick. "Look, there's no time to explain… Yeah, I'm sure. I know when a woman's in labor. This isn't my first rodeo, cowboy. Just meet us at the hospital. Okay, okay … yeah, hold on." He held out the phone to Jane.

She exchanged phones with him and pointed to the highway sign ahead. "Turn up there. The service has me on hold while they try to reach my doctor."

She lifted Nick's phone to her ear. "Ryan?"

"What happened? Is everything okay? Did he upset you?" Ryan fired questions at her in a strained voice. "I swear, I'll kill him if he had anything to do with this," he spat.

Jane paused to listen to Nick's conversation. "Yes. Jane Keegan. We're on our way now." He flicked a glance her way. "Okay, Jane. Your doctor's on her way to the hospital."

She smiled weakly at Nick then turned her attention back to Ryan. "My water broke right after Nick showed up, but he didn't have anything to do with it. It was actually good that he was there. We're almost at the hospital, and Dr. Murcia is on her way, too."

She heard footsteps in the background through the phone. "I just got to my car. I should be there in just a few minutes. Everything's going to be fine, *Querida*. You know that, don't you? I promise you, everything will be fine."

Ryan's voice soothed her, but she wondered if he believed his own words. She wasn't sure she did.

"I know it will," she said, trying to hold it together as another wave of pain caught her off guard. "Please hurry. I love you," she said, and ended the call. She didn't want Ryan to hear the anguish in her voice.

Jane shouted directions to Nick through a series of painful contractions until they finally reached the hospital. He screeched to a halt at the curb at the Emergency Room entrance and threw the car into Park. Jumping out, he ran to the entrance and grabbed one of the wheelchairs inside the glass doors. Wheeling it to the passenger side of the car, he opened her door and shot her a tight smile. "I gotta say, I'm glad we got here. I was afraid I'd have to deliver your baby on the side of the road." He helped her into the wheelchair.

"Bet you're smacking yourself now for making a pit stop to visit me," Jane said in a desperate attempt at humor as he wheeled her inside.

"I'm glad I was there for you. Makes up a little for the times I wasn't." Nick stopped the wheelchair just short of the reception desk. "This is Jane Keegan. She's in labor," he shouted.

The receptionist tapped the keyboard. "Yes, you're Dr. Murcia's patient. We're to send you straight to Maternity. Wait by those double doors. An attendant will be right there to take you up."

Nick followed directions and pushed her to the designated spot.

Jane looked up at him from the chair as she clutched her belly. "You don't have to stay with me. Ryan will be here in a minute. You have a plane to catch."

His gaze bounced from Jane to the exit and back to her. "I've left you alone when you've needed me before, and I'm not going to make the same mistake again. As long as it's okay with you, I'm staying with you until Ryan gets here."

She nodded. "Okay. I'd like that," she said, ignoring how strange it was that Nick's presence was giving her a sense of comfort.

An attendant appeared, smiling. "Looks like someone's ready to have a baby. Let's get you upstairs," he said to Jane, and nodded to Nick. "You can follow us."

Jane opened her mouth to explain that they were waiting for her baby's father, but she was gripped with another agonizing pain. Speech was beyond her; all she could do was try to implement the breathing methods she'd learned when she had Tyler.

A nurse met them as the attendant wheeled her onto the Maternity wing. "Is Dr. Murcia here yet?" Jane asked, gasping for air.

The nurse nodded calmly. "She's here. I'll get you prepped, and Dr. Murcia will be right in," she said. "You can follow me, Mr. Keegan."

He paused. "I'm not ... I mean, I am, but I'm not—" Nick stumbled.

At any other time, Jane would have enjoyed witnessing Nick ramble on in embarrassment. But not now. Not now.

"I'm sorry. You're not Mr. Keegan?" The nurse glanced at Jane, just as another wave of pain stabbed at her belly.

"He's … oh … oh," Jane said, clenching her teeth.

"I am Mr. Keegan. I'm just not—" He pointed to Jane's stomach.

"He's not the baby's father. I am," Ryan said, and knelt in front of Jane. "Breathe, *Querida*."

Jane sucked in a breath and forced it out between her teeth. She shook her head, and a strand of her hair stuck to the sweat on her cheek. "It's too soon. It's too early."

"Not according to our little girl."

His voice was as smooth as warm honey on a summer's day. Jane sucked in a breath and managed to let it out more slowly. She reached for his hand. "I'm so glad you're here."

The nurse's gaze skipped over all three faces. "Well, I hate to break up this little party, but I need to get Ms. Keegan prepped for delivery. When you two figure out who should be in the delivery room, you can put these on and come on in. We'll be in Room Three." She slapped a package of scrubs onto the counter, took command of the wheelchair, and rolled Jane into the room.

Another contraction ripped through her body, and sweat beaded on her upper lip. "That was a bad one," she gasped when it finally eased. "They're getting worse."

The nurse helped her into a gown, settled her on the bed, and was just starting an IV when Ryan stepped into the room, wearing a pair of green scrubs.

"Dr. Murcia will be in soon," the nurse said as she left them.

Ryan came to the bedside. "So, what makes you think we're about to have a baby?" he teased gently, stroking the hair back from her forehead.

"Can't imagine," Jane's voice broke from worry and pain. But she tried to muster a grin for Ryan's sake.

Dr. Murcia knocked once before opening the door. "Baby decided to come early, it seems," she said, followed by a tight smile. "Let's see what we're dealing with." Dr. Murcia examined Jane with quick efficiency and checked her cervix. "Okay. Considering that your water broke and you're nearly one hundred percent effaced and dilated, keeping this baby *in utero* is no longer an option. In fact, it should only take you a few pushes to get the baby out." Dr. Murcia consulted the fetal monitor and turned to the nurse. "Page Dr. Blake, please." Her gaze moved to Jane. "We're going to have the Neonatologist on standby."

"What's wrong?" Jane asked. Another contraction started, and she grabbed Ryan's hand.

"Is everything okay with the baby?" Ryan asked.

"The baby's heart rate is decreasing." Dr. Murcia moved to the foot of the bed. "All right, Jane, get ready to push."

Chapter Thirty-One

Doctors and nurses skated around Ryan in a precise, synchronized dance. Every person in the room had a purpose and a job to do, except Ryan. For the first time in his life, he felt absolutely helpless as he wiped Jane's brow with a cold cloth while she braved another wave of contractions. He gazed into her worry-filled eyes, searching for the right thing to say. This baby was heading into the world much too early, and Jane's unrelenting labor offered her little respite from the pain.

Ryan would take every last bit of agony from her if he could. Since that wasn't possible, he asked, "Can't you give her anything?"

Dr. Murcia shook her head. "She's too far along. It would slow things down, and your child can't afford that. We need to get this baby out now. Okay, are you ready to push, Jane?"

Jane clenched her teeth and nodded.

The nurse picked up one of Jane's legs and caught Ryan's gaze. "Go to the other side and hold her leg, just like this."

Ryan moved to the far side of the bed and used one hand to hold Jane's leg as the nurse instructed, while he clasped Jane's hand with the other.

"That's it. Now, Jane, push on the next contraction," Dr. Murcia said from the foot of the bed.

Ryan couldn't understand how she could stay so calm. His focus was on Jane, but he was also willing his body to not pass out, which was becoming an all too real possibility.

Jane squeezed his hand with a strength he'd no clue she possessed.

"You're doing great, *Querida*. I'm so proud of you," he murmured.

The strain around her eyes seemed to ease as he spoke, and Ryan felt an ache in his heart at the sight of her trust in him even now, when she was pushed to her limit.

"Yes," Dr. Murcia chimed in. "We're almost there, Jane. We just need a few more strong pushes."

A sobbing breath escaped through Jane's pale lips. "I can't," she whispered. "Oh, Ryan, I'm so sorry…"

"Sorry? Ah, *Querida*," he murmured, the words bordering on prayer, "don't you realize? There is nothing you cannot do. I will spend the rest of our days trying to deserve you. You are my brave, strong love," he vowed, kissing her whitened knuckles. "My brave, strong love. Fight now, Jane. Fight for our child, *Querida*."

****

A blast of energy surged through her veins at the sound of his voice, and she lunged forward, giving it everything she had, squeezing his fingers as she held her breath and bore down through a long, sustained push.

For an instant, everything was silent. Then Dr. Murcia turned, with a bloodied bundle in her hands. "Okay, team, we have a Code Pink," she said, and passed the motionless body to the neonatologist.

"She's not crying," Jane protested, gasping for breath. "Ryan, why isn't she crying?"

Dr. Murcia placed her hand on Jane's leg. "You have a very tiny, very beautiful little girl. Because she was born early, her lungs aren't fully developed, and she's having trouble breathing on her own. Dr. Blake's team is taking over her care."

"Oh my God, Ryan," Jane said, and fought against the sea of sobs that rose in her chest as she watched the flurry of urgent actions taking place in the corner of the room. One of the nurses shifted, and Jane caught a glimpse of the tiniest person she'd ever seen. Their baby lay completely still, her skin a pale blue.

Jane wished she could unsee the vision. She wanted to look away and then glance back to the sight of a pink, plump baby screaming angrily over being roused from her warm and safe spot in Jane's womb.

But she couldn't look away. She could only stare at her daughter's fragile body.

"Our baby," Jane said weakly, clinging to Ryan's hand. They watched powerlessly while the doctors and nurses inserted tubes and lines into the infant's tiny body. *How can something so small handle all that?* Jane wondered wildly.

"Move her to the NICU," Dr. Blake ordered, and turned to them. "Dad, you can follow us or stay here. It's up to you."

Ryan's gaze moved to Jane and the anguish she read in his face practically tore her apart. "Go to her, Ryan. She shouldn't be alone."

"But you need me, too," he insisted, and his voice hitched.

"My life's not on the line. Our daughter's is." Jane squeezed his hand. "I don't want our little girl to be alone if she…" Jane couldn't finish that sentence, but she realized that she didn't have to. It was clear that Ryan knew all that she was implying, and that he was haunted by the same fear.

He cupped her face within his palms. His thumbs brushed along her damp skin, and she closed her eyes.

"Look at me, *Querida*."

Jane rallied to meet his gaze.

"Whatever happens," he swore to her solemnly, "whatever the outcome, you and I will always have each other. We will get through this together. Do you hear me? We're in this together."

Jane nodded, doing her best to ignore the fresh tears that streamed down her face. "Together," she promised him. "Forever. Now go to her."

****

Ryan had to move quickly to keep up with the team heading to the neonatal intensive care unit. The first thing he noticed when walking into the NICU was a symphony of beeps and buzzers. The lights were dimmer and the temperature was warmer than elsewhere in the hospital, and he blinked to adjust his vision as he watched his daughter being attached to even more machines as she was placed in an incubator. Tubes and lines invaded her mouth, her tiny arm, even her umbilical cord. His only relief came from watching her pale blue skin slowly take on a rosier pink hue.

The neonatologist checked the monitors before walking to Ryan's side. "Your daughter is stable, Mr. Keegan. She's out of the woods for now."

Ryan's gaze remained glued to the incubator. "It's Zeigler. Ryan Zeigler." Suddenly, the mix-up of names seemed unbearable. It was bad enough that Nick had been the one to drive Jane to the hospital, and now he was being addressed with his name.

"My apologies, Mr. Zeigler."

Ryan nodded. "Will she be okay? Is she going to make it?" He was afraid of the answer, but he had to know. If the news was bad, he wanted to be the one to prepare Jane for the worst.

"She's very small. We haven't weighed her yet, but I estimate her to be under two pounds. Her lungs haven't fully developed yet, so she won't be able to breathe without a ventilator, at least for now. The next few days will be crucial, but I'm encouraged that she'll respond well."

Ryan stepped forward and crouched down to get as close as he possibly could to his daughter. Her skin was almost translucent, her tiny veins and blood vessels visible beneath it. Never in his life had he seen something so small and fragile. Other than her little chest moving up and down in rhythm to a song only she knew, she was motionless.

As he watched her, a warm hand came to rest on his shoulder. "You've been given a gift today. This little girl is a gift." Ryan listened to the voice of the woman behind him, a steady voice with a lilting Irish accent. "She's in good hands—mine," the woman said with a chuckle. "I'll take good care of her."

Ryan looked over his shoulder.

A stout nurse stood behind him, with graying hair and a crooked nametag with the name "Doreen" printed in block letters. "You need to have faith that all will be well with her. Go to your baby's mum. She's the one who needs you now. Come back with her when you can. We'll be waiting."

Ryan blinked back tears as he straightened and nodded. "Thank you," he said, and walked slowly to the door. He turned back for another look at his daughter, etching the vision of her into his memory, hoping for a sign that everything would indeed be okay.

The baby's hand moved slightly.

If Ryan had blinked at that moment, he would have missed it. But he saw the movement, almost as if she were reaching to him.

It wasn't much. But it was enough.

****

Dr. Murcia was still in Jane's room when he returned.

Jane pinned him with her stare, reading him without words. "She's okay," she breathed, more of a statement than a question, and he sensed that any other answer would break her heart.

"She's stable," Ryan answered.

"And she'll be okay."

Ryan tried to stay strong. He so wanted to promise that everything was going to be all right, but it was out of his control. He took a shaky breath. "I don't know. She's so tiny, *Querida.* So incredibly small."

As Jane listened, her eyes filled with tears.

A sense of helplessness overwhelmed Ryan, breaking down the wall of courage he had tried so hard to build. He crumpled next to Jane and embraced her. He knew they both needed to be brave for their daughter, but, in order to do that, they needed to let themselves feel the fear honestly, so that they could work through it. Together, they cried softly, drawing strength from being in each other's arms.

Ryan wasn't sure when Dr. Murcia left the room, what time it was, or even how long he and Jane held each other before they ran out of tears, but renewed bravery filled his core when he lifted his head and looked into Jane's clear eyes.

"Let's go see our daughter," Jane said, with a watery smile.

"Are you sure you don't want to rest a little?" Ryan asked. Dark circles stained Jane's pale complexion. She looked as if she were in desperate need of sleep.

"No, I want to see her. I *need* to see her," Jane said in a strong, clear voice. Her strength and conviction fueled Ryan even more, and he shot her a grin. "Your wish is my command. I'll be right back."

Striding out to the nurses' station, he said, "I'd like a wheelchair for Jane Keegan. She wants to see to our daughter."

Daughter. He loved the way that sounded.

A nurse pointed down the hallway and nodded. "You can grab one over there. I'll be right in to help."

Ryan pushed the chair into Jane's room. "Your chariot awaits," he said, and was reminded of the night he'd met her, and how he had fallen in love with her on Uncle Pascal's gondola.

When the maternity nurse arrived and helped Jane out of bed, Ryan was alarmed to notice how unsteady Jane was on her feet when she tried to stand. "You're worrying me, *Querida*."

Jane winced as she moved into the chair. "I can handle some discomfort. I'm sure it's nothing, compared to what she's going through. She needs me. She needs *us*."

"Only for a few minutes, this first time," the nurse cautioned. "You've lost a lot of blood. You need to rest and build your strength."

Taking over, Ryan pushed Jane's chair toward the NICU, wondering how many sets of parents had walked that same path, and how many times he and Jane would have to follow it. In that moment, he truly realized that life would never be the same.

A serene vibe he hadn't noticed before seemed to overlay the unit as they approached their newborn. Ryan's gaze sought out Doreen, waiting for them just as she had promised.

"Ah! You're back, and you've brought Mum," she said with a warm smile.

"This is Jane. I'm Ryan."

She nodded. "I'm Doreen, and I'll be taking care of this little princess, most days."

"How is she?" Jane asked as her gaze moved to the small form in the incubator.

"Her heart rate is strong. She's doing well, for being one pound and seven ounces."

Ryan pushed Jane's chair closer.

"She's so little. So many tubes and wires," Jane whispered. "Why isn't she moving?"

Doreen came to join them. "Babies born this early generally don't move very much, dear. It's perfectly normal. Preemies save their energy, and use it to help develop vital organs first. Nature is a beautiful thing."

"May I hold her?"

"Not yet, I'm afraid. But as long as there are no complications, you should be able to hold her soon. But it's all right for you to touch her though. Would you like to?"

Jane nodded. "Of course. Yes."

Doreen took Jane and Ryan through the procedure for preparing to handle a baby in the NICU, and rolled Jane's chair closer to the baby. Jane tentatively reached over the enclosure and touched her baby's warm skin. She traced her finger lightly down the baby's tiny arm, from her elbow to her hand. "I've never seen fingers so small. But she's warm. So warm." Jane placed three fingers on the baby's side. "I can feel her heartbeat."

"Aye. I told you, it's strong," Doreen agreed, and turned to Ryan. "Would you like to feel it?"

He gazed at his daughter's tiny form. "I don't know. I almost feel as if I could break her just by touching her."

Doreen chuckled. "You'd be surprised by how much strength preemies possess. It's deceiving. You won't break her, I promise. Go ahead."

He reached in and slid his finger down her leg to her foot. "Look at her toes." She flexed her foot, and Ryan laughed. "I think she's ticklish," he said, turning to Jane, and felt his heart leap at the sight of Jane's smile.

"And what is her name? Or shall I continue calling her Princess?" Doreen asked with raised eyebrows.

Jane and Ryan looked at each other. "The fair Princess Zeigler needs a name," Jane said.

"That she does." They'd discussed and even debated baby names, but hadn't been in a hurry to decide on any finalists since they thought there was plenty of time.

Jane gasped. "Raya. I'd like to name her Raya." Her smile grew bigger when the baby's hand moved toward her.

"Raya." It wasn't a name either of them had mentioned before, but it was perfect. "How'd you come up with it?"

Jane tilted her head. "It just came to me, as if she just came into the world like a ray of sunshine. Plus, it's a combination of yours and your sister's names. She's little and spunky, just like Maya, but I'll bet she has your eyes."

"Raya it is."

Jane's gaze followed the tubes to a host of beeping machines next to the isolette. "So many machines." He watched as her glance moved across the room to the other isolettes, each holding a tiny baby. "Look at all these little lives."

"Yes, and as long as you two are okay here, I'm going to check on my other little ones," Doreen said, and headed to a nearby baby.

Jane shook her head. "I can't believe Raya's here. She should still be *here*," she said, and touched her belly with her free hand. "She's so different from Tyler as a newborn. He was a fat little baby who wouldn't stop moving. I had no clue there were babies who were born like this."

"The only baby I remember being around was Isabel, and all I really remember about her, as a newborn, was all her hair. She had so much of it," Ryan laughed. "And I remember how fast she grew. Raya will grow fast, too. Before we know it, she'll be walking and talking and driving."

"And going on dates," Jane joked.

Ryan shook his head. "Never," he intoned with exaggerated solemnity. "She'll never go on dates."

As Jane giggled in response, the door opened, and the maternity nurse walked to their side. "She looks like she's doing well. You'll be able to see her again later tonight, but I need to get you back to your room now."

Jane and Ryan pulled their hands from the incubator. Then, hesitating, Jane kissed her fingertips and pressed them to the clear plastic barrier. "We love you, little Raya."

Ryan rested his palm on Jane's hand. "She's small, but she's a fighter. Just like her mom."

"More like her dad," Jane laughed. "I thought you were going to throw Nick through a wall when you got here. You didn't, did you?"

Ryan had almost forgotten about his exchange with Nick. "No. I guess I should be glad he showed up at the house when he did. Why was he there, anyway?"

He listened as calmly as he could, while Jane explained the reason for Nick's visit on the way back to her room. Then he helped her back into her bed, and smoothed her hair back. "You look absolutely exhausted, *Querida*. Why don't you get some sleep? I'll call our families."

Jane nodded as her eyelids closed. "Don't forget to call Char."

"How could I ever forget Charlotte?" Ryan kissed her softly. "I'll be back later," he promised, and made himself leave.

He followed the signs to the Emergency Room, since his car was still parked in the ER lot. More tired than he cared to admit to himself, he made his way through the waiting room toward the exit.

"Ryan!"

Startled, he turned to see Nick waving his hands. "What are you still doing here?"

"How are Jane and the baby?" Nick asked.

"Jane's fine. The baby's on a ventilator, but she's doing well, considering how early she is."

"So it's a girl? Jane was sure she was a girl," Nick said, and smiled.

"Yeah, a girl she is. But why are you still here? Jane said you were on your way to a golf trip. We figured you'd be halfway to Arizona by now."

Nick shrugged. "I couldn't leave without knowing everything was okay."

"That was decent of you, Nick," Ryan said, and slapped him on the back.

"Yeah, well, I've made some poor decisions in my life. I'm trying to make up for a few of them." He brightened. "But hey, congratulations are in order. Can I buy you a drink?"

"I don't know. I'm bushed, and I have a lot of calls to make. I was heading home."

"Fair enough. How about if I grab a six-pack and meet you there? I can call Jane's side of the family."

"That would help. It's kinda weird … but 'weird' seems to be the way we do things." The two men laughed and walked out of the hospital together.

****

Ryan took a long, cool sip from his beer bottle and stepped onto the patio, finally finished making the calls to the Zeigler-Rosales side of the family.

The conversation with Maya had taken the longest. She'd wanted every last detail of the birth and Raya's status, and she'd cried when Ryan told her the baby's name. It had taken a concerted effort to talk her out of planning a huge family party for Raya. "Let's take it one day at a time, for now. She has a long road ahead of her," he'd said to his sister.

"Done with the Keegan calls?" Ryan asked Nick.

"Tyler, Beverly, and Charlotte," Nick said, holding up three fingers. "Charlotte gave me the third-degree about being here. She wanted to know my intentions. Can you believe that? Was I really that much of an asshole?"

Ryan grinned. "Women stick together. You should know that by now." He took a seat next to Nick and stared into the flames.

"Hope you don't mind that I started a fire. This thing's beautiful," Nick said, pointing to the fireplace.

Ryan scanned the patio. "The place was a mess before Jane got here. I never came out here. But Jane loved it, right from the start, even when the only thing on the whole patio was a beaten-up table and a couple of chairs. She fixed it up and strung some old Christmas lights into the trees." He smiled at the memory. "She has a knack for making a house a home. I had this fireplace built as a surprise for her."

"You make her happy," Nick said, and took a pull from his beer. "I was jealous as hell when she told me about you. She had a sparkle in her eye when she talked about you. I never made her sparkle. But you do," he conceded, and held his bottle out to Ryan, who met it with a clink.

Ryan shrugged philosophically. "I never would've met her, if it hadn't been for you. So I guess I have you to thank." He set his bottle on the table. "I'm going to head back to the hospital. You're welcome to stay here for the night, if you'd like."

"I'll take you up on that. I've got a flight out, in the morning."

"If I don't see you before you go, have a good trip."

Nick stood up, looking sheepish. "Look, I've been meaning to thank you."

"For what?"

"For being what I couldn't."

Ryan shook his head. "We all have times when we aren't who we want to be. Sure, I was there for Jane when you weren't, but maybe you'll be there for somebody else when they need it the most." He held out his hand. "See you around, Nick."

"See you around," Nick echoed, and they shook on it.

Chapter Thirty-Two

"Whoa there! Where are you going, Ms. Keegan?" the nurse called from behind the desk.

"To see my baby," Jane answered, her gaze glued to the door leading to the NICU.

"You need to use your call button when you want to leave your room," the nurse scolded as she scooted around the desk and grabbed a wheelchair.

Wheelchairs. Jane would be thrilled never to see one of *those* again, too. "I'm perfectly able to walk. I don't need that thing." She waved her hand dismissively.

"You gave birth just a few hours ago. We don't want you passing out and hitting your head. Please take a seat, and I'll take you right over," the nurse insisted, maneuvering the chair into Jane's path.

"Women have been having babies and returning to work in the fields for decades. I should be fine to walk a few feet to visit my baby," Jane grumbled, but slumped into the chair. She hadn't a clue when or where those legendary women were who went back to working in the fields after popping out their babies, but it was the only argument she'd been able to muster on such short notice.

"Wait just a second while I find coverage for the desk," the nurse said, and headed around the corner.

Jane huffed out a frustrated breath and lowered her arms over the sides of the chair. Grasping the metal rims around the wheels, she pushed down.

A wave of accomplishment filled her as the chair inched silently toward the neonatal unit.

A dozen pushes later, Jane breathed a sigh of relief as she gazed through the window from the hallway and saw that Raya was exactly where she had been, a few hours before.

"There you are. You shouldn't have left without me. Watch your hands," the nurse scolded. She took over, pushing Jane into the NICU, where Doreen looked up from one of the incubators. "Call us when she's ready to go back," the nurse said to Doreen, and disappeared into the hallway.

"You're back already. Couldn't you sleep?" Doreen asked, as her fingers tapped away on the keyboard of her rolling laptop.

Jane grabbed the wheel rims again and rolled herself to Raya's incubator, grateful that Doreen didn't try to stop her from doing it on her own. "I slept a little, but then I woke up in a panic. I had to be sure she was okay."

Doreen moved to Jane's side and squeezed her shoulder. "She's doing just fine. You can always call us from your room, you know."

"I didn't think of that. This is all new to me." Jane shook her head. "My son Tyler was so much simpler. He was born, we stayed in the hospital a few days, I dressed him in his 'going home' outfit, my husband strapped him into his car seat, and we drove home. Back then, the only thing I worried about was when he'd finally sleep through the night." She gazed at little Raya. "Now there are so many more things to add to the worry list." Jane choked back a sob.

"You're not the first mother to cry in here, and you won't be the last. It's okay. Sometimes it helps, just letting it out," Doreen said. Her soft voice and Irish accent soothed Jane's nerves. "I just made some tea. Would you like some?"

Jane smiled. "That sounds perfect. Thank you."

Doreen patted Jane again and ambled off, returning a minute later to hand Jane a Styrofoam cup.

Jane took a sip. "This is delicious," she said in surprise. "What is it?"

"A breakfast tea that's only available in Ireland. My sister sends me some, every month or two. It's the only tea I'll drink."

"I can see why. Do you get back to Ireland often?" Jane asked, taking comfort from the normalcy of the conversation.

"Not as often as I'd like. My husband, Nathan, and I left our families and came to the United States almost forty years ago. We promised to return and visit every year, but it didn't happen. Back then, money was tight. Now, we're too set in our ways to travel a lot. We go back for special occasions. Weddings. Funerals." Doreen sighed. "Sometimes, life takes over our plans."

Jane nodded. "I know that all too well. If anyone had told me, a year ago, that I'd be sitting in a Texas hospital, watching over my preemie daughter, I would've called them crazy."

"Well now, no one expects to have a preterm baby, dear," Doreen said.

Jane smiled at the older woman. "I didn't mean it like that. About a year ago, I divorced Tyler's father. When I married him, I thought we'd grow old together. He was perfect. At least, that's what my mother told me." Jane shook her head. "Eighteen years later, I found out he wasn't the man I thought he was, and then I turned into someone I didn't recognize. When we divorced, I thought that was it for me. I'd had my shot at love, and I didn't expect another chance." Jane sipped her tea.

Doreen leaned back in her chair. "You don't seem the type to give up."

"Oh, but I did. I gave up on love entirely … until I met a cowboy who smelled like fire and midnight. He reignited a flame that I thought had been snuffed out

forever. It was that fire and his love that created her."
Jane tilted her head and stared lovingly at her little girl.
"Raya is a miracle. Doctors told me, years ago, that I
couldn't have any more children." Jane turned to face
Doreen. "I never dreamed I'd be sitting here now, madly
in love with two people I never knew existed a year ago."

Doreen's gaze moved from Jane to Raya. "That
may be the most beautiful love story I've ever heard," she
murmured.

But Jane couldn't help feeling a pang of guilt
when she stared down at Raya's tiny form. "But how did
this happen to her? What did I do that caused her to be
born so early? Maybe I worked too hard. Maybe I
shouldn't have carried the groceries. Maybe I shouldn't
have traveled so much." A fresh batch of tears rolled
down her face.

Doreen plucked a tissue from a nearby table and
handed it to Jane. "Don't do this to yourself, dear. You're
not to blame. No one is. For some reason we'll never
know, this was her time to be born."

Jane dabbed her eyes. "How will I be able to
leave her here?"

"It won't be easy, but at least you know she's in
the best possible hands," Doreen said with conviction.

"True, and I'm grateful, but I'll worry about her
whenever I'm not here. I'll never stop worrying."

Doreen held her cup of tea between her palms,
and smiled at Jane. "I've taken care of babies like yours
for almost forty years. I've seen hundreds of them come
and go. I've seen happy homecomings and excruciating
heartbreak. I've come to know pretty quickly which
babies will thrive and which won't. I'm hardly ever
wrong, even though at times I wish I was." Doreen's gaze
moved to Raya. "This little girl is a fighter. She's a
survivor, just like her mum. Mark my words, she's going

to open those eyes and demand to breathe on her own, soon. She's going to grow and gain strength, day by day. Before you know it, she'll be home. Of course, I should warn you, she's not going to be easy. This child has a fire inside her. She's going to challenge you, every day. But it will be worth it. She's going to grow up to do very good things. Very, very good things."

Jane shook her head in amazement. "How can you know all that?"

Doreen patted her hand. "I'm not sure. I just do, dear. I just do. Now, let's get you back to bed. You're going to need your rest," she said, and walked silently to the nurses' station.

"Doreen?"

"Yes, dear?" Doreen asked as she lifted the phone receiver to her ear.

"Thank you." It didn't seem like enough. In the course of a single conversation, Jane had spilled out all the thoughts, worries, fears, and guilt she'd kept bottled up. Now, a sense of peace flowed through her body, and she knew in her heart that Raya would be okay. She had to be. There was no acceptable alternative.

Doreen nodded slowly as though she understood the richness of those two little words.

****

Jane pulled on a pair of yoga pants and a hoodie before taking the short walk to the neonatal unit. The nurses had finally stopped insisting on pushing her in a wheelchair. Jane was physically well enough to go home, and therefore was well enough to visit her baby on her own.

But her heart was heavy as she walked the short path from the maternity unit to the NICU for the last time as a patient. After she was discharged, she'd be required to check in at the reception desk in the lobby, then zigzag through corridors and ride an elevator up to see Raya.

Doreen smiled when Jane pushed open the door. "I almost don't recognize you without your bathrobe."

"It feels strange to be dressed. I've been on bed rest for so long, I've almost forgotten what real clothes are like." Jane gazed at Raya's incubator as she washed her hands and slipped into a paper gown. "Ryan's on his way to take me home. I told him to meet me here." She shook her head. "It's so hard to leave without her."

"Ah, but I have some good news to make it a little easier. Dr. Blake was just here, and she says Raya is cleared for you to hold." Doreen raised her eyebrows. "What do you think? Are you ready to hold your daughter?"

Jane's heart soared. "Really? Yes!"

"Well now," Ryan's velvety voice said from the doorway, "I haven't seen that beautiful smile in a long time. What's the occasion?"

She turned to Ryan and resisted the urge to run into his arms, since she'd just finished prepping to handle the baby. Instead, she flashed him a wide grin. "We can hold Raya," Jane said, taking a seat in a nearby chair. She'd watched with envy as other parents of preemies held their babies, so she knew the drill.

Doreen reached over the top of the incubator, lifted Raya's little body, passed her to Jane, and covered the baby with a blanket.

Intellectually, Jane knew that Raya weighed less than two pounds, but she was still amazed by how lightweight the baby felt in her arms. However, Raya's body seemed to emit the warmth of someone many times her size. Her heat fueled Jane's soul as she smiled down at the bundle in her arms.

As if in answer, Raya made one of those special baby noises Jane remembered from when Tyler was a newborn. Carefully, Jane pressed her index finger against Raya's impossibly small palm, and felt her little fingers wrap around her fingertip in a way that tugged at her heart.

Ryan joined her, after Doreen helped him wash his hands and don a gown. "My two beautiful girls," Ryan said, beaming at Jane.

"Would you like to hold her?" Jane asked after a few minutes. She knew there was a limit to how long Raya should be out of the incubator, and she wanted to be sure Ryan had time with her, too.

"I'm kind of nervous about it. You sure I can't break her?"

"Nonsense. I've told you, this little girl is a tough one," Doreen said, and took Raya from Jane so they could switch seats.

Jane's heart felt as though it would burst with happiness as she watched Ryan take his daughter in his arms for the first time.

Their time holding her drew to a close all too soon, and Doreen returned Raya to the safety of the incubator, while Jane and Ryan promised they'd return the next morning.

Ryan wrapped his arm around Jane's shoulder as they rode the elevator to the lobby. "We just held our baby," Ryan said.

Jane nodded still feeling the warmth of her baby. "There's so much life in her little body!"

"I felt it, too. She looks frail in the incubator, but, wow, holding her in my arms is a whole different experience. It was like she was telling me she's going to be okay. She's going to be just fine, *Querida*. She'll be just fine."

Jane looked up at him. "I know she will. Come on, my handsome husband to be. Take me home."

Epilogue

"Your chariot awaits, *Señorita*." Uncle Pascal smiled proudly as Jane approached the dock with Charlotte.

"*Tu eres muy ... guapo*," Jane said unsure of her wording. "You are very handsome," she repeated, admiring Ryan's uncle in a suit.

"Your Spanish is coming along. It looks like your lessons with Rosa are working." Pascal's wife, Rosa, had been helping Jane with her Spanish. Jane discovered Rosa knew how to speak English better than she'd let on when they first met on New Year's Eve.

"Rosa's wonderful. Thank you for suggesting it." Jane kissed Pascal on the cheek before he helped the two women into the boat.

The last time Jane had ridden a gondola to Marriage Island, she hadn't realized the significance of that short journey, just a few yards down the river. But as she glanced at Pascal busy rowing her to their destination, and at her own simple white dress which she'd purchased just a few days earlier with Charlotte, she realized her life was a maze of journeys, each with its own starting and ending point. Some had dropped her off in unfamiliar places, leaving her with a feeling she wasn't supposed to be there, while others returned her back where she had started, but pushed her in a new and different direction.

She turned to Charlotte, sitting beside her. "You're quiet. I thought you weren't done saying 'I told you so' yet." Charlotte had been a whirlwind of help over the past few days. Their shopping spree had borne fruit in the form of dresses, shoes, and flowers. Charlotte organized the wedding official, a three-piece blues band, and a photographer, all while chanting "I told you so," every step along the way, or so it had seemed to Jane.

Charlotte championed herself sole credit for Jane and Ryan's paths meeting almost a year ago from that exact day.

Charlotte offered her a smile, with tears shining in her eyes. "I was trying to distract myself so that I wouldn't cry, but then I stopped myself and my thoughts moved on to wondering what would happen if Pascal flipped the boat. What would we do? I don't swim very well, you know."

Jane peeked over the side of the gondola and spotted the floor of the riverbed. "Don't think you have to worry about that, Char. I'm pretty sure you could just stand up, here."

"Well, that's a relief. Seriously, though, I was thinking about how happy I am about how happy you are. I was kidding around with you, saying I was the one who got you back in the saddle, but the truth is that you did this all on your own. You took control of your life at a really tough time, and you made something beautiful out of it. You deserve all the happiness in the world, my friend." She wiped her eyes and shrugged. "You're my hero."

Jane blinked back a tear of her own. "Thank you. You're always there for me when I need it most. I only hope I can return the favor, one day."

Charlotte squeezed Jane's hand as the hypnotic whoosh of the water pushed by Uncle Pascal's paddle propelled them ever closer to everyone Jane held dear. Soon, he began to sing. It was soft, at first, but his rich voice grew louder as they approached Marriage Island.

His song was slow and filled with emotion. Jane understood bits and pieces of it, because he sang in Spanish. It had something to do with family, love … and maybe a cow, but it sounded lovely. Her glance moved beyond Pascal to focus on the old cypress. The island, she saw, had been decorated with yellow and purple flowers. She pointed and turned to Charlotte. "The flowers…"

"I can't tell you how hard it was to find them on short notice, but I wanted them to match the painting on your patio fireplace."

Jane smiled. "You are the best friend ever."

The first faces she saw were the men she loved most: Ryan and Tyler. Tyler, so handsome in his suit, stood proudly alongside Ryan. The two had become fast friends. Tyler had taken Ryan up on an offer to learn the restaurant business. Even though he wasn't old enough to drink it, he'd learned all he could about wine, and Ryan offered to take him on a winery trip to Napa Valley when he hit twenty-one.

Jane's gaze scanned the group of wedding guests. It warmed her heart that everyone important in their life was in attendance.

She giggled as she spotted Isabel waving so frantically that her basket of flowers dropped to the ground. Tyler bent down to help her gather the petals back into the basket. She wore a white dress, similar to Jane's, and Maya had woven tiny daisies along with ribbons into her hair.

Then Jane's eyes met Maya's. The younger woman stood stoically alongside her husband. Jane and Maya would always be connected by the secret Jane had promised to keep. Jane exchanged a heartfelt smile with her as they floated closer to the dock. Maya had surprised Jane when she asked her for help in completing an application for a teaching certification program at the local college. She couldn't be prouder of her soon to be sister-in-law.

Jane craned her neck, looking for her mother, and finally found her smiling face. She'd almost missed her because Beverly was the only one seated. Jane worried about her mother's health, but she was happy that Beverly was well enough to have flown out to spend time with Raya and, as an unexpected bonus, to attend the wedding.

Finally, she returned her gaze to Ryan. The sight of him, so tall and handsome, holding their beautiful daughter in his arms, left Jane breathless. In all the years she'd been with Nick, she had never known love like the love she shared with Ryan. It was as if he had opened a hidden section of her heart, and a landslide of respect, trust, and pure love had poured out in response.

Ryan passed Raya to his sister and strode to the dock as the gondola approached.

Pascal threw the rope to Ryan. "I have the great honor of delivering two of the most beautiful women on the river to you, Reyo." Pascal held his hand out to Charlotte. "And I didn't even tip the boat," he said with a wink.

Ryan secured the rope to the dock and helped Jane from the gondola. "*Querida*, my love, you are absolutely stunning," he said, and held out his hand to her.

"You two are going to make me cry," Charlotte said, taking Pascal's arm as she followed behind Ryan and Jane to take her place alongside her boyfriend, Jacques.

Ryan offered Jane his arm, just as he'd done on the first night they'd met, and Jane slipped her hand around it. Her life with Ryan was always a game of opposites. He made her feel brave yet protected, independent yet cared for, an individual yet part of his team. Most of all, he made her feel loved and part of something beautiful.

They stood in front of the cypress tree, just as so many couples had done before them, and spoke their vows in front of their loved ones. Jane couldn't take her eyes off Ryan until she heard the words, "You may kiss the bride." As Ryan cupped her face in his palms and brushed his lips against hers, she closed her eyes, savoring the moment, searing it into her brain forever.

Then he drew back slightly, just a breath away from her face. "I feel like my life began the first night we stood in this exact spot together. I will love you for the rest of my life, *Querida*."

She smiled at him through her tears. "I thought my life was over, that night, but that wasn't true at all. You gave me a second chance at love, and together we've created a new life, and for both those things I'm eternally grateful. I love you, Reyo Rosales Zeigler. I'll love you forever and always."

A cloud of yellow and purple petals fluttered around them as they were surrounded by the love and well wishes of family.

The End

www.sandrareneeappet.com

ACKNOWLEDGEMENTS

Achievements are rarely attained alone and books are no exception. Many people and places, both directly and indirectly, helped shape this story, including...

My agent, Liz, who read, reread and helped fine-tune Jane and Ryan's story.

Judy Myers, whose keen eye on the early version of this story helped the manuscript shine for submission.

Beta readers Leisha, Janis, Liz, Lori, Kathryn, and Hillary. Your insights and perspectives were invaluable.

My Bookalicious Babes book group. I love and appreciate you all more than you know.

My assistant, Tai. Thank you cheering me on and waiting patiently for this book. I promise, the McAvery Brothers are next.

Ravenna Tate, for her expertise on all things in the NICU. You brought Nurse Doreen to life.

Stephanie Evanovich, my partner in crime at our annual writing getaways and random textfests. Your unwavering support and friendship means so much to me.

The incredible team at Evernight Publishing, especially Stacey, Christine, Karyn, and Jay.

The magical city of San Antonio for the inspiration of Vine and Ryan.

Finally, the members of my wonderful family who have been there every step of the way.

SANDRA RENEE APPET

EVERNIGHT PUBLISHING ®

www.evernightpublishing.com